Double On The Murder

AUTHOR

D.A. Helmer lives in the San Francisco Bay Area. He also spends time in Los Angeles, Montreal and Berlin. He was in Berlin in 1989—when the wall came down. One of his most spellbinding moments was meeting the writer William Burroughs, in San Francisco in 1981.

A multiple Pushcart Prize and Best Of The WEB nominee, D.A. Helmer's fiction is published internationally. Some of his fiction has appeared in *Drinkers Only Magazine, Otoliths Literary Journal, Erotic Review, Literary Yard, Close To The Bone, The World Of Myth Magazine, Alien Buddha Zine, Writers Club e-Zine,* and in Year's Best Hardcore Horror Anthology. *Double On The Murder* is his first novel. He is currently working on the manuscript for his second crime noir novel, while simultaneously working on his first collection of short crime fiction.

PRAISE FOR D.A. HELMER

D.A. Helmer does a great job evoking classic noir with a fresh voice, and the action scenes are cinematic and brutal in all the right ways

— **Thriller Magazine**

Double On The Murder reads like a crime noir movie. It's a juicy mystery novel, with more twists and turns than *Dead Man's Curve*

— **Thomas Andrae, Ph.D.**

For a debut crime noir novel, *Double On The Murder* is indeed a page turner. The writing is unique and vivid

— **Scott Waters, Author**

Double On The Murder

D.A. HELMER

Close To The Bone Press

Close To The Bone Press
an imprint of Gritfiction Publishing
Northampton
Northamptonshire
NN4
www.close2thebone.co.uk

First published in Great Britain in 2026 by Close To The Bone Press

ISBN 979-8-9950843-0-3

Cover design by DAH

Photo credit : Ambroo / Pixabay

First Printing, 2026

Double On The Murder

1

The man staggered into my office like a drunken fool. His face looked weary, and he needed a shave. His damp black suit, grey shirt and maroon tie smelled of old laundry, and his messy dark hair dripped rainwater on my oak floor.

The man sat down hard in the straight back wooden chair in front of my desk. It was an armless chair. He slouched, spread his legs out, and let his droopy eyes focus downward to a crack in the floor. That's where they stayed, downward, eyelids half closed.

I waited, giving the man a chance to say something. His lips didn't move. I was tired of waiting.

"What can I do for you?" I asked with authority, while sitting behind my desk.

"I need help." His words were loaded with anxiety. He looked up, but not directly at me. I could see that his dark eyes had a drugged dullness to them, or maybe he was exhausted.

"What kind of help?"

"The kind that finds people," he said in a low, unsteady voice that seemed to drag through the air.

He dug a cigarette out of his coat pocket. When it was in his mouth, his eyes went back to the crack in the floor.

Then his body leaned hard to the right. He looked ready to collapse.

"You need the police?"

"I called them. Said they'd check it out. Said they'd get back to me. That was this morning."

His voice sounded dry, as if his words were scraping over his tongue.

The man straightened up in the chair, pulled a book of matches from another pocket, struck a match, lit the cigarette, shook the match dead, then dropped the smoking match to the floor. He took a long drag from the cig, burning a quarter-inch of tobacco, then exhaled a fogbank of smoke. For a few seconds I couldn't see his face, like it had vanished from his head.

"Next time, use the damn ashtray on my desk," I said irritably. "Did the police get back to you?"

"Yeah. They called in the afternoon, asking more questions." He looked at his cigarette, as if wondering why he was holding it. He frowned and said: "They wanted her parents phone number. Told me to stick around town." The man exhaled another long, hard breath. His teeth were chattering now. He stuck the cigarette between his teeth. The chattering stopped.

Since stumbling into my office, the man had not looked at me.

"Where did you get my name?"

Taking the cigarette out of his mouth he said: "I remembered a business card somebody handed me." His anxiety felt like it was reaching out for me to turn it off. He pulled the card from his pants pocket and read out loud: "Joe Stone, *Private Dick*."

I nodded with a grin asking: "Who gave you the card?"

"The woman I'm looking for." He paused. "She might be dead." That was the first time he looked into my eyes. His expression was grave, his tone flat. "I was told you were at the club one night, left your card on the bar. She gave it to me. I stuck it on a shelf."

I was suspicious of him. Maybe it was his disoriented behavior and his messy hair. Or maybe it was his rumpled look and his slurred words. I watched him while he stared at the floor again. Muscle spasms rolled over his face like small, lapping waves, until the tension piled up in his jaw. His lips were pulled in tightly. There was something off about this guy. Yet, I felt compelled to push forward with more questions.

"With all the private detectives in Los Angeles, why come to me? I mean, you could've gone to Lew Archer."

"Because I was able to walk here," he said half-whispering, as if talking to himself. "I don't know. I don't know what I'm doing." His voice raised slightly, channeling frustration. "I–I don't know. I *just* don't know."

This guy was falling apart, was about to crack. He dragged on his cigarette in three quick bursts like he wanted to swallow it. When he exhaled, his face turned pale and sweaty, and he was trembling. I looked over at the thermostat. It was seventy-five degrees.

Looking back at him, trying to make eye contact, I asked: "Other than the card, have you heard of me before?"

"I remember you saved a missing teenager last year, a girl, Ana Dia. Was headlines for a while. You were in all the papers, on all the T.V. news." He still wouldn't look at me.

"Let's get back to the missing woman. You said that she might be dead?"

"Yeah, maybe. I don't know." He gave me an uneasy side-glance and quickly looked away again. Then he stood up and stumbled over to the window, saying: "It's all so damned confusing."

"What did you tell the police?"

"That she was missing," he said irritably. "That she was supposed to be taking inventory at the club this morning." He was looking down at the boulevard. Red neon glazed his face and clothes. The half-smoked cigarette dangled from his lips. He tilted his head sideways to get away from the smoke. Then he pulled the cigarette from his lips, ashes fell to the floor.

"Why not tell the police what you told me?"

"I don't know. It's all so… fuzzy. I'm not sure about anything." Almost whispering again, he added: "Could I have imagined that she was dead?"

I didn't respond to that question.

Standing up from behind my desk, I looked out the window. Red and blue neon spilled over the wet roads like liquid candy. The intersection at Hollywood and Vine was nearly empty, in a ghostly way.

I watched the man's reflection in the window. Had sized him up already while he was sitting in the chair: early forties, five-ten, a hundred and seventy, strong build and wearing quality clothes. And he had the type of good looks that gets one through life with a smile and a yes at every turn.

The man left the window and sat back in the chair, still not looking at me. I sat down at the desk again.

"You said there might have been a murder, but there's no stiff. Who is she?"

"She works for me," he replied. "I own a whisky club a few blocks from here, on the Boulevard at Wilcox." He was still looking down at the floor.

"Is she just an employee?"

Looking at me now, a little surprised, he asked: "What do you mean by that?" His thick eyebrows lifted to the middle of his forehead and stayed there, until he let go of the muscle tension.

"I'm trying to get the story straight. If you want my help, I need to ask some personal questions with answers placed under the light."

"Yeah, okay, we're lovers. Is that what you wanted to hear? Is that *under the light* enough? Or do you need details of our sex life too?"

I ignored his two-bit sarcasm and asked: "What's your name, the name of the woman, and the name of club?"

He leveled his strained eyes on mine and answered with a hard tone: "I'm Scott Drum. Her name is Patty Walker. The bar is The Open Blouse." Then he looked at the cigarette in his hand, as if it was there to back up his answer. The smoke swirled upward around his face, like a phantom, until it disappeared altogether. Then I thought back to a female client I had a few months ago:

I had tailed a husband for a suspicious wife. The husband led me to The Open Blouse, a whisky club for men. It had a glamorous ambience: copper engraved ceilings, crystal chandeliers and plush furniture. The Open Blouse clientele was made of well-heeled men suffering from generational wealth. The men got to hang out with the desirable club-employed girls. While there, I learned that only educated, single girls in their twenties were hired, and that most of the girls were eager for a silk-stocking life. It was an affluent playground, where the women looked like stars and the men were in troubled marriages.

"How old are you?"

"Forty-three." He answered quietly this time, eyes working the floor again.

"And Miss Walker?"

"Twenty-four," he said, still looking down.

"Are you married?"

"Listen, Mr. Stone!" he snapped, glaring at me. "I'm tired of this ceaseless third degree. Can you help me or not?"

"Without answers to my questions, then no, I can't help you, Mr. Drum." I got up, walked to the door, opened it and said: "I hope you find what you're looking for. Good night." I waved my hand out the door.

Scott Drum sat straight up in the chair, his body rigid, and his face pinched with tension. He took another aggressive drag from his cigarette, stressing the tendons in his neck, then, slouching back into the chair, he turned his head and looked straight into my eyes.

"Yeah, I'm married. Ten years. No children," he said. His eyes narrowed down on me while he stretched his legs out again. Cigarette ash fell to his pants.

"Does your wife know about your relationship with Ms. Walker?"

"Not as far as I know. Don't think she'd care anyway," he said with a dismissive wave of his hand. He leaned his head back, eyes looking towards the ceiling. "Patty and I have been involved for several months, since the time I hired her."

"What about enemies, Mr. Drum? Does Miss Walker have enemies?"

"I don't know," he said while shrugging his shoulders, looking at me now.

I walked from the door to the window, opened it wide. Moist fresh air blew into the office. Standing there, looking out the window, my visit to The Open Blouse came back to me:

It was a soft-core strip joint, where the girls were lean and fit, and uninhibited about opening their blouses, upon request. It was almost a topless joint, but not really. The girls were required to have firm mounds, and the men were forbidden to touch the braless girls. Violation of this rule got you barred from the club. If a patron and a girl wanted to take their association further, they needed to meet on their own terms, away from club property. No exceptions. By talking with a few of the girls, I learned that patrons and club-girls had met many times. Divorce filings and courtroom dramas frequently followed.

I turned from the window, looked at Drum and said: "Describe Miss Walker. Height, hair, eyes, you know."

"Five-six, long blond hair and bright blue eyes. She has a great figure and her face is divine. I've never met a woman like her, gorgeous and educated, with a disposition as sweet as spring."

I nodded and said: "Tell me about your wife. Her first name, maiden name, age, looks, and what she does for work."

"Mya Regis. She uses her maiden name. She's thirty-nine. Five-seven and lean, with long red hair, green eyes and good lips. Work? Never. She's a socialite. Her job is to be seen."

"Regis?" I asked, surprised. "Any connection to Regis Fabrics?"

"Yeah. Milo Regis is her father. And according to Mya, he is the only *real man* she knows."

His voice was bitter with sarcasm. I could almost taste it.

Milo Regis was *the* West Coast fabric baron and one of the wealthiest men in Los Angeles. He arrived from France forty years earlier with pennies in his pockets, and he had built a kingdom with those pennies. A ruthless double-dealer, it was common news that Regis ran his business with an iron fist and his personal life with a bad temper. Last year his wife had an affair with Moe Merrit. Regis' then attorney. When Milo Regis found out about the affair, he beat Moe Merrit to within an inch of his life. A month later Merrit shot himself in the forehead. He was found dead in a cheap motel room along Sunset Strip. And three days after Merrit's death, Mrs. Regis jumped from the roof of Milo Regis' four-story Garment District warehouse. It appeared to be a clean suicide. There was no lengthy investigation.

In more ways than one, my gut told me not to take this case, to stay away from anything that was connected to Milo Regis. I should have walked Scott Drum out the door, turned out the lights and gone home. But there was something I had come to like about Drum, something that made me want to help him out of his confusion. What that something was I couldn't say, but I was willing to give him the benefit of the doubt. I felt that he was a good man, who had become burdened with somebody else's trouble.

"Okay, Mr. Drum. Over the next few days, I'll look around. The fee is a hundred and twenty a day for my services, plus sixty per day for each of my two associates. The first three days are paid up front. Will that be a problem?"

"No problem at all. I have the cash on me." He paused, leveling his tired eyes on mine, and said: "Mr. Stone, Patty means everything to me."

I nodded and asked: "Did you kill Patty Walker, Mr. Drum?"

"Huh? I mean, no. Of course not. Why would you ask?"

"Just covering all the bases. Tomorrow morning, bring some photographs of Patty Walker and a few photographs of your wife. Say, around nine o'clock. One more question, why do you think Miss Walker might be dead, Mr. Drum?"

"Because Patty was lying next to me on the bed. We were in the apartment I keep above the club." He was talking fast again. "I was out cold. It must have been a mickey because I only had one Scotch and water. I woke up groggy and disoriented. Patty was lying next to me. Her face was bone-white and her throat was bruised. I tried to get up but passed out again. Not sure for how long I was out the second time, but when I came to, Patty was gone. That was last night. I've phoned her a dozen times today. Even went to her apartment. She's gone, Mr. Stone."

His grave expression returned and his shoulders slumped. He leaned forward and rapidly crushed his cigarette in the green glass ashtray sitting on my oak desk. He gave me another sideways glance, then looked away quickly.

"And you withheld most of this information from the police, by only telling them that she didn't show up for inventory?"

"Yeah, that's right," he said. He leaned back and slouched in the chair. His chin hanging low to his chest.

"Why?"

He shrugged his shoulders. "I don't know why, Mr. Stone. I'm confused, tired, worried. That's no excuse. But that's all I can tell you."

"You assumed Miss Walker was dead because of the bruises on her throat?"

"Yeah. But I was doped. I think. Could I have imagined it?" His eyebrows pulled together and his eyes moved rapidly, as if searching the air for answers.

"Where is Ms. Walker's apartment?"

"700 Laurel Canyon Boulevard, Apt. 20." He looked up at me with strained red eyes and a sagging face, a face that seemed to have aged ten years, since he first came into my office.

"What did your wife say about you not coming home last night?"

"She was out of town. Left yesterday morning. Told me she was going to Ojai for a few days, to stay at a spa." He paused to take in a breath and said: "Anyway, we're separated. It's been like that for nearly a year."

I nodded while taking a few notes. "You got a name for the Ojai spa?"

"No, I don't." His voice was sounding old and tired.

"Okay, Mr. Drum. Go get yourself cleaned up, and get some rest. We'll talk tomorrow morning, that is, if I need any additional information. And you'll be staying where to-night?"

"At the apartment above the club. That's where I've been living since the separation." His face drew lines of deeper strain, and his complexion seemed to be greying around the edges. "I'm going to close the club, until this confusion is cleared up." Reaching into his pants pocket, he pulled out a wad of money and counted a thousand dollars in one-hundred-dollar bills. "This should cover you for the next few days." His voice was hollow, and his face had turned ash white.

Before he left, I gave Scott Drum an umbrella for the rain and a receipt for what he paid me. I wrote down his phone number, turned off the lights and left the office.

It was a wet January night. The kind of night that would feel good to be at home, and tucked in with a fifth of Jack Daniels, the phone off the hook, and Coleman Hawkins blowing his bluesy tenor sax through my stereo console.

2

After Scott Drum dropped off the photographs the next morning, I sent my associate Arnie Bender to Ojai with a color photograph of Mya Regis. The photograph was slightly blurred, but it was easy to see that she was an attractive woman.

Later that day at the courthouse, I pulled the file on the beating of Moe Merrit by Milo Regis.

I was curious about the details of that case.

The assault and battery charges against Regis were dropped, over a temporary insanity filing by his new lawyer, due to the adulteress circumstance. I was willing to bet that Milo Regis waved a wad of green in front of the district attorney, to make the case go away. Regis had great power of persuasion over some of the city officials. Most of whom were more greedy than honest.

Next, I pulled the file on Mrs. Amy Regis' suicide. I read that there were no witnesses and no goodbye note. The incident happened on a Sunday morning around five a.m. Businesses in the area were closed at that hour of day. The report also said that Milo Regis was in the building at the time of the jump.

Regis stated that he and Mrs. Regis stopped by the warehouse to pick up some paperwork. They were planning on an early breakfast at a nearby restaurant. Regis said that while he was in his fourth-floor office collecting the papers, his wife went to the rooftop to watch the sunrise. The report stated that it was the last time Mr. Regis saw Mrs. Regis alive.

Then I read the file on Moe Merrit. His family said that he was not suicidal. They said that he was scared and in physically bad shape from the beating, but he was not despondent, and he didn't own a gun. The district attorney filed Moe Merrit's death as a suicide: shot dead-center forehead at close range. A chrome Colt .32 Snub-nose revolver, with a spent round in the otherwise empty cylinder, lay at his side. Next to the gun was a typed note stating that the affair with Mrs. Regis was morally wrong, and that he couldn't live with himself because of it. There was no handwritten signature. The pistol's serial number at the bottom of the butt was filed off, as well as the serial number inside the frame. Suicide. Case closed.

Leaving the courthouse, I drove to Abe's Deli on Vine Street for a quick lunch. Back at the office, I spent a few hours on paperwork for some other cases. Then I took a nap on the office couch and slept until six-thirty. That's when the phone woke me.

"Joe Stone, Private Investigator."

"Hey, Boss, it's Arnie. Been in Ojai for a few hours now. Went to all the spas, flashing the mug shot of that Regis dame. Nobody recognized her and nobody was registered in any of the spas under that name. Went to all the hotels, restaurants and whisky clubs. Same dead end. Want me to stick around here?"

"Good job, Arnie. I have a feeling that Mya Regis never left Los Angeles. Go get some dinner, then come back to the city. I'm sure your lovely wife Millie would like to have you home tonight."

A few hours later, I parked my car on Hollywood Boulevard at Wilcox Avenue, across the street from The Open Blouse. Thought I should get another look at the club, now that Scott Drum was my client. It was a square, two-story stucco job, painted dark grey with light grey trim. There was a solid bright blue front door set off to the right. The building had a flat roof that tilted slightly back and down. On one side of the building there was a small parking lot. On the other side there was an eight-foot concrete wall running along an alley. A tall lemon tree stood at the front end of the alley near the wall.

There was a *CLOSED* sign in blue neon on the inside of the front picture window. There was a larger blue neon sign above that window on the outside of the building that read: *THE OPEN BLOUSE*. The inside of the club was dark, but there was a dim light in one of the two windows in Scott Drum's apartment above. Unexpectedly, a silhouette appeared in one of the shaded windows for a few seconds. Somebody in a coat with a large hood over their head. The light went out. The apartment turned dark. I looked at my watch: nine fifty-seven.

I walked along the alley to the rear of the building. The alley was poorly lit and mostly dark. There were tipped over trashcans with two mangy mutts gulping down the garbage. A line of rats scurried along the concrete wall to the backside of a dumpster. The dogs scattered when they heard me coming. The rats couldn't have cared less.

A wooden staircase led to the apartment. At the top landing, a dim bulb was lit above a light blue door. The door had a diamond-shaped curtained window. I stood next to the dumpster in the shadows, looking up at the top landing of the stairs. The air around me smelled like a decomposed animal.

Around ten p.m. the apartment door opened. Somebody came down the stairs in a black ankle-length hooded coat. With the hood up, I couldn't get a fix on the face, but I got a glimpse of white tennis sneakers. There was athletic strength to the person's movements, but I couldn't tell if it was a man or a woman because of the wide coat. The dark alley didn't help any.

The hooded figure ran down the alley towards the boulevard and hailed a taxi. The person slid into the back seat of the cab, which spun around, heading west. Maybe I should have followed the cab, but I was tired, and went home instead. The comfort of my flat and a bottle of bourbon were calling me. It was that kind of a night.

Over a glass of whisky, I studied the case information about Scott Drum. If Patty Walker was missing, there were at least two people who'd possibly want her gone. One of them was Drum's wife Mya Regis, because of conceivable social embarrassment. The other was her father Milo Regis, out of rage over Scott Drum two-timing his daughter, although they were separated. But what if the person who came out of the apartment was Patty Walker?

I looked at my watch: ten-fifty. I reached for the phone, but my hand stopped in midair as if hitting a barrier. I decided to question Scott Drum in the morning, about the mysterious activity at his apartment. I closed the case folder, turned out the light, then found the bed. I think I stubbed my toe, but the whisky was a decent pain-killer, so it was hard to tell. Sleep came like a gentle kiss.

The phone woke me at nine the next morning. It was my other associate, Dave Wells. Besides working for me, Wells was a part-time forensics photographer. He was at The Open Blouse.

"Morning, Boss. I was called in to pop some photographs. You might want to get over here as soon as possible."

When I pulled up to the club twenty minutes later, squad cars lined the street. Red lights flashed their edgy warning. The club and the alley were cordoned off. Uniformed cops stood guard along the sidewalks like Roman sentries.

I saw Homicide Detective Harley Jewels standing at the front of the alley, next to the lemon tree, talking to a group of people. Detective Brick Woodhouse was in the middle of the alley talking to a uniformed cop.

Jewels, Woodhouse and I go back over twenty years. We were on the LAPD homicide unit before I quit. We still spend time together hitting the whisky bars. They also spend a lot of their time in my office. It's their hideout for breaks from L.A.'s homicidal madness. Their supervisor, Captain Doug Roberts, allows me to tag along on investigations. Captain Roberts appreciates my way of thinking. Most cops hate private detectives, but this is a different situation.

When Jewels saw me, he came over and shook my hand.

"Hi, Joe. How's it going?"

"Things were going okay until this. Harley, what's going on here?"

"Follow me." While we were walking, he added: "Dave Wells said you just started working a case for this joint."

"Yeah. Somebody's girlfriend is missing. The boyfriend hired me to poke around."

As we headed into the alley, I shook hands with Detective Woodhouse. We chatted a bit, then Jewels and I walked to the back of the alley. The trashcans were still spilled over, but the dogs and rats were gone, and a more putrid odor was clinging to the air. At the back of the alley behind the dumpster was a body, partially eaten by the rats. From what was left of the face, I could see it was Patty Walker. Her bright, blue eyes were open, but the lights were out. There was a bullet hole dead-center forehead. A Colt Snub-nose .32 caliber revolver was next to her. It was shiny chrome.

Jewels asked: "You know her?"

"Yeah. She's the girlfriend I was looking for." I was beginning to feel aggravated.

"Well, congratulations, you found her," he said flatly. "Who's the boyfriend, the one who hired you?"

"Scott Drum. He owns this joint."

"Okay..." Jewels replied with a nod, "let's take a walk upstairs."

When we entered the apartment, Dave Wells was there popping camera flashes from different angles. We nodded at each other, then I followed Jewels into the bedroom. The coroner was in there, getting ready to stab a corpse with a liver thermometer.

"Is this the boyfriend?" Jewels asked.

"Yeah. That's Drum."

"The one who hired you?"

"Yeah," I said, with even more aggravation.

Scott Drum was on the bed, spread-eagle, on his back. A chrome-plated Colt .32 Snub-nose revolver was at his side. A bullet hole was dead-center forehead. He was wearing the same clothes as the night before.

For a few chilling seconds, I stared at Scott Drum's dead body, then glanced around the room. A glimmer from under the bed caught my eye. It was a diamond earring, one of those dangly types. When Jewels had his back to me, I bent down, like I was tying my shoe, reached under the bed, palmed the earring, and dropped it in my coat pocket. I looked around some more, then walked back to the living room.

Dave Wells was photographing a beige Olivetti typewriter that had an apparent suicide note in the carriage. The note read:

Mya,
Patty and I decided that this is the only way.
I'm sorry,
Scott

There was no signature.

"Dave," I said to Wells, "when you're finished here, let's go down and look at the stiff. See if she's wearing earrings."

"Sure, Boss." Wells popped a few more living room photos. The harsh exploding magnesium was like a whiteout, leaving my eyes with short-lived, multicolored spots. After my eyes cleared up, Wells and I headed down the stairs to the alley. The medics were ready to load Patty Walker's sheet-covered body into the ambulance. They accommodated Wells' request to look at her ears.

I walked around the dumpster, poking trash on the ground with the toe of my shoe, when I spotted a large black button mixed in with the trash. It was clean and didn't look like trash at all. I picked it up, dropped it in my pocket, and walked towards the front of the alley. Dave Wells told me that Patty Walker had earrings in both ears.

I was heading out of the alley, when Detective Jewels called out to me.

"Joe. Hey. Wait up."

"What 'cha got, Harley? Anything pretty to add to this ugly scene?"

He smiled faintly and said: "The coroner puts Scott Drum's death around eight to ten p.m. last night, but the girlfriend's killing happened maybe a day and a half ago. Rigor mortis stiffened her like a carriage bolt, and she was pretty chewed up by the time we got here. Must've made a good meal for the rats." Jewels' expression was grim.

"Who called it in?" I asked.

"The cleaning lady called in Drum's body. One of my uniforms found Walker's body."

"Where is the cleaning lady now?"

"In rough shape at General, under sedation. Her sons are keeping the coppers away."

"Any witnesses?"

"No one saw anything, but three of them said they heard what sounded like two cars backfiring. One around nine thirty, the other at nine-forty," Jewels said.

"Is there a club manager?" I asked. "Somebody you can talk to about getting the staff together for questioning?"

"Yeah," Jewels replied. "His name is Bryce Parker. I'll call you once we have the meeting set up. It would be good to have you there, listening in."

I nodded while my hand played with the button and the earring in my coat pocket.

Dave Wells walked over to me, asked what he should do next. I told him to look around the plush hotels in the city, flash a photograph of Mya Regis, and to make a lot of noise when questioning the concierges and bellhops, mentioning that Joe Stone is looking for her.

Wells replied: "If Mya Regis is in town, I'll have no problem flushing her out. No problem at all." His white-enameled smile glistened with confidence, like he knew something that I didn't.

"Call Arnie's house," I said to Wells. "He should be back from Ojai by now. Have him go to Milo Regis' warehouse in the Garment District tonight, to watch who comes and goes. Let him know that a few hours there should be enough."

After leaving The Open Blouse, I had a gut feeling that I should have sent both Arnie Bender and Dave Wells to the Regis Fabrics warehouse. Milo Regis' bodyguards were known to be hostile.

3

Later that day I was staring at the diamond earring lying on my desk. The black button was in my hand twirling between my fingers. The phone rang.

"Joe. Brick Woodhouse here. The forensics and autopsy reports came in fast on Drum and Walker. The Colt found on Scott Drum's bed was the pistol that killed Drum, and Patty Walker's plug in the head was from the other gun lying next to her. The serial numbers were filed off both weapons, and get this, her gunshot was post-mortem. The cause of Walker's death was strangulation, which most likely occurred somewhere else, and not in the alley."

"Scott Drum said Patty Walker looked dead, lying next to him on the bed. He told me that Walker had bruises around her throat. Drum was passed out for a while. When he came to, he said he felt drugged. After looking at Walker, he passed out again. When he came around later, Walker was gone."

"He could have been right, about Walker being dead at that time," Woodhouse said, then added: "The typewriter and the suicide note left in the carriage were wiped clean.

The only prints found in the apartment were Scott Drum's and Patty Walker's."

"Drum didn't mention seeing a bullet hole in her forehead," I said. "Walker must have been shot while she was lying dead behind the dumpster."

"My thinking, exactly," Woodhouse replied. "Forensics found traces of chloral hydrate inside two drinking glasses with Drum's and Walker's prints on them. And this is intriguing: both pistols had one used round in the otherwise empty chambers. Same as the Moe Merrit case.

"Well, that's something to keep in mind. Okay, Brick. Thank you."

I thought about the backfire sounds that the witnesses heard. Most likely they were gunshots plugging the bodies just before I arrived at the alley that night. Thought about the person in the hooded coat who ran from Drum's apartment, who took a cab and headed west.

Feeling hungry, I started to dial Abe's Deli, when the office door opened wide and leisurely. I hung up the phone in what felt like no movement at all, and just sat there feeling as brainless as a piece of wood.

With a black raincoat draped over her right arm, Mya Regis stood in the doorway, and she was by far more beautiful than Scott Drum's description. Her dazzling, bright green eyes worked me over like a summer hot spell, and her dark red-painted lips seemed to be wet with anticipation. They were full, moist, glistening, and slightly parted, like she wanted to say hello, and her long red hair had a fire-like radiance. She wore a knee-length black silk dress with long sleeves, and there were black silk gloves at the ends of those sleeves. The dress was perfectly tailored, and she had plenty of curves that accented the perfect tailoring.

"Mr. Stone," she said with a spellbinding voice that was a little deep and smoky in tone, "I've been told you were looking for me." Her green eyes flashed as if delivering the words with an electric charge.

"Ah, yes, I–ah…" Her voice took hold of me like an opiate streaming through my head.

"When a woman enters a room, Mr. Stone, a gentleman offers her a chair. Preferably the most comfortable one."

I almost stumbled across the room, feeling as if I was tripping over loose shoestrings, but managed to pull the big pink-cushioned chair away from the window and up to the desk. She draped her coat over the back of the chair, then presented her gloved hand for me to guide her to the seat. A light scent of intoxicating perfume surrounded me. I inhaled slow and steady, taking in its fragrance. It smelled expensive, like the kind that spells trouble for any man.

There was a smooth confidence in the way Mya Regis lowered herself into the chair, and in the way she sat on the edge of the cushion, maintaining regal poise. The crossing of her legs slid the dress up several inches, revealing an inviting length of black silk thigh. She was not subtle about crossing her legs, nor was she shy that the dress skimmed the edge of her nylons. Ms. Regis had my attention.

"I understand that you are investigating my husband's death." Her tongue ran slowly over her upper lip, adding a more glistening effect. When she looked at me, her head lifted slightly then tilted a bit to the left. My head tilted with hers as if she was controlling it. She appeared to be a sophisticated operator, cool and suave.

I had yet to say anything that wasn't like a stutter with a drool.

Taking in a deep breath, I exhaled slowly, and answered: "Yes, ah, I was assisting the, ah, homicide detectives. I'm a private detective and not…"

"Then what is *your* business with *their* case, Mr. Stone?" Her eyes widened with bright green light.

"Your husband hired me to find a missing employee. He was, ah, concerned for her welfare. She didn't show up for work, and..."

"Scott hired you to find his lover, the dead girl in the alley, who turned out to be Miss Walker. Isn't that right, Mr. Stone?" Her tongue moved slowly over her top lip again, like it was looking for something to taste. From the light coming through window, her long, red hair had the shimmering effect of wet autumn leaves on a breezy day.

"I'm sorry, Ms. Regis, but I–I cannot discuss any more client information with you."

"Then why were you looking for me?" Her eyes fixed hard on mine. They were penetrating, as if accelerating into my eyes with a gripping determination to command the interview. I had to take control.

"Why did you lie to Scott Drum about staying in Ojai?"

"That is my business, Mr. Stone. Is there anything else?" Her expression tensed.

"How long have you known about the affair?"

"I knew about it from the beginning." Her face was relaxed now, and her voice was softer, and she seemed more comfortable answering this question. "I met Miss Walker the day Scott hired her. I was at the club which I rarely visited. Scott and I were going out for dinner, as we occasionally did." She paused for a moment to reflect on that night. "There was the flirtatious way Scott spoke to Miss Walker, and the almost intimate attention he gave to her."

She paused again, and looked towards the window for a few seconds, as if searching her memories. Then she looked back at me and continued: "I felt something about Miss Walker that I can't explain, like there was a connection between us. And then there was the physical resemblance between Miss Walker and Jill Sabin. Jill was another girl who used to work at the club. She was fired for violating employee rules. Anyway, the resemblance between Miss Walker and Jill Sabin was uncanny. But then, most blonds look alike. Wouldn't you agree, Mr. Stone?"

I didn't answer that question and asked: "Did you speak with Patty Walker?"

"No. It was all very quick. I was only there for a few minutes before Scott and I left the club."

"Did you see Miss Walker again?"

"No. That was the only time."

"Do you know where she was from?"

"The club's manager, Bryce Parker, told me that she had moved to Los Angeles from the Bay Area. I think from San Rafael."

She licked her upper lip again. Obviously, a nervous habit. It glistened like polished red porcelain.

At that point she asked in a deep, soft tone: "Have I satisfied your needs, Mr. Stone?"

Her head lifted with a slight jerk, as if signaling that she was done with me.

"Just a few more questions, if you don't mind."

She tilted her head to the left again, and screwed up her mouth, obviously annoyed by my persistence.

"Did your father know about the affair?"

"You should be asking him, Mr. Stone."

"I am asking you, Ms. Regis. Did he know?"

"Yes. I told him."

"His response?"

"He asked me if he should handle it."

"Handle it how?"

"I don't know."

"Did he ask for Miss Walker's name?"

"Yes."

"Did you give it to him?"

She sat up straighter, eyes flaring at this question. "Why wouldn't I?" Tilting her head to the left again, her eyes narrowed down on mine with an exasperated force.

I shrugged my shoulders at that question and asked: "Did your husband and your father get along?"

"They were different men with different convictions and different principles."

"But did they get along, or…?"

"They avoided each other. Father saw Scott as a financial burden. Scott saw my father as a tyrant. Father wanted me to have a prenuptial. I disagreed. Scott wanted us to move as far away from my father as possible. I disagreed to that also."

"You don't appear to be upset over your husband's death, Ms. Regis."

"I am wearing black, Mr. Stone. Is there anything else?" Her tone was curt, distrusting.

Looking into her eyes I said: "Tell me about the affair you are having."

"I do believe that we are finished here, Mr. Stone." Her mouth closed tightly then twisted, pulling off to one side in a fit of anger. Tension spread over her face like a tight drum skin, and her bone structure seemed to swell up, protruding along the cheek bones. The lack of subtleness in Mya's temper gave her some edginess. I liked it. It pulled her off her pedestal, bringing her down to earth with the rest of us. Her face was flushed. I liked that too.

When Mya Regis rose from the chair, her eyes fixed hard on the diamond earring, lying on the desk behind the phone. She pretended not to notice it, then she turned swiftly to leave the office.

There was great hostility in her body language. Stopping at the doorway, she turned towards me in a controlled manner, and with a forced easiness said:

"I can see you are a good man, Mr. Stone. I remember how you saved that teenage girl, Ana Dia, last summer. It was a touching story." She paused for a few seconds then said: "In a more pleasant situation, I am sure we could be friends."

I didn't say anything.

She turned and left the office, leaving the door wide open. I watched her walk down the hallway, high heels clacking hard and loud. I took pleasure in the way her hips moved, like a bongo player's slow rhythm, and in the way the tight dress gripped her slender body. I think she left the door open for my eyes to follow her along the corroder. It worked.

I stood up and walked over to the window, in hopes of seeing who was driving her. From my second-floor vantage point, I watched Mya Regis walk down the boulevard, then turn right at Vine Street. Several seconds later, a dark green Lincoln came from Vine Street, crossed Hollywood Boulevard and continued north on Vine. In the passenger seat I could make out Mya Regis' gloved hands and her crossed legs. But all I could see of the driver were the arms of a grey tailored suit with black-gloved hands on the steering wheel. I also saw a bit of his light brown or maybe blond hair.

I walked over to close the door, then sat down at the desk, thinking it was odd that Mya Regis didn't say anything when she noticed the diamond earring. Most women have something to say when they see diamonds.

The wall clock showed four forty-five. I headed over to Abe's Deli, around the corner on Vine, and ordered ham and cheese on rye with a glass of beer. Thirty minutes later I left the restaurant and walked back to the office.

Detectives Harley Jewels and Brick Woodhouse were standing in front of my building. Jewels was pacing in little circles on the sidewalk with his hands in his pants pockets. His fedora was pulled low over his eyes. Woodhouse leaned with his back to the building, chewing on a toothpick. His hat was pushed up and back on his head. The sole of one shoe was pressed against the wall, his arms hung down at both sides. Jewels said they saw me in Abe's Deli paying my bill, and decided to wait for me at the office. They wanted to take me to a crime scene. We headed to the Garment District in their car. They were unusually quiet.

4

On Paloma Street at Milo Regis' warehouse, a few patrol cars and several uniformed cops were spread out a block wide. It was nearing early evening. The air was colder. A chill ran along my spine, needling the back of my neck.

The warehouse alley was cordoned off at the entrance. A squad car and some uniforms stood guard. Down the street, a crowd of gawkers had formed like a pack of wolves in waiting.

Jewels and Woodhouse grabbed my arms, and rushed me across the street to the back of the alley. There were more uniforms standing around, along with two medics and the coroner. An agitated red light was flashing from the top of an ambulance. The only other light was from a patrol car spotlight, aimed low to the ground. A soft rain sparkled in that harsh light, falling on a sheet-covered stiff lying face up in a puddle.

When I saw the brown wingtips sticking out from under the sheet, I nearly lost my breath, then my balance. My body turned dead-cold. When I lifted the sheet, Arnie Bender's head laid there in blood and water. His eyes were open and clear. He had been shot dead-center forehead. A chrome Colt .32 Snub-nose revolver was at his side, submerged in the puddle. There was no sign of struggle, no sign of a mugging gone wrong. It looked like murder to me.

I stood there frozen to the spot, looking at my friend of ten years. Blood crystalized along my spine and my gut threw itself upside down. Staggering to the side of the alley, I puked up ham, rye and beer, then fell to my knees, feeling like a defeated man.

Woodhouse came over, gave me a hand getting up and walked me out of the alley, back to the car. I staggered and stumbled while Woodhouse kept me from falling over. With Jewels in the driver's seat, we drove to a whisky joint on Sunset Boulevard. By the time we left the bar an hour later, I was passed out drunk in the back seat. Jewels drove us to my Echo Park flat, where the two of them got me out of my damp clothes and put me to bed.

I didn't remember dreaming that night, but I remembered the cold emptiness in Arnie's open eyes, and how his mouth was open, too, as if trying to breathe.

Next morning the phone screamed like it was taking a beating. My eyes were glued shut, my mouth wouldn't open, and my throat was parched. There was sour bourbon coating my tongue. It tasted bad. Then my eyelids opened a little, and I made out the bedstand clock. It was ten-ten. The phone stopped. I lifted my torso up by my elbows, and swung my legs off the bed, to sit up. I sat there for a long time with my head hanging to my stomach. I felt dry and hot, in need of water. I stood up, stumbled to the bathroom, turned the cold water on, and stepped into the icy rush, gasping. A few seconds later I was out of the shower, shivering like a hairless cat. The phone was ringing again. I answered it.

"Joe. Brick Woodhouse. Been trying to get a hold of you all morning. How are you feeling?"

"Like I crawled out of a crap house." My voice was raspy.

"I'm sorry about Arnie Bender. He was a funny guy, always had me laughing. Damn it! Dave Wells is with Millie. She was in rough shape, hysterical. The doc gave her sedatives. She's resting at home."

"Thanks, Brick, for everything. Thank Harley, too."

Harley Jewels and Brick Woodhouse were honest cops. They had been with the LAPD homicide division for twenty years, and there wasn't a corrupt bone between them.

It was Jewels and Woodhouse who wanted to keep the investigations into the suicides of Moe Merrit and Amy Regis open. They smelled stench coming from the bottom of the pit, and they wanted to dig deeper to find the source of the rot. The rot smelled like Milo Regis. But Police Commissioner Daniel McKenna, Regis' golfing buddy, ordered the case closed.

Commissioner McKenna was a hardboiled bastard. He ran the department with dirty hands and a short-fused Irish temper. To cross him once was to lose his respect. To cross him twice was the end of your career as a Los Angeles cop. As an LAPD homicide detective, I crossed McKenna once, when he was my Captain. He played dirty with a murder involving a mobster's son. I had the son pretty much strapped to the hot seat for killing his girlfriend's lover in cold blood. But the prime evidence had disappeared from the evidence room. I called out Captain McKenna on his crooked move and shook the filth in his face. From that day on he made my cop-life miserable, until I had nothing but contempt for him. To get McKenna out of my life, my only choice was to resign from the force. That's what I did. That was twelve years ago.

"The other reason for calling," Woodhouse continued, "was to say that we're having a meeting with The Open Blouse staff tonight, at eight o'clock at the club. We'd like you to be there."

"Okay," I said, my voice still raspy.

"One last thing," Woodhouse said. "The Colt .32 used on Arnie had one spent cartridge in the otherwise empty cylinder. The serial numbers were filed off. It was the same setup as Drum and Walker. This killing pattern doesn't look good."

"Alright. I'll see you at eight tonight." My voice lacked expression.

"Joe. There was a typed suicide note in Arnie's pants pocket."

"Brick, we know damn well it wasn't suicide," I said exasperated.

After hanging up the phone, I headed into the bathroom. Took a hot shower this time, then got dressed and left the apartment.

Wobbling down the sidewalk, I made it to Star-Struck Café a few blocks away. After two black coffees, the grogginess was knocked out of me, but my head was filled with Arnie.

"I'm going to get the killer who did this," I said under my breath.

Leaving the café, feeling steady enough to drive, I headed to the Garment District. I parked a block from Milo Regis' warehouse and sort of staggered the rest of the way to the alley.

The heavy, wet air and grey winter light fit my somber mood.

5

Standing across the street from the Regis warehouse, I saw a patrol car with two cops leaning against the front fender. They were keeping the alley blocked while Arnie Bender's murder was under investigation.

Icy drizzle filled the air. The moisture was dense enough to dampen my hat and shoulders. The cold air felt as heavy as a broken heart.

Leaning against a telephone pole, I lit a cigarette and was thinking about Arnie. A chill rattled my spine, making me shiver uncontrollably, until a warm childlike voice came from behind me saying: "People can't fly."

I snapped out of my cold thoughts and turned around.

A bag lady stood there holding two canvas bags crammed with stuff. Her clothes were tattered, which made her look like a cat-scratching post. She was about five-foot-five, with long, grey hair that was both frizzy and matted. Her large brown eyes sparkled with innocence, but the deep lines around them were like scars of chronic sadness. Her face was pancake-flat and wide. Small yellowish teeth filled her spacious mouth. She looked to be in her sixties.

"People can't fly. They try, but they can't fly," she said again with a voice so sweet, so warm, that it drew me in.

"Have you seen people trying to fly?" My voice had turned animated.

"Oh, yes. She tried. The man helped her, but she crashed."

"The man?"

"Oh, yes. He pushed her to help her fly."

"What did the man look like?"

"Big round face. Lots of white hair." She spoke slowly, clearly.

"Where were you when you saw the man push her?"

"Hiding in the alley, behind the dumpster."

"Why were you hiding?'

"Bullies steal my coffee. I hide to drink it," she said with confidence.

Without another word the bag lady waddled off like a penguin on ice. Three grey pigeons flew down from a building's ledge, landed on the sidewalk and waddled down the street behind her. Their heads bobbed in the same rhythmic motion as the bag lady's.

I could hear a man yelling at the cops. I walked down the street to get a full view of the alley.

"When will this carnival end?" The angry man yelled.

"As soon as the investigation is completed, Sir." A young cop answered respectfully.

"Investigation? Into what, a drunken fool killing himself? Shut this bullshit down. I've got trucks that need to come and go. I've got a business to run!"

I looked up to the top floor of the warehouse. Milo Regis' round face was sticking out of an open window. He had a full head of white hair. He slammed the window shut when he noticed I was watching him.

It was time for me to question the hot-headed Regis about Patty Walker. But today was not the day. Feeling exhausted, I drove to the office and slept on the couch for the rest of the afternoon.

At five o'clock, I woke from a restless sleep. Was dreaming about Arnie. A sudden emptiness blew through me and hollowed my bones. I shook it off and stood up from the couch, stumbled over to the small sink and threw cold water on my face. Still suffering a little from the hangover, I decided to go for a cocktail, thinking that what I needed was to get back on the horse that threw me.

I changed into the fresh shirt, tie and suit that I kept in the office closet, and grabbed a clean hat and headed out the door for a whisky bar in Santa Monica, called Five In The Afternoon. It's a cedar shake, rustic joint with outside deck seating along the beach. Getting into my '61 maroon Buick Electra, I headed west on Santa Monica Boulevard.

This wintery night, the smell of ocean, and the breaking waves, lifted me out of my despair. I had just finished a Scotch and water, when my heart popped like a hot balloon over the sudden excitement. Mya Regis walked through the door of Five In The Afternoon. She was wearing a skintight knee-length, light grey silk dress with small black buttons from the neck down to the knees. It had long sleeves and a Nehru collar. Her hair was tied in a Samurai ponytail, with loose strands of hair falling on both sides of her face, like red lightning bolts. When she noticed me, her light green eyes sparkled as she walked over to my table. My breath felt like it was jammed in my throat.

"Mr. Stone, how lovely to see you again, and so soon."

"Hello, Ms. Regis. Is this a coincidence, the two of us here at the same time?"

"I don't believe in coincidences, Mr. Stone," she said with a warm smile.

Smiling back at her I asked: "Would you like to join me?"

"It would be rude of me to take you away from your work. Unless, of course, you are not here for sleuthing. Although, I can't imagine otherwise." Mya's vibrant eyes were magnetic, pulling my eyes into hers.

"I'm here as a patron, off the clock until eight. Please join me," I said.

I stood up and pulled a chair from the table. With her hand in mine, she sat down as gracefully as she did in my office. While sliding her chair up to the table, I could feel the heat radiating from her body. It was a lot of heat. It hit me like a Santa Ana wind had moved through my blood. I sat back down. The waiter came over immediately.

"Ms. Regis, how lovely to see you. The usual?"

"Thank you, Ken. Yes, the usual, please."

"You're a popular woman," I said playfully. "You must come here a..."

"I own this bar, Mr. Stone."

"Oh. I thought Sherry Miller was the owner."

"Sherry is the general manager, the visible boss that I've created. I'm the silent boss. Sherry runs this place pretty much on her own."

Mya's drink, a Famous Grouse Scotch Blend with water on the rocks, came to the table. When she lifted the glass to her lips it was like she was seducing it. She caught me staring at her mouth, and her eyes told me that she wanted me to stare.

"Mr. Stone..."

"Please, call me Joe."

"Okay, Joe. How is the investigation coming along? And please, call me Mya."

I smiled warmly. "I'm not here as an investigator. I'm here having a drink with a beautiful woman, whose company I'm enjoying. Let's talk about you and the reason behind your silent boss arrangement."

She blushed slightly, and said: "It is a way for me to have a drink with a handsome man and to not have it spread across the gossip columns. Believe it or not, Joe, I cherish my privacy." She paused for a few seconds, then continued: "My father has no idea I own this bar, nor did Scott. Are you married, Joe?"

I shook my head several times and raised my eyebrows. Couldn't say why I raised them. I just did.

"No. Never found the time to cultivate a relationship into marriage." I stopped, took in a slow breath and said: "Um, look, Mya, ah, would it be inappropriate to have lunch together, after the investigation is completed?"

"I would prefer dinner at my place in Bel Air. This is my apology for snapping at you the other day in your office." She handed me a card. "Call me. And if you don't, I'll show up at your office again."

The look in her eyes had me dialing the number in my head. I nodded, smiled, and tipped my glass towards her. We talked some more. She told me that she and Scott Drum had lived separately for the past year. Her father was unaware of their separation, because she and Scott were not sure of where the marriage was going. She said that they had grown apart and were headed in different directions. After the separation, Mya stayed at their house in Bel Air. Scott Drum was content with the apartment above the club. They stayed married for many reasons, but passion for each other was not one of the reasons. Mya said that they were good friends. I sensed that she hurt deeply over Scott Drum's death, though she hid it well.

When I was ready to leave, Mya took my hand and turned her cheek for me to kiss.

6

At The Open Blouse, only five of the nine employed girls showed up for the inquest. Manager Bryce Parker was also there. He was a good-looking young guy with cropped blond hair, and was dressed in sporty clothes. Standing five-seven, Parker was lean and fit with dark blue eyes on a handsome face.

Of the four girls absent, Jill Sabin was the only one in town. Earlier in the day Bryce Parker had called Sabin at her home, to tell her she needed to attend the inquest. He told me Sabin had replied contemptuously, 'I don't work there anymore, you asshole'. Jill was fired for hand-jobbing a patron in a back booth. The patron had slipped her two hundred bucks. They got caught in mid-act by a bouncer, who threw the patron out the door, and Bryce Parker fired Sabin. Parker told me Sabin had kept the two-hundred bucks.

Also absent was a Ms. Kimmie Turner, who had worked at the club for about month. She was out of town. Two of the other absent girls were back in their Midwestern hometowns, deciding it was safer to live there.

The inquest lasted about two hours. Jewels, Woodhouse and I talked to each employee separately. They had alibis, except for Bryce Parker. He was home alone.

"Did anybody stop by your house?" I asked.

"No, Mr. Stone," Parker replied. "I went to bed early."

"Do you live alone?"

"No, Mr. Stone," he replied politely, never losing his engaging smile. "I live with my mother."

"Will she vouch for you?"

"No, Mr. Stone. She was out with friends. I was in bed before she got home."

The club's employees knew about the relationship between Scott Drum and Patty Walker. They said it was low-key.

"Patty was smart and strong-willed," Bryce Parker said with a firm voice. "She knew what she wanted in life and was going for it. She had a degree in business. Scott saw an opportunity to use her business smarts to benefit the club." Parker lowered his voice and said: "There was talk of Scott making Patty general manager." He pulled his lips tightly together and shook his head and Parker's face morphed into an old man's expression, heavy and sad. Darkness swept over his eyes. I could see there was something taxing his mind. He shook it off and smiled again, but the smile was artificial this time.

"One more thing, Mr. Parker, we'll need Jill Sabin's address."

"I have it in the office, Mr. Stone. Let me get it for you." Bryce Parker's behavior reminded me of a submissive child, eager to please his parents.

When Parker returned and handed me the paper with Sabin's address, I was startled by what I had read. Detective Jewels saw the look of surprise on my face, but before I could hand him the note, the club's phone rang. It was for Jewels. He and Woodhouse were needed at Griffith Park. Jewels' expression had changed to a frown. He asked me to follow along. I absentmindedly stuffed Jill Sabin's address inside the pocket of my overcoat.

Below the Griffith Observatory stood the Lincoln. It was parked in the dense darkness of a redwood grove. It looked like a boulder until my headlights caught the green metallic finish, making it sparkle. I got out of my car and Jewels and Woodhouse got out of theirs. We walked over to the Lincoln and looked inside.

Mya Regis lay across the back seat, face up. Her open green eyes held a paralyzed stare, like the unmoving glass eyes of a child's doll. There was a bullet hole dead-center forehead. One of her arms hung over the seat and down to the floor, like she was reaching for something. A revolver lay at her finger tips. Her light grey button-front dress was unbuttoned up to her waist, and her legs were spread apart. Her panties were missing, and her green silk bra was partially exposed along the top of the dress, where a few buttons were undone.

Beside her on the seat was a typed suicide note. It read:

Scott,
I could not go on without you
I will always love you
Mya

There was no signature.

A quick chill splintered my chest. My heart felt like it was collapsing. I struggled to keep my balance while walking back to the car. Sitting behind the steering wheel, my head felt hammered and cracked open. Pulling a pint of Scotch from the glove compartment, I watched the disturbing scene of Mya Regis' body lifted from the Lincoln, plopped onto a gurney and slid into the back of the ambulance. A white sheet was draped over her, like a cheap slipcover over a used couch.

Possibly, she drove herself to this location. Maybe to meet somebody. The keys were still in the ignition. Time of death was about two hours ago. That would have made it shortly after I had left Five In The Afternoon, where Mya and I had drinks together, made plans together.

When the ambulance left the scene, there was no siren, just a blinking red light floating down the dark road, like a firefly alone in the woods. With the silence that followed, my chest turned tight as a bowline knot.

I chugged the whisky. My body turned numb.

Three days later, after a media frenzy over the tragic death of the well-known socialite, Mya Regis was laid to rest in Westwood Village Cemetery next to her mother Amy Regis. It was the vault section of the graveyard, loaded with bronze plaques of famous dead people.

It was raining lightly and the grey sky was a testament to the collective sadness that had gathered for Mya.

The funeral was a dense crowd of politicians, movie people, throngs of socialites, a gaggle of reporters, and a horde of desperate onlookers. There were also a few employees from The Open Blouse, including Jill Sabin. Bryce Parker pointed her out to me. She wore a long black wool coat with a black head scarf and large black sunglasses.

Surrounded by several giant bodyguards, Milo Regis stood next to his daughter's casket. Before the casket was slid into the vault, his right hand reached out and touched the top of the oak coffin, as if feeling for a heartbeat. Then he touched the bronze wall plaque with his wife's name inscribed on it. Milo Regis looked weak and undone, like he had unraveled from his head to his feet.

A forensic sweep of the Lincoln, and the surrounding area where it was found, had turned up nothing useful. There were some spent camera flashbulbs scattered around the ground. Most likely from tourists.

During the autopsy some blond hair was found tangled in Mya Regis' red pubic hair. It was not the short and curly type. It was more like head hair. It made sense then that the dried, whiteish gobs found on her pubis were identified as saliva. As with the other murders, the pistol that killed Mya Regis was a chrome Colt .32 Snub-nose revolver. The serial numbers were filed off and there was one spent cartridge in the otherwise empty cylinder.

A menacing killing pattern had emerged on the streets of Los Angeles, and it was beginning to feel personal. Now, along with tracking down Arnie Bender's murderer, I would have to find justice for Mya Regis, too. Because her eyes told me that we could have been good together.

7

Four days after Mya Regis' funeral, I stood in front of the Regis warehouse on Paloma Street. It was a 1930s four-story red brick building, with floor-to-ceiling metal-framed windows. A massive red, white and blue porcelain painted sign hung over the front entrance. It was designed like a waving banner and read: *REGIS FABRICS*.

Had a three o'clock appointment with Mr. Fabric Baron himself. Clicking my tongue against the roof of my mouth, I straightened my posture and walked towards the building. Doubt about the meeting with Milo Regis had slipped into my head. I tried to shake that feeling loose. It wouldn't budge.

At the door, a two-hundred-fifty-pound, six-foot-seven body guard, with the voice of an old bullfrog, ordered me to hand over any weapons. I surrendered my Ruger.

Inside the large lobby, another guard of the same stature gave me the once-over two times. The second time was slower, more feely. I think he liked touching men. He then led me to a cage-style elevator, where another giant waited to ride with me. We rode in silence while the old machine rattled all the way to the fourth floor. The giant never took his menacing eyes off me.

When I stepped out of the elevator, another giant patted me down quickly, only once. He ordered me to sit in a plush grey chair inside a small, square room. It had bare white walls and no other furniture. I waited in silence, inside this windowless box, bored by the sophomoric minimalism, while the guard stood with his back against the door, holding his disdainful eyes on me. After five minutes a wall intercom buzzed. The guard picked up the receiver, listened to the message, hung the receiver on its base and said with a loud, brassy voice: "Mr. Regis will see you now. Follow me."

He was not friendly.

We walked to a multi-locked steel door at the end of a short windowless hallway. The giant opened the door and announced in a pleasant tone: "Mr. Stone is here to see you, Sir."

When I entered his office, Milo Regis didn't bother to stand up, nor did he present his hand to shake mine, though mine was extended. In front of his massive dark oak desk were two plush dark grey chairs. He didn't offer me a chair, he just glared at me, like I was an intrusive moron. I dropped my hand to my side. It twitched a little. My other hand held my hat.

The white walls of his office were decorated with photographs of him, standing or sitting, with famous people. There was also a photograph of Milo Regis and Police Commissioner Daniel McKenna standing together on a golf course. There were no photographs of his wife or daughter.

Behind him was a floor-to-ceiling, wall-to-wall metal framed window with a view of Paloma Street. The smaller window to my left looked down on the alley, where Amy Regis and Arnie Bender had died.

"You get one minute with this bullshit. Get on with it!" His vulgar tone cut into me, with what felt like a dirty edge. It almost made me feel grimy.

"Mr. Regis, first, I'm sorry for your loss, and..." He cut me off clean and sharp, yelling:

"I don't need your worthless sympathy! Why are you taking up my time?"

I tensed up, then realized it was time to take this miserable bull by the horns. Dropping my hat on a chair, I walked up to his desk, placed my fingertips on its polished surface, and switched my voice to an interrogative tone.

"Where were you on the night Patty Walker went missing?"

"The audacity of *you* to ask *me* a question like that! I could have you bounced down to the street in seconds." His face turned red and he was pulling hard for breath. He started dry coughing, which was part choking, part wheezing, part gasping for air. He sounded like an old goat with asthma. He finally caught his breath and composed himself. I stepped back from the desk, thinking he might be contagious. Then I took a solid stance, and threw a dirty question at him, hoping to provoke an incriminating answer.

"Wouldn't it be faster to drop me from the roof?" My sarcasm was bold and stupid. He jumped up from his chair, pulled a black Colt .32 revolver from behind his back and aimed it at my forehead. I didn't flinch, keeping my eyes on his, until he lowered the weapon. Then he belly-laughed like an idiot, sat down again and laid the pistol on the desk. His eyes were opaque and colorless.

"Who the hell is Patty Walker? Why should I know her?" Regis growled in a low, crackly voice.

"She worked for your late son-in-law Scott Drum. She was..."

"I still don't know who you're talking about." A dark, murky layer spread over his eyes like spilled black paint, as if to cover over his shameless dishonesty.

"Scott Drum was involved with Walker."

"What does Drum's two-timing my daughter have to do with me? And why are you asking me questions about a dead tramp?" he said with a bitter, sarcastic tone. "Are you too dumb to notice that the cops found her?"

His breathing was heavier, and his dark eyes darted around the room as if trapped insects looking for an escape. He was losing patience again, and rapidly thumped the butt of the pistol with the tip of his thick, hairy index finger.

"Scott Drum paid me to find out why she was missing."

"Like I said, shit for brains, never heard of her, and…"

"Your daughter told you about the affair, told you the girl's name. You asked her if you should handle it. What did you mean by that? What did you mean by handle it?"

"Get out of my office, you babbling moron!"

His hairy finger pressed a small chrome button on his desk. The giant came in, and with a vice grip for a hand, grabbed my arm around the bicep, nearly cutting off the blood flow, and pulled me to the elevator. Then he sent me to the first floor. At the front door, the giant that I encountered coming in shoved my weapon into my gut. It was a hard handoff intended to crack a rib, but I had anticipated the blow, and pulled back from the force of the impact. Making sure I had an unpleasant exit, he shoved me from behind. I stumbled across the sidewalk and almost fell into the road.

The meeting lasted less than a minute, but I had caught Milo Regis in a brazen lie.

Leaning against my Buick, I wondered what Regis was hiding by lying about not knowing of Patty Walker. And did the bag lady really see Amy Regis fall from the roof after being shoved?

I looked up and down the street hoping to see the bag lady again. Then I remembered the note Bryce Parker had handed to me at the inquest. The one with Jill Sabin's address. I pulled the folded paper out of my overcoat pocket and read: *700 Laurel Canyon Blvd. Apt. 30.* The same building Patty Walker had lived in.

8

Wind gusts buffeted the Buick while I was parked in front of Sabin's building. Sitting there in the car, the chassis jerked with the clumsiness of a vibrating bed, and the Mexican fan palms, on both sides of the building, rattled like cold skeletons. A dark sky covered the area with its heavy lid, suppressing most of the daylight. I sat there and waited for the weather's attitude to let up, and thought about Arnie Bender and his great laugh. About Mya Regis, and the way she walked out of my office, and how her fluid motion made my eyes float along with her.

My heart raced. Memories can do that, make the heart race.

A sudden gust hit the car with a tight punch that knocked me back to the present. It was a solid punch, followed by heavy raindrops pelting the Buick's roof. Having had enough of this prize-fighting rain, I put on my hat, pulled up my coat collar and ran the twenty feet from the car to the building's entrance. I slipped, almost fell, as the wind shoved me sideways. By the time I reached the awning over the front entrance, my coat and hat were dripping wet.

The three-story apartment building was a plain, light grey stucco job with white trim. There were ten lemon-yellow doors on each floor, with black numbers tacked to the doors. The exterior hallways were guarded with thin black wrought iron railings, and there were lofty yucca trees all around the front end of the building.

I usually took the stairs, needing to work off the steak, fries and booze, but on this stormy day, the dry elevator was a refuge.

I stopped at the second floor. The doors rattled and drew open with a worn-out scraping sound. Struggling against the rain and the wind, I walked the outdoor hallway to Apartment 20. Patty Walker's former place. Detectives Jewels and Woodhouse had said they swept the apartment, found nothing of interest.

Looking through a window, I could see that the apartment was empty, except for two painters rolling out the walls with fresh white paint.

I gripped the slippery handrail and decided to climb the stairs to the third floor. Maybe I needed the challenge, or the feeling of accomplishment. Either way, I gained nothing but more wet clothes from the climb.

At Jill Sabin's door, I knocked gently, waited ten seconds, then knocked again, harder this time.

"Yes? Hello?" From somewhere deep inside the apartment, came a woman's thin tentative voice. She sounded anxious.

"Jill Sabin?" I kept my tone relaxed.

"Yes. Who are you?"

"Joe Stone, a Private Detective, Miss Sabin. I have a few questions about Patty Walker."

"Look. Listen. The police were already here. I told them what I know." She sounded irritated.

"I'm a *private* investigator. Could we talk about The Open Blouse, about the staff?"

"I don't work there. I can't help you." From the sound of her voice, she was now standing behind the door.

"But you did work there until you were fired for violating employee rules. Please open the door, Miss Sabin, so we can talk under better conditions."

The hammering wind nailed me to the building. Sabin opened the door, but kept the chain lock attached while she stayed out of sight.

"Miss Sabin, please unlock the door."

"Why should I?" She sounded suspicious now.

"Scott Drum hired me to find Patty Walker before they were both killed."

The chain-lock slid. The door opened slowly.

Entering the apartment, I was stunned by the strong resemblance between Jill Sabin and Patty Walker. Sabin's watery blue eyes and her fine facial structure were like Walker's.

On a table in the dining room was a photo of her and Walker with identical smiles, sitting at a beach. Except for Sabin's cropped blond hair, the resemblance seemed intentional, like somebody had played with cloning.

Then I remembered what Mya Regis had said in my office: *Most blonds look alike. Wouldn't you agree, Mr. Stone?*

Except for a dozen boxes taped shut, Jill Sabin's apartment was nearly empty. Aside from the table and chair in the dining room, there was no other furniture. In the bedroom I could see an unmade mattress on the floor with scattered blankets across the room.

"Why are you moving?" I asked politely.

"I don't have enough money for this place." She was agitated.

"Where are you moving to?"

"Boyle Heights, with a girlfriend, until I can get a job, then a place of my own." She stopped talking, and looked at me with distrustful eyes. "How did you know I lived here?"

"Bryce Parker gave me…"

"To hell with Parker!" she snapped. "He's the reason I'm jobless. He's a backstabbing hypocrite."

"But you violated employee rules."

"I needed the money," she retorted shamelessly.

"Yes, of course. Maybe you could help me un…"

"Look, if you're here thinking that I'm going to give you a hand-job well, you can leave right now. I'm not in the mood."

"No, Miss Sabin. No, not that. When I saw that you and Patty Walker lived in the same complex, I was curious. How did that come about? Who lived here first?"

We stood a few feet apart. I was in my wet coat, holding my wet hat, and Jill Sabin was in a white tee shirt and braless. The tee shirt accented her small, buoyant breasts, and her tight red mini shorts drew my attention to her shapely legs. White bobby-socks stuck out of white tennis sneakers. Altogether, her body was lean and strong looking, and her movements were graceful, like that of a trained dancer.

The space heater was set on high. I could feel sweat forming under my arms.

"I was living here first and was working at the club first." She spoke fast, with anger. "When Patty started working at the club, she was renting a room in a women's boarding house. We became friends at work, and a place came up here for rent."

"You seem angry," I said.

"Angry? I'm so angry, so goddamn angry!"

"At who?"

"At Bryce Parker. He's a deceiving asshole. Behind his happy-go-lucky face, Parker is a jealous bastard and a heartless hypocrite."

"If you don't mind me asking, how so?"

"Parker is a sleazy womanizer. He took advantage of the new girls who came to work at the club. When I started working there, he hit on me at the right time. I needed sex." Her head bobbed back and forth, and she rolled her eyes. "We screwed behind the bar after closing. Unfortunately for me, it was anticlimactic," she said coldly. Sabin pulled her lips back tightly then shook her head from side to side, while speaking through clenched teeth. "Together, we broke two rules: no sex on club property and no sex with other employees."

"So that's why he's a hypocrite. I get it now."

"Look, Mr. Stone, I've got hours of cleaning to do, so..." She waved her open hand towards the door.

"Yes, of course, I'll be going. What about your relationship with Scott Drum? Was it professional? Friendly? Intimate? I mean, you look so much like Patty Walker. And how was your relationship with Mya Regis, was it...?"

She cut me off cold and hard: "You need to leave now or I'll call the manager." Her blue eyes were incandescent and jittery.

After leaving Jill Sabin's apartment, I drove to Abe's Deli. A hot lunch and a glass of beer filled my stomach, but my mind was on Mya Regis. I ordered another beer. Maybe to kill the feelings I had developed for her.

I drove back to my apartment, took a hot shower and turned up the heater.

Thinking about Arnie Bender's murder and feeling disturbed, I poured a glass of Scotch and threw it back with infuriating force, wishing it would knock Arnie back to life.

At seven forty-five I crawled into bed exhausted. Or maybe I just needed to turn off this menacing world for a while.

9

Ten thirty the next morning at the office, I was troubled by the thought that some people are inherently evil, and they bring that evil into the world at birth, hiding it between the folds of their baby fat, until it shoots out like venom into the lives of others.

The ringing phone pulled me out of my agitated head.

"Hey, Boss, I... ah..." It was Dave Wells.

"How's the diamond necklace case, Dave?"

"Got it figured out. Should wrap it up in a day or two. Listen. I stopped by Millie's house to see how she was doing. She didn't answer when I knocked. Tried the door, it was unlocked. I found her unconscious on the couch. The cops and medics are here now. She mixed whisky with sedatives. Millie is dead, Joe."

For twenty years Millie had been in my life. We tried to be a couple, tried living together. We were good lovers but lousy homemakers. Our friendship meant more to us, so we stopped pretending we could hold a domestic relationship together. I introduced Millie to Arnie Bender. They fell hard for each other. The three of us became like family, and we were together most days. Yet, since Arnie's murder, I had been neglecting Millie, putting my suffering first. Should have pulled myself together. Millie needed me to hold her in my arms, while she fell apart.

I could barely breathe, needed to go outside!

Stumbling down the office stairs to the street, I walked fast. People, cars, buildings zoomed by in a dense, glaring blur of light and sound. Four blocks later, I slowed down, caught my breath and looked around. I was headed in the direction of Wilcox Avenue. The Open Blouse was in view. It looked strangely artificial and real at the same time.

On the other side of Hollywood Boulevard, the bag lady sat on a park bench. Before crossing the street to sit with her, I stopped in a café, ordered two coffees to go. I was shivering. My teeth chattered. The waiter said my face was dead-white, asked if I was alright, if I needed help. I dropped a pile of money on the counter and said: "I must be coming down with something." His dull grey eyes narrowed down on mine with skepticism, as he stared at me with an unsettled expression, like I was a junkie, hopped on drugs.

When I approached her in the park, the bag lady's eyes were closed, her head faced forward, and her knobby chin jutted out. She appeared to be sleeping, but there was no slack-jaw, no snoring. She sat perfectly still like a weathered statue. A few head-bobbing pigeons waddled around her feet, pecking at croissant crumbs.

"Good morning. I hope I'm not disturbing your sleep," I said in a low voice, not to startle her.

"I'm not sleeping," she answered with a childlike response. "I'm communing with my pigeons, but I'm finished now." She opened her eyes and looked down at the pigeons. "These three follow me around." Her voice was lyrical.

"They seem like good company. Have you named them?"

"Oh yes. I call them Fah, Sol and Lah." She giggled. "See how they looked at me when I said their names."

I nodded, smiled, then handed her a cup of coffee.

She took the cup, rose quickly from the bench, and said: "Come. We'll hide behind these bushes to drink our coffees."

"It's okay. I'm with you. The bullies will stay away. Please sit and enjoy your coffee."

She sat back down, holding her cup with both torn-gloved hands. She placed her nose to the rim of the cup and said: "Ah."

Her layered clothes were frayed: she looked like a ball of yarn coming undone. I sat next to her while we sipped our drinks together like trusted friends.

From the park bench, The Open Blouse was in view. I watched Bryce Parker pull into the parking lot. He got out of his car and carried a large grey paper bag into the club. It contained something that filled it completely.

"You look tired, maybe a little sick. Your face is pale," the bag lady said in sweet rising and falling tones.

"I've had a rough couple of days."

"Too much booze, not much sleep?"

"Yeah. Something like that." We drank more coffee, sitting in silence again. My breathing was still fast and shallow. I kept shaking and trying to hide my distress over Millie's death from the bag lady.

I turned my head to look at her and noticed a new addition to her bric-a-brac. Sitting there on top of a bag were two rectangular pieces of brown cardboard, about 11" x 14", held together with white string. Sandwiched between the cardboard were sheets of white paper.

"What do you do with that?" I pointed at the cardboard.

"I'm an artist. I draw. Sometimes every day, sometimes not so much. But I'm still an artist, even when I don't draw." I couldn't help smiling at her jubilant conviction.

She placed the bundle on her lap, untied the string, lifted the top cardboard, and proceeded to flip through her drawings with pride. I was surprised to see colored pencil drawings of the streets, buildings and people of Los Angeles. People with big heads and small bodies. Pigeons, dogs and squirrels with human faces, and sidewalks made of eyes and mouths. One of the drawings was of Milo Regis' warehouse. The windows were menacing eyes, and the front entrance was a human mouth with viper fangs. Unexpectedly, I was startled by a drawing of Milo Regis, perfectly rendered, pushing Amy Regis off the roof of his warehouse. Another drawing was of Amy Regis lying in the alley on her stomach. Tiny black wings were coming out of her back. The bag lady saw my bewildered expression.

"She crashed. Her wings were too small for her to fly," the bag lady said, her eyes heavy with sorrow.

With urgency in my voice, I asked: "When did you draw these?"

The bag lady looked at me shocked. Her expression froze and her eyes widened with alarm.

"When I was hiding behind the dumpster in the alley. Hiding from the bullies." She was scared.

I softened my voice and said: "I'm sorry. I didn't mean to frighten you."

We sat in silence again. She sipped her coffee, watching me, while I looked at the Regis drawings that were now sitting on my lap.

Amy Regis' light purple dress and dark purple coat were perfectly detailed. Thinking back, there was no account of the colors of her clothing in any of the newspaper articles that had covered her death. The only place these details were described was in the file at the courthouse. Yet, the drawing of Amy Regis lying in the alley was exact, almost like a forensic photograph. Even the white scarf around her neck was accurate. There was no way the bag lady could have known this, unless she had seen Amy Regis lying dead in the alley.

"Where do you live?" I asked politely.

"Here today, or down there tomorrow," she was pointing. "Or maybe not around here. Maybe someplace that I can't see from here." Her sweet response made me smile.

"Can I pay you for these two drawings?" I pulled five twenties from my wallet and handed her the money. She refused the cash, saying that her art wasn't for sale, but I could borrow the drawings, if I promised to return them. I promised.

Looking in the direction of The Open Blouse, I watched Bryce Parker walk back to his car, still carrying the large grey bag. It seemed empty now.

I stood up from the bench and said: "I have to go. What's your name?"

The bag lady rose slowly, gathered her belongings, and without answering my question, she waddled down the street. Fah, Sol and Lah waddled behind her, until the four of them turned a corner.

10

Had to walk fast to reach Bryce Parker before he got to his car. The coffee sparked some heat, made it easier for me to move. Still, my stomach felt like it had gone through a gut grinder. Millie. Arnie. Yeah, through a gut grinder. I walked faster. My heart seemed to be lodged in my throat, choking me like a thug. I loosened my tie and shirt collar. A fist of cold air hit my neck and face. I pulled the air in, was able to breathe properly again.

"Parker. Hey, Parker!"

When Bryce Parker turned and saw me, his eyes were suspicious and his faced sagged with deep dark lines, then his mouth dropped open, like he was caught in the act of some crime. He rolled the bag up tightly and held it close to his body. Suddenly, his face changed to an engaging expression. His eyes brightened and his sagging face pulled in tightly. Yeah, this All–American boy could turn on the charm. But I needed to grill him, to shake him out of his cover. I suspected he knew something about the murders of Scott Drum and Patty Walker, though I can't say what my reason for this suspicion was. It was just there, nagging my mind.

We shook hands, and Parker took my hand with a feminine touch, then he pulled his hand back quickly without losing the happy face. While we exchanged small talk, he clutched the grey bag tighter, almost protectively. When I asked about its contents, he said it had contained extra clothes that he kept in his locker, at the club.

Bryce Parker was a little taller than Jill Sabin, and I was surprised at how much they resembled each other, down to the cropped blond hair. Even their faces had similar lines and form.

The grey sky turned a shade darker, light rain had started. I tucked the bag lady's drawings inside my overcoat and said: "Let's go inside the club. I have a few questions."

"Oh, Mr. Stone, I'm sorry, but I'm in a rush and…"

"Look, Parker, it's either with me now, or the homicide bulls will send you an invitation for a sit-down at their house. What's it going to be?" His eyes held a dull somewhat drugged look. He grimaced, and his face became pale. It was an empty threat, but he bought it.

Inside the club it was dark and chilly, and it smelled of stale booze, old tobacco, and rank cologne. All the chairs had been placed on top of the tables, and the barstools on top of the bar. Parker flipped on some bright lights. We sat at a table near the only window.

Bryce Parker did everything he could to appear as small as a rodent. He clutched the rolled-up bag closer to his body and made his eyes big and innocent-looking. His posture was slouched and his chest was pulled in, like he was hiding something in there.

"With Scott Drum dead and the club shut down, why do you have a key?"

"I'm the new general manager. I have to keep the club in good condition, until it reopens." Parker's voice was faint, as if he was about to run out of breath.

"Reopens? When?"

"As soon as Mr. Regis takes over the title. The club was in Mya's name, not Scott's. We'll be open for business in about two months." He sat there drawn in and still, with only his jaw moving when he spoke. His eyes were unsteady, darting around the room, like they were running from a menacing darkness.

"Always the model employee. That's you Parker, the model employee," I said sarcastically while thinking about Jill Sabin's upsetting situation. "Tell me what your relationship was like with Scott Drum?"

"He was my boss. It was like that. Boss and employee. He trusted me and I trusted him." His eyes were still avoiding mine.

"Did you respect him or did you envy him?"

"Envy him? I'm confused, Mr. Stone. What are you trying to say?" He was looking out the window now. I could see our reflections in the glass pane of the picture window. We were eyeing each other.

"Scott Drum had a beautiful wife," I said, "and he was having a relationship with the equally beautiful Patty Walker, while running this successful whisky club." I stopped to watch Parker's face in the reflection. His eyes were flying all around, landing on nothing. I needed to rattle him, to bust him open.

"Parker," I said with a stern voice. "You were menial, a peon in Drum's world of success, and you resented that. And you wanted to have sex with Patty Walker, the way you had sex with some of other new girls you hired. But Walker was off limits to your horndog bullshit. You took offense to that, and you turned bitter enough to break the employee rules behind Scott Drum's back. You backstabbed your boss and continued carrying on like a model employee." My voice remained steady. "You goddamn hypocrite. You screwed Jill

Sabin behind the bar on the dirty floor. Then you sacked her for breaking the same rules that you broke with her. What kind of bullshit were you dishing out?"

Parker inhaled hard, caught his breath in his throat and held it there, like he was suffocating on it. When he answered, his words pulled themselves over a lump of saliva. They sounded thick and wet.

"Jill wanted nothing to do with me after that one time," he said in a whiny voice. "She avoided me like I was contaminated. Yeah, I was crazy for Patty, but Scott moved in on her, and she fell for him." He stopped talking and wiped his mouth with his sleeve. Shaking his head, he said bitterly: "I couldn't stand having both girls ignoring me at work." His facial muscles tightened like constrictor knots, then his tone drew fire. "I canned Jill Sabin to get one of them out of my life. I had the chance to do it, and I did it. Is that what you wanted to hear?" Parker put his right-hand palm facing up on the table, and spoke through clenched teeth: "Look at me, Mr. Stone. I'm a twenty-eight-year-old nobody who lives with his mother. This club is all I have." His eyes pooled. But I needed to keep pushing, to make him spill.

I pulled the diamond earring from my coat pocket and dropped it on the table.

"Whose earring is this?" I demanded.

Parker was spilling tears now. "It belonged to Mya Regis," he said flatly, almost whispering.

I had to press him harder. My instinct told me that Bryce Parker could be a key player in this fatal tragedy.

"How do you know it belonged to Mya?"

"I saw her wearing them." His sudden weakened tone made me think that he was lying.

"What was your relationship with Mya Regis?" He didn't say anything. His eyes were looking away from me again. I thumped my fist on the table, and the loud, heavy sound reverberated throughout the room.

"Answer me, Parker!" His body jerked back into the chair, as if I had swung a blade at him.

Speaking in a taut whisper, teeth clenched, he said: "I liked Mya. She liked me. We were friends." He paused to swallow the saliva lump in his throat. "Imagine, a nobody like me and Mya let me into her life. She invited me to her house in Bel Air. She introduced me to her friends." Tears dripped along his cheeks, dangling off the end of his chin like glass raindrops, until they fell to the bag, creating dark blotches.

"Who wanted Mya Regis dead?" My tone was severe, and my determination for an answer was persistent.

Bryce Parker sat up straight, yelling at me, with spit flying from his mouth: "Get out, now, or I'll call Mr. Regis!" His contorted face was in a panicky sweat, and his blue eyes were bulbous and hot, like fireballs aimed at me. He jumped up from the table, rushed to the telephone behind the bar, and maniacally dialed a number. When I was heading out the door, I heard Parker on the phone: "Hello! Mr. Regis…"

11

On Hollywood Boulevard the wind laid dead, like somebody had gutted it. A drizzle blurred the air in front of me. I pulled my hat low, and shoved my hands into my coat pockets. I was walking fast. The grey sky was holding a cold indifference. It felt like the end of so much.

Millie. Arnie. There was no way for me to come to terms with their deaths without avenging Arnie's murder: to watch the killer's eyes, my hands on his throat, his last breath exhaled into this double-crossing world.

The deaths of my friends had thrown me off kilter emotionally, even mentally.

My mind raced with this hot-headed thought: the world was full of wicked people who tear into the existence of others, taking everything, even their lives.

My heart was smoldering with bitterness. Scott Drum, Patty Walker, Arnie Bender, Mya Regis, and Millie Bender, dead. And for what?

Needing to steady my nerves, I stopped walking. As my breathing settled down, I found myself in front of a liquor store, thinking that life is nothing more than a slap in the face and a lonely funeral.

I walked inside the store, bought a bottle of Old Grand-Dad. At least that was something I could hold on to, until I decided to kill it.

It was two-thirty when I got back to the office. Dave Wells was sitting in the pink-cushioned chair with his boots on the low windowsill. His eyes were closed. Dave had pulled an all-nighter on the stolen jewelry case.

It seemed like another lifetime when we were in the Army together. We were both assigned to the Criminal Investigation Department on the same base. After we left the Army, we stayed in touch.

A few years back Wells called from Bozeman, Montana. Said he was bored with investigating missing goats, cattle, sheep and stolen farm equipment. I invited him to come to Los Angeles to work for me. Though I got him to shed his cowboy clothes for slick city suits, he refused to wear anything but snakeskin cowboy boots. He had thirty pairs made from different vipers.

Dave Wells was a former rodeo cowboy and one hell of an investigator. Though with a full head of blond hair and bronzed skin, he looked more like a surfer. Standing six-one at a hundred-and-ninety pounds, he was built with the strength of an oak tree. Nothing shook him. Nothing backed him down. Wells was a good friend to have on your side. But for some reason we were not as close as Arnie Bender and I had been. And it was easy for me to see that Wells was jealous of that friendship.

When I intentionally slammed the fifth of bourbon on the desk, Wells jolted while instinctively reaching for his .357 cowboy rod. We laughed and shook hands. I hadn't seen him in a few days.

"A little early for the firewater, Boss?"

"Maybe. Maybe not." I stood behind the desk looking at him, and confessing: "I just can't get a reading on these killings. Arnie Bender's murder digs into my gut like a rusted fork. Now Millie Bender's suicide. It's all a senseless waste of life."

"Maybe it's time to let the homicide dicks work it out on their own. We've got that new theft case of that Picasso drawing to keep us busy, and that other..."

"If Arnie Bender hadn't been murdered, I'd agree with you. But I can't let it go. And then Mya Regis' murder. Why?" My frustration was like electric tension, just short of combusting.

"Joe, listen, I get that you were mesmerized by that gorgeous dame. Maybe you even fell for her. Maybe she fell for you. I don't know. But you've got to get your head on straight and let that case go. I'm telling you, Joe, let it go."

"I can't, Dave. I'm sorry," I said shrugging my shoulders, then added: "You'll have to finish up the art theft yourself."

Wells didn't say anything to that. He just stared at me with unmoving eyes.

I opened the whisky and poured two drinks. We nodded at each other and threw them back.

That's when the office door opened slow and wide.

One of Milo Regis' giants filled the door frame. I recognized him as the guard who shoved me out the front door of the warehouse.

Wells got up from his chair. I sat down in mine. The giant ducked under the door header and entered the office with his massive form, filling the small space like a two-story house.

"I's gots a message from Mr. Regis." The giant's voice sounded like a dying bullfrog in a dried-up swamp. "Stays away from The Open Blouse, ya has no business there. And stays away from the staff. Yous catch me drift?"

His dark eyes resembled abandon coal mines, deep and bottomless, and his thick, black eyebrows were like smeared coal dust across his forehead, shading the eyes even more.

I said: "What if I don't. What if I don't give a damn about your drift?"

Stretching a threatening grin across his misshapen face, the giant pulled his rod and aimed it at my head. Dave Wells stepped towards him. Startled by Dave's confidence, the giant turned and fired at Wells. BLAM! Wells had anticipated the shot, throwing himself into the pink-cushioned chair. The slug hit the wall with a puff of dust and a thud sound. With the giant distracted, I pulled my .38 from the desk drawer. The giant saw my quick move, he turned, aimed his pistol at me. BLAM! I gave the giant a third eye, but it didn't match his other two. This one was red and wet, with a red tear running down to the bridge of his nose in a slow-moving line. He stood there for a few seconds, with a dumb-struck expression, trying to figure out what had happened. Then his knees buckled and he dropped on his back, hitting the floor with the whump of four concrete sacks, enough to shake the entire office. The gun blast had echoed around the room, ringing my ears, rattling my teeth, and the odor of nitrocellulose stung the inside of my nose, and in my hand the black gun barrel was still smoking, like a burning cigar left in an ashtray.

Wells and I stared at the dead man. The giant's thick skull stopped the slug from exiting: there was no discharge leaking from the back of his head. It would be an easy cleanup.

Waiting for the police to come, we discussed hiring another investigator. Wells said he knew of a private dick, Max Lee, who would fit in with our posse. Occasionally, we looked at the fallen giant. His dark eyes were open, fixed on a crack in the ceiling.

This was not the first time Wells and I had sat together with a dead man staring at a ceiling.

We were Lieutenants investigating an Army base drug problem involving a Captain and a Master Sergeant. With enough evidence against them, Wells went off to cuff the Sergeant, while I headed off to collar the Captain. Somehow, he got word that I was coming, and he ambushed me. He had me on my knees with his .45, pushing the barrel into my skull, telling me I should've stayed out of it. He was standing in front of me when Wells entered through the back of the house, coming up on the Captain from behind. The Captain caught Wells' reflection in a glass pane. He turned quickly and shot twice. Wells dropped, spilling blood. After the second shot, I sprang from the floor like a flying monkey, and grabbed the Captain's head, twisting it until his neck snapped. When I lowered his body to the floor, I was thinking that Wells was dead too. But he was lying there, smiling and grimacing, his eyes spiked with pain. He'd taken a slug beneath the clavicle. It went clean through. The other shot missed him. He said he'd had a gut feeling that I was in trouble.

Waiting for the Military Police, Dave Wells and I sat on the floor leaning against a wall, drinking the Captain's 25-year-old Delmore Scotch and watching the dead man. Every so often Wells would moan, and I would fix him up with another glass of that expensive whisky.

We gave our statements to the uniformed cops, while the dead giant was being hauled off to the morgue. Soon after the commotion died down, Dave Wells left for Santa Barbara, to make inquiries about the art theft.

Detectives Harley Jewels and Brick Woodhouse came to the office to investigate the shooting. After the excitement was over, I showed them the bag lady's drawings.

"Who drew these?" Jewels asked. His eyes widened, lifting his eyebrows nearly to his hairline.

Both detectives stood around my desk staring at the drawings. Woodhouse was holding a cigarette, while picking tobacco from his tongue. Jewels sipped a glass of water.

"They were drawn by a bag lady, who saw Milo Regis push Amy Regis from the roof."

Woodhouse laughed from his belly, and the air came out of his mouth as if somebody had pumped his gut. He picked up one of the drawings and chuckled.

"Let me get this straight," Woodhouse said with a crooked grin. "Some street urchin tells you she saw Milo Regis toss his wife from the roof, with the only proof being her word and these drawings, and you want us to reopen the case?" He snorted loudly with his mouth closed. The air came out of his nostrils this time.

The office smelled stale. The odor of the dead thug's five-and-dime cologne, along with cigarettes and bourbon, had mixed into a nasty stench. The room smelled like a dank floor mop in a run-down roadhouse. I got up from my desk, opened the window, then stood there inhaling the fresh air while looking outside. The dark grey layer was still gripping the sky. Red, blue and green neon spilled like dayglow paint over the rain puddles, and the streets were as empty as a rained-out Dodger's game.

I could see the detective's reflections in the top window pane. I turned to look at Woodhouse and answered: "Yet, you still believe that Milo Regis is guilty without any proof. Isn't that right, Brick? Isn't that what you said several months back, that you were sure Regis killed his wife?"

I walked backed to the desk and continued: "And here you are with a possible witness, and you're laughing it off because she's a bag lady?"

Woodhouse poured a bourbon and slammed it back. I could hear the whisky knocking his tonsils around. He sat down in the wooden chair with a thud, leaned into me from across the desk and said in a low raspy voice: "Commissioner McKenna ordered us to close this case, Joe. Our balls are in a vice. If I mention these drawings, McKenna will tighten the vice. I like my balls. I don't want them in McKenna's ball crusher." His head moved slowly from side to side while his face drooped, with what seemed like the expression of a tired geriatric.

I knew what Woodhouse was talking about, having had my own balls in McKenna's ball crusher. It was emotionally disturbing.

Detective Jewels shook his head in agreement and said: "By the way, the thug you put down was Vincent 'Bullfrog' Rotello, a greaseball with a rap sheet longer than his body. He was charged with four murders over the past several years, but none of the charges stuck. He has been one of Regis' strongarms for the past five years. Regis will not take this sitting down. There could be hell to pay, Joe. It's best you stay holstered day and night." Then he added: "I'll call in a clean-up crew for this blood spill."

I nodded at Jewels.

"Can we have these drawings?" Woodhouse asked.

"They don't belong to me." I was irritated. "I have to give them back to the artist."

After the detectives left the office, I sat at my desk with a stack of troubled thoughts. But one thought was more troubling than the others: *things might turn even more hostile.*

I poured a whisky, then realized I hadn't eaten since breakfast.

Grabbing my overcoat and hat, I headed out the door, leaving the untouched glass of whisky on the desk, and the office door unlocked for the cleanup crew.

12

At Abe's Deli I took my time eating, while chatting with a few locals. Left Abe's two hours later. Rain hammered the city like it was trying to tenderize the concrete.

While burning a cigarette under an awning, I noticed a black Cadillac parked in the middle of the block. Two men were slouched in the front seat. The driver straightened up when he noticed me.

I took my time smoking, and kept my eyes on the Caddy. After finishing the cig, I flicked the butt in a puddle and watched the hot orange tip turn black and cold. Pulling up my coat collar and tugging my hat low, I headed back to the office thinking that the window was still open.

When I started to walk, the Cadillac's engine turned over with a steady purr. I watched the Caddy's reflection in a store window. It moved towards me with its headlights off. I unholstered my Ruger, slipped it into my overcoat pocket and gripped the butt.

When I stepped inside the street entrance of my office building, the Caddy pulled up to the curb, stopped for a few seconds, then drove off. Its headlights came on, blurred by the rain. I relaxed my grip on the Ruger then walked upstairs to the office. The window was closed and locked, but I knew I had left it open. I pulled the pistol out of my coat pocket, flipped on the lights and scanned the room. There were raindrops on the floor near the window, but the blood stain was gone. I looked around some more. A sheet of paper stuck out of my black Remington typewriter. What was typed on it made my heart race.

What's the point in living in a world with so much loss?
It makes no sense. This is the only way out.
Forgive me,
Joe Stone

I was startled by the ringing phone. It rang about four times before I answered it.

"Hello!"

"Joe, it's Dave Wells. You alright? You sounded startled. Were you sleeping?"

"I'm okay. Was doing paperwork. Reading a few things. How's it going with you?"

"I'm still in Santa Barbara. The weather is stormy. It's going to be worse tomorrow with hours of rain coming hard and steady. Going to lay low until it passes."

"Okay."

"Joe, what's going on? Your voice sounds different."

"I'm tired, Dave, just tired."

"Okay, Boss. Get some rest. I'll keep you updated on the art theft."

"Sounds good. I'll see you in a couple of days."

My eyes returned to the typed note, then moved around the office to the door, the window, the closet. With the .38 in my grip, I walked towards the closet door and yanked it open. Nothing but clothes, shoes and ties. I exhaled long and heavy and walked over to the window. The Cadillac was parked in front of the building now. A cigarette glow lit the face of a man sitting in the passenger seat, turning his features savage red. I recognized him as one of the goons from Regis' warehouse. Stepping back from the window, I checked the cylinder of my .38. Four rounds left, after plugging Bullfrog. I flipped off the lights, walked back to the desk, pulled out a box of rounds from a drawer, loaded one in the empty chamber and put a handful in my coat pocket. One more look out the window. The Caddy was gone.

I sat down in the pink-cushioned chair and my mind flipped to a despairing thought: *We are all born on death row.* Then a chill grabbed my spine. I shivered violently.

The best thing for me to do right now was to go home. I was exhausted and needed sleep, and plenty of it.

Before leaving, I called the cleaning agency. They confirmed closing the window. And no, they didn't see anybody around the building. Then I noticed that the whisky glass I had left on my desk was empty. I asked the cleaning agency about that. Said it was sitting there full when they arrived, and no they didn't drink it.

I locked the office door and walked down the stairs, leaving the typed note in the typewriter, wanting Detectives Jewels and Woodhouse to see it.

When I stepped outside, two men rushed me from behind, pulled a hood over my head, threw me into the back seat of a car and held me down. As we sped away from the curb, I recognized the steady purr of the Caddy. It was a finely tuned purr, and it felt like it was going to be a nice ride, until somebody clobbered my face. Behind my eyes a bomb's red glare exploded. Then the red faded to black, like a burning cigarette dropped in a rain puddle.

When I came to, the pungent odor of oil and dry rot filled my nose. Could hear steady rain hitting a tin roof, loud and sharp-sounding. It jabbed at my ears, making them ring. My hands were tied behind me to a metal chair and there was cold water around my ankles. I was damp and shivering. Through the loose mesh of a hood, I made out a bare light-bulb hanging from a rafter by a wire. Don't know for how long I was out, but my head felt like a silk stocking with a tear in it. One side of my brain wanted to stay awake, the other side wanted more sleep. My lids turned heavy, then slid in slow motion over my eyes, like curtains closing at the end of a show. First there was a soft, far-off darkness, then the darkness became harder, coming closer, pushing into me with its blackhole wide open, like a buried man's dirt-filled mouth. Then there was light and people and warmth:

Mya Regis stood at the ocean's edge facing the sunset. Lapping waves were at her ankles. Her naked body pulsed like an exposed nerve. I could hear Arnie Bender's voice but couldn't make out what he was saying. Millie Bender walked over to Mya and said: 'He wants you'. Mya answered: 'I am waiting for him'. Arnie said: 'Look, Dave Wells is here'. Wells wrapped his naked body around Mya's body and they had sex standing up. The contrast of their hair color was striking. Mya called out in pleasure, but it could have been pain. Arnie rushed over to her, then he dropped to the ground on his back. A black mamba tunneled into his forehead. Bryce Parker floated on the water. His eyes were set with a contemptuous glare. A large black button was dead center between his lips. He sucked on it like it was a pacifier. When I looked back at Mya, she was gone. Dave Wells was standing with Jill Sabin and Patty Walker. Walker and Sabin held twin babies. Millie Bender said to me: 'It's in front of you'. I looked down. The black button was in the sand. When I looked up again, I was alone, but could hear a man's voice coming from somewhere in the distance.

"Hey, private dickface, wake da fuck up. C'mon buddy. Open yer purrty eyes."

Somebody kicked the metal chair with such force that my bladder busted open. I pissed my pants hard. The hot urine flooded my crotch, running down my left leg, and my head was pounding like somebody was striking it with a brass doorknocker, over and over, striking it. I drifted off.

"Hey! Wake up, dickhead." The chair was kicked one, two, three times. I jolted awake and could see that the hood was off now. My eyes were open, but everything looked fuzzy. Then my head drifted down to my chest, and I could see the water at my feet slowly come into focus. The piss had turned the dirty water a sickly yellow color around my left ankle. Without warning, a large hand grabbed my chin, lifting my head roughly. There was a huge, bloated face a foot away from mine, and a fist the size of a streetcar coming straight at me. It hit my jaw like a head-on collision. My mouth filled with hot, salty bitterness. I gagged, coughed and spilled blood. The giant let go of my face and my chin dropped to my chest. He lifted my head again until I was looking into his squinting black eyes. He squeezed my cheeks with his enormous forefinger and thumb until my mouth opened and he filled it with whisky. The flavor of blood and bourbon sloshed over my tongue. It tasted like rotten corn mixed with rusted iron. I gagged, then puked all over myself. The giant's laugh was cruel and sloppy as he poured more bourbon into my mouth. This time I swallowed it, to clear the burning vomit jammed in my throat. The giant held my head up again until we looked into each other's eyes, but my eyes drifted downward to the nasty yellowish-brown water around my feet.

"Hey, dickface. Now dat 'cha all hydrated, listen ta dis. Dat was jus'a love tap to gets yer attention. Next time I's-ill follow through and bust yer face. Look-a-me when I talks-to-ya."

I looked up at the giant with half-closed eyelids. "Mr. Regis says he aint mad a'cha for popping Bullfrog, who was only suppos'ta gives ya a message. I hated dat asshole, and Mr. Regis says Bullfrog skimmed cash. So yous done-us all a favor. Now, lis'n good. Stays away from anythin' that has anythin' ta do with Mr. Regis. Or da next time ya poke a'roun, I's-ill kill ya myself. Ya gots dat?"

I nodded slowly, painfully.

Holding a large knife in his hand, one that could gut a whale, the giant walked behind me and sliced the rope that bound my hands to the chair. The knife's blade sounded like it was whispering to the rope as it sliced through the strands. Then my arms fell to my sides and dangled like two dead bodies hung from rafters. The giant handed me the whisky bottle. I reached for it, palmed it, but my arm fell back to my side, and the bottle tipped upside down, spilling the whisky into the dirty water. My jaw throbbed. My breathing labored. I spit out more blood. Cold piss dampened my crotch, and my shoes were soaked through from the dirty water.

With my eyes partially focused, I saw the inside of a large dilapidated wooden warehouse. Had no idea where I was, or for how long I'd been here. But the giant thug was gone. Sitting in my wet clothes in dull pain, I lifted the whisky bottle to my mouth, forgetting it was empty. I dropped the bottle, and sat there for what felt like Hell-eternal, while the rain banged the tin roof with nerve-wracking intensity.

Through partial-fuzzy eyes, I looked at my watch. It could have been four a.m. My blurred vision made me dizzy and my head felt like a deserted balloon adrift in some cold, vacant space. Then a warmth drifted up from somewhere, and it led me into a deep, dark space, where I couldn't feel the cold.

13

Around seven a.m. my eyes opened again. My vision was still fuzzy and my mouth tasted like a rusted drain pipe. Lifting myself out of the chair, I wobbled for a few seconds, caught my balance, then exhaled long and hard, as I hobbled towards a small hinged wooden door cut into a larger sliding door. My shoes made squishing sounds when I walked, and my clothes smelled like a nest of dead rats. Daylight was streaming through the cracked planks of the building.

When I pushed open the small wooden door, the icy air hit my face like a sharp slap. I almost shivered out of my skin. The rain must have stopped during one of my blackouts, and the lingering dampness, mixed with the pungent odor of dry rot and oil, nauseated me. And I could taste it on my tongue. It tasted bitter. The morning sky held dirty white clouds smeared with light grey, dark grey and black. The grim sky mirrored itself in the large rain puddles that had collected in a huge muddy parking lot. Putting my hands in my coat pockets to keep them warm, I found that my Ruger and the slugs were still there. My car keys were there, too. There was a typed note wrapped around the keys:

I don't want to kill you Mr. Stone.
Mind your own business, so I won't have to.
Go to the back of the warehouse.

Through mud and puddles, I hobbled over to my maroon Buick, parked behind the warehouse.

Sitting in the car, motor running, I remembered a pint of Scotch in the glove compartment. Reaching for the whisky, my bruised body complained loudly. With a grip on the bottle, I filled my bloodied mouth with the whisky. Barely had the strength to lift the bottle to my lips the first time, but I struggled and lifted it again.

With the heater cranked up like a smelting furnace, I put the car in gear, and drove through some potholes, wincing and groaning over bumps and dips until reaching a paved road. A street sign read East 4th Street. I was somewhere in East Los Angeles along the river.

After driving for several minutes, I spotted a phone booth at an auto service station. Called and left a message for Jewels and Woodhouse, to meet me at my office in forty minutes. Back in the car, I remembered my dream, but was in no mood for cryptic nonsense. I needed straight answers, not baffling riddles. I looked at myself in the rearview mirror, and saw a face that was terribly pale and bruised and old-looking. Then my heart hammered my ear drums. I was hot and sweaty. Saliva flooded my mouth.

I pushed the door open and heaved once, twice, three times. A surge of chills raced through my bones, knocking them together. I chugged more Scotch just to clear the puke stuck in my throat. Feeling too exhausted to drive, I put the car in gear anyway.

Started to think about Arnie Bender, about the first time we met, at Abe's Deli ten years ago: the joint was packed, and all the tables were taken. I was reading the L.A. Times. And standing next to my table was this thin guy dressed in a classy light brown linen suit, with a yellow and black checkered silk shirt, a red bowtie and a brown fedora. Glancing down, I noticed his polished brown wingtips, then I heard: "Would you mind, Sir, if I shared your table?" There was something captivating in his politeness.

I invited Arnie to sit down, and, at that moment, we became nearly inseparable as friends. With his humorous personality, Arnie should've had his own television talk show. He had a way of making you feel special, and he never lost that gift. Arnie had a small p.i. business that was not doing well. I offered him a job sleuthing for me. After a week of talking about him to Millie, the three of us had lunch together, and Millie and Arnie formed an immediate connection. It was that fast. Maybe it was a coincidence that he was a private investigator and chose my table. But as Mya Regis once said: I don't believe in coincidences.

I finally pulled up to the office with open car windows. Harley Jewels and Brick Woodhouse were standing outside. Woodhouse leaned with his back to the building, hands in his pockets, eyes looking down at the sidewalk, his hat pulled low to his forehead. Jewels stood near the curb, his hands in his pockets, tapping his foot against the sidewalk. His hat was pushed up, away from his forehead. When they came over to the car to greet me, they snapped their heads back, like somebody had punched their faces.

"What in the hell, Joe!" Woodhouse said. "Jesus H. Christ. You smell like a rotting corpse."

I opened the door and dry heaved several times, until my stomach felt like it was packed with barbed wire. My eyes were fuzzy and my ears were ringing like warehouse alarms.

"Milo Regis thanked me for plugging Bullfrog." My voice was raspy and shaky. "He had a few of his thugs deliver a thank you note." I stopped talking, looked down to catch my breath, noticed how destroyed my shoes were, and said: "Harley, in my closet there's fresh clothes and shoes. Bring them to the shower room." My voice felt heavy, thick, as if cut from wet walnut. With a grimace and a groan, I tossed the keys to Jewels.

Holding on to the car, it took a minute to stand up. I steadied myself and yanked the soiled seat cover out of the car and into the road.

Bent and limping, I shuffled my battered body into the building. Woodhouse stayed at the bottom of the stairs with the entrance door wide open. Step by step I made it to the second floor. My breathing labored and the exhales smelled like rancid beef. Down the hall Jewels was holding my fresh clothes. When I got to the shower door, he laid the clothes on a chair and backed away.

Standing under the hot shower was all I could do, gulping down water until my stomach bloated. My head-pulse was like a steel stave ramming my skull. When I turned the water to cold, it shocked me out of my sluggishness.

Jewels was sitting in a chair in the hallway. Woodhouse was off getting coffee. With help from Jewels, I made it to the office and sat motionless in the pink-cushioned chair. I just stared out the window, too uncomfortable to move.

A few minutes later, Woodhouse came back and handed me a coffee and buttered toast. Still staring out the window, I sat in silence. Jewels and Woodhouse watched me, while they sat on the couch smoking cigarettes. After a few minutes, the phone rang. I nodded at Woodhouse to answer the call.

"Joe Stone's office. Detective Woodhouse speaking." There was a pause. "Hey, Wells."

Woodhouse looked at me. I gave him the I'm-not-here sign.

"No, Joe's not here. He's at Abe's picking up food." There was another pause. "Okay, I'll give him the message." Another pause. "Okay, I got it. Good-bye." Woodhouse said to me: "Dave Wells will be back from Santa Barbara in a few days. Said the leads on the art theft haven't panned out. Said he was going to nose around some more. He also said that you both have an appointment with a Max Lee in two days."

I nodded, but it felt like my head hadn't moved at all.

While working on my coffee, I told Jewels and Woodhouse about the Cadillac outside of Abe's Deli, about finding my suicide note after returning to the office. Told them about being abducted and beaten, and about the filthy warehouse scene.

"I'll have the typewriter and paper dusted," Jewels said. He dialed headquarters. "You need to see a doc?" he asked.

"I'm okay, nothing broken. My face hurts. Some sore muscles." I sat back against the pink-cushioned chair, trying not to moan.

"We can pick up a few of Milo Regis' goons," Woodhouse said with a smirk. "Put 'em in a lineup, make 'em feel uncomfortable." Speaking through clenched teeth he added: "I'd like nothing more than to pistol whip a few of those thugs."

"If you do that, Brick, they'll come at me again, and I'll be a corpse lying in a gutter. Milo Regis made it clear that he'd have me killed, if I surfaced on him again." I offered him the typed note that was wrapped around my car keys. He came over and took the note from me and read it, while shaking his head in disbelief.

Shifting my body to the left side and releasing a grunt, I said: "We need facts with impact. If Milo Regis is directing The Open Blouse killings, then we need a way to throw him off his hinges." I shook my head and added: "But what motive would he have had for killing his daughter?"

I shifted in the chair again, grimacing.

While Jewels was on the phone, Woodhouse walked over to the window, opened it and blew his cigarette smoke outside, only to have it come back in his face.

"The dusters will be here in thirty minutes," Jewels said. "Until then, let's talk about this."

Holding up the L.A. Times, he showed me the morning's headline:

UNKNOWN KILLER ON RAMPAGE
FOUR DEAD IN LOS ANGELES

"Who in the hell wrote that?" I snapped.

"A journalist looking for the spotlight," Jewels said. He slapped the paper on the desk. "He never mentioned that these murders are linked to The Open Blouse." He frowned pulling his eyebrows down at the edges. His mouth tightened, expressing frustration.

Woodhouse picked up the newspaper, looked at the headlines and said: "By the end of the week, this'll be the city's living nightmare. There will be wack jobs packing weapons and hurting the wrong people." Woodhouse took a drag from his cigarette and exhaled while speaking, the smoke trailed with his words: "Commissioner McKenna's office brought the press in and fed them this horseshit. He's a crooked bastard, that McKenna." He slammed the paper on the desk, pulled another drag from his cigarette, and walked back to the window again, with more smoke trailing out of his mouth.

"Who is this Max Lee we keep hearing about?" Jewels asked.

"We need another associate. Dave Wells says Max Lee is the one."

"Never heard of him," Jewels replied.

"He's from Detroit, looking for a change of scenery. Wells said that Max Lee loves palm trees."

"Loves palm trees, huh? Good luck with that," Jewels replied with a grin. Then he looked over at Woodhouse: "There's a stack of paperwork at the station waiting to waste our time. Brick, let's go."

Jewels opened the door and left the office. Woodhouse scowled, then crushed his cigarette out in the green glass ashtray on my desk, and followed Jewels down the hallway.

After guzzling a glass of water, I continued to stare out the open window. The clouds hung like dark mesh over the city. Cold air blew in. I stood up and closed the window, then sat back in the pink-cushioned chair, and had a wrestling match with restless sleep.

Thirty minutes later, still exhausted, I pulled myself together enough to drive to my flat, where Jack Daniels nursed me into dreamland.

14

For the rest of that day and the next, I stayed at my place in Echo Park, a few blocks from the lake, on Logan Street. It was a second-floor flat in a light green stucco building, trimmed in white, and built in the 1920s.

Sitting on the couch, my feet up on the coffee table, I didn't want to move, just wanted to be left alone. My face was bruised, but the severe pain had let up.

Before leaving the office yesterday, I called the hotel in Santa Barbara where Dave Wells was staying, to return his call. The hotel clerk said that Wells never checked in.

Around three o'clock my phone rang.

"Joe Stone."

"Hey, Boss. I'm calling to remind you about our meeting with Max Lee, at two tomorrow."

"Okay, Dave. So, the hotel wasn't right for you?"

"What'd'ya mean?"

"I returned your call. The desk clerk said you never showed up."

"Oh, right. Forgot to mention that I'm staying at a rooming house. I guess I forgot to leave the phone number.

I felt I would've been too close to the subject by staying at the hotel."

"Sounds like the right move then. Any progress with the case?"

"It's leading back to Los Angeles. To a Spanish art dealer, living on his yacht at Cerritos Yacht Anchorage in Wilmington."

"Sounds like you're closing in. Anything I need to do before you get here?"

"Nah, I got it. I'll see you tomorrow at two o'clock. You're going to be impressed with Max Lee."

"Alright then. Tomorrow it is."

Ready for some sleep, I walked into the bedroom and slid under the blankets, until the phone pulled me out of bed.

"Joe Stone."

"This is Woodhouse. You need to get over here."

I wrote the address down and headed out the door.

The Bel Air mansion had captivating attributes: armless Greek statues stood on both sides of the shiny, double brass gates. Two huge "Rs", crafted out of abalone and silver, were attached to the centers of both gates.

As I approached the entry, a young cop stopped me to check my identification, then he checked a list he was holding, and waved me through.

I drove along a winding road paved in grey granite slabs, lined with lofty Asian palms and guarded by more armless statues. On the final turn of the road, the three-story mansion of Mediterranean design came into view. It had white stucco walls and ornately crafted wooden trim painted Santorini-blue. Even in the dark light of the oncoming storm, the magnificent 1930s structure seemed to radiate a theatrical brightness.

Parked along the horseshoe driveway in front of the mansion were two squad cars, two black unmarked police vehicles, and the coroner's black station wagon. Two officers were standing guard at the mansion's double-front glass doors. I parked my car, got out, and one of the officers came over to me right away.

"Mr. Stone, this way please. Detectives Jewels and Woodhouse are on the third floor. The elevator is over here," said the overweight, middle-aged cop. His fleshy face sagged like a rubber pouch filled with dough.

"I'll take the stairs. I need the exercise."

The officer laughed, said he understood, and patted his big belly. It jiggled just enough for me to notice.

By the time I reached the third floor, it felt like I had walked through a European museum.

There were dozens of paintings, drawings and sculptures by the world's masters. All of this in a mansion whose floors were black and white marble, inlaid with thin silver lines.

Down the hallway, a tall, lean older cop stood in front of an open door. He had a military haircut, a tight, unlined face, and a jaw like chiseled rock. With an emotionless command, he waved for me to come.

When I stepped into the bedroom, Jewels and Woodhouse came over to me. In a dejected tone Jewels said: "Here we go again." He wagged his head slowly, and his eyes were heavy with grief from what he had seen.

A raven-haired woman was lying nude on her back. There was a bullet hole dead-center forehead. Her eyes were open but clouded grey, like a heavy fog had moved in. Her expression was pleasant and relaxed, as if she had been expecting us. Next to her right hand was a Colt .32 Snub-nose revolver. A typed suicide note was in the carriage of a black Corona typewriter, sitting on a desk.

Dear Mother and Father,
I am a failure. Forgive me.
I love you,
Kimmie

There was no signature.

Kimmie Turner was the embodiment of the All-American beauty. At twenty-years-old, she had moved to Los Angeles from the small factory town of Ilion, New York, to pursue an acting career.

She had an agent and an acting coach. Now, at twenty-one, she was a beautiful corpse.

"Who found her?" I asked.

"The window cleaner," Jewels replied. "He called the police immediately. Right now, he's sitting outside by the pool. A young guy. Nerve-wracked. He's from Mexico, doesn't speak much English."

"This is what we found to be of interest," Woodhouse said. "It was in Miss Turner's coat pocket." He handed me a business card from The Open Blouse. It was Bryce Parker's. His home phone number was written on the back.

I nodded and asked: "Whose *palace* is this?"

"Robert Rollin," Woodhouse said with a crooked grin cutting up the right side of his face.

"*The* Robert Rollin, the film producer?"

"The one and only. Rollin Productions. The forty-five-year-old head honcho," Woodhouse replied, still grinning.

"Where is he?" I asked.

"In Mexico with his twenty-five-year-old assistant Marsha Brook," Jewels said. "They left two days ago, to look at locations. His wife is in San Francisco with their two kids, visiting her parents. We spoke with her on the phone. It was important for her to let us know that her husband and Miss Brook are only in Mexico together for business."

This time I grinned and asked: "Why was Kimmie Turner here?"

"The house manager told us she was going to do a photo shoot around the pool, today," Jewels answered. "She was set to be the femme fatale in Rollin's next crime film. He offered his estate to her agency. Miss Turner arrived last night. Her agent dropped her off."

"Where is her agent?"

"Being questioned at his home," Jewels replied and then added. "The house manager told us that Kimmie Turner was alone after her agent left, which was around five p.m. He said there were no sightings of anybody else coming or going."

Woodhouse was across the room talking with the coroner. He walked back to us and said:

"Turner's lights went out sometime between two and three a.m." Woodhouse wiped his face with his big hand, from his forehead down to his chin. He looked tired, and his six-foot frame slouched a little.

"Did the house staff hear the shot?" I asked.

"No," Jewels said. "The bedrooms are soundproof. The house manager and the rest of the staff have their own quarters, about fifty yards behind this one. Ms. Turner was the only person inside the mansion, at that time."

"So, nobody heard the shot," I said. "What about a car coming or going? There must have been a car."

"When we asked the house manager about that, he said the only car that came through the gate was her agent's," Jewels replied, then added: "There is a twenty-four-hour guard at the gate."

"Then it's possible," I said, "that the killer parked somewhere along the road and scaled the ten-foot wall at another location, away from the guardhouse. It's also possible that Kimmie Turner was waiting for his arrival, and she let him in."

Jewels nodded while cupping his chin in his hand, then he pulled the skin with his fingers and said: "The gate guard was questioned. He didn't see anything unusual, as far as strange cars in the neighborhood goes. We asked about the possibility of scaling the wall. He said it might be possible for somebody who is six-feet tall and in good shape."

Woodhouse added: "The press will run with this one. They're going to turn the city into a hellhole of fear." The lines around his eyes grew deeper and darker. He sighed, and pulled on his lower lip with his thumb and forefinger, while looking down at the floor. He seemed a bit unsettled about the murder of another young woman. Maybe because he had a teenage daughter. Jewels and I tightened our mouths, nodding in agreement with Brick's assessment of the likely press response.

I took a sideways look at Kimmie Turner, lying dead on the bed. It was a distressing scene.

The three of us were silent as we watched the medics wrap Turner's body in a sheet. They placed her on a gurney and rolled her out of the bedroom. The coroner followed behind them, while jotting down notes. His bulbous body seemed to float out of the room like a large human bubble.

"When will Bryce Parker be brought in for questioning?" I asked.

"As we speak," Jewels replied. "You want to listen in?"

"Wouldn't miss it."

"One more thing," Woodhouse said: "Kimmie Turner was wearing a red silk bra. It was on the floor next to her clothing. But her panties are missing." He shook his head slowly and added: "We've searched the bedroom, the bathroom and the other rooms. They're missing, just like Mya Regis' panties were missing from her murder scene." After delivering that information, Woodhouse looked even more troubled.

"Well, that's something to think about," I said. "It sounds perverse to me."

Driving from Bel Air to the Hollywood Police Station, I thought about a passage from a Zen book I had read: Delusion is an illness of all humans.

My thoughts gathered quickly: We are all burdened with a desperation to please ourselves, and some of us will go to any length to reach that pleasure point, even if it comes down to knocking others out of the way.

This killer is probably stuck in the subsurface of delusion, where his demon tortures his mind day after day. He might even be a self-hater, but is too much of a coward to turn his anger against himself. Maybe he blames others for his wicked ways, and murdered his victims out of revenge, or for just plain satisfaction. Maybe he blames his parents for the way his troubled mind works. Maybe he even killed his parents, and his dog. His goldfish too.

15

From behind the two-way mirror, I watched Bryce Parker in the interrogation room, pacing from corner to corner, like a mouse in a snake cage, and the snake was hungry. Parker's face was sloppy with perspiration. He loosened his tie, until the knot hung like a cowbell at his stomach. His dress shirt was unbuttoned halfway, and he pulled at his tee shirt, to get the wet fabric off his skin. It seemed that Parker had become a pressure cooker with a jammed release valve. He had a hard time breathing, as if the air was stuck to the ceiling and he couldn't suck it into his lungs.

Having been warned by Milo Regis to keep away from his employees, I stayed behind the mirror, out of sight. But what I wanted was to shake the truth out of this punk, just a couple of good shakes, to make him spill his guts.

Detective Jewels entered the room, yelled at Parker to sit down. Parker sat quicker than a drowning man breaking water. He squirmed, shivered and rocked back and forth in his chair, while Jewels read the police report in silence. Parker's eyes bulged out of their sockets, like badly tempered ball bearings ready to crack. The chair made squeaking sounds while he rocked.

"Sit still!" Jewels demanded, slapping the metal table with the file folder. The sharp sound made Parker's body jolt and his head snap up and back.

"I have to use the bathroom," Parker whined. He was holding his crotch and shaking uncontrollably.

Jewels got on the intercom: "Officer, take this asshole into the bathroom. Stay in there with him."

The assisting officer came in and escorted Parker out of the room. A short time later the officer brought him back. But Parker didn't make it to the urinal in time. He was dressed in some old ragged pants that were too big for him, and he was carrying his wet pants in a brown paper bag. Parker was shivering, and his red eyes flared under the ceiling lights, like hot distress signals.

Detective Woodhouse entered the room, walked over to Jewels and whispered in his ear. Jewels nodded, then his lips pulled in like a tightly closed clam, his eyes narrowed down, and his forehead contracted into corrugated folds. Jewels gave Parker a sideways look with an added smirk, his head nodding.

"Tell me what he said," Parker demanded.

"That's police business, asshole. Tell me about your relationship with Kimmie Turner."

"Never heard of her," Parker answered rudely. "Can I go now?"

"Your business card was in her pocket. Does that ring a bell?"

"I don't know her." Parker was heating up with spineless indignation.

"Detective Woodhouse just reminded me that at the inquest, you said Kimmie Turner worked at The Open

Blouse for about a month." Jewels was grinning now. "Tell me again how you don't know her."

"Huh? Who? Where?" Parker was more frazzled. His hands were like nervous spiders crawling over each other on the table. Sweat pooled beneath them.

"Parker, we got you in a goddamn lie, and we're going to nail you for this murder. Now tell me what happened." Jewels raised his voice: "Why did you kill Kimmie Turner?"

"What? Dead? Kimmie's dead?" Tears filled Parker's eyes. His voice lowered to a whisper. "She called me to say she got into Rollins' movie. Dead? No. No." He moved his head from side to side in quick jerking snaps, his eyes were tightly closed.

"Ah, so you do know her," Jewels said, puckering his lips and nodding rapidly.

Parker sat motionless now with his head low to the table.

"When did you last see her?" Jewels asked.

"After she quit the club, we stayed in touch." Parker lifted his head and looked at Jewels. "I saw her about a month ago. Maybe two. I'm not sure." His voice was tremulous. He started talking fast. "She called me yesterday, said she was staying at Robert Rollins' mansion. She was giddy. Said that she had a new lover who was staying with her for the night. Said she met him at a whisky joint on The Strip."

"What was his name?"

"I don't know."

"What else did she say about him?"

"That he wore the coolest black cowboy boots."

"What else?"

"That he was rugged and hot, and older than her."

"What was his name?"

"I said I don't know."

"Did you have sexual intercourse with Miss Turner?"

"What?"

"Answer the question."

"Once or twice," Parker said softly. He shrugged his shoulders and asked: "What does that have to do with anything?"

"Well," Jewels demanded, "was it once or twice?"

Parker lowered his head again. His thin upper lip was pulled in tightly, beaded with sweat. His nerves were hot, but he was motionless, and the sweat held steady to his skin. Then he lifted his head, looked Jewels square in the eyes, and said through clenched teeth: "Once. Only one time. That's all she wanted." His eyes stayed on Jewels' eyes as if looking for sympathy.

With a calm voice, Jewels asked: "How bitter were you that it was only once?"

"I was disturbed by it," he growled. "Because I fell for her."

"And?" Jewels probed.

"And what?" Parker snapped. "What? What do you want me to say? Yeah, I was angry over it, okay? Is that what you wanted to hear?" Parker's lips moved in and out rapidly like a pink sea anemone, then his mouth and jaw tightened, squeezed by anxiety, and his breathing labored with a hyperventilating force.

"Angry enough to kill her?" Jewels asked with a level voice.

Parker caught his breath and his voice raised: "Huh? What?" No. No. No! You're wrong. You're not pinning that on me. I want a lawyer!"

"Where were you last night?" Jewels inquired with the same level tone.

"Home."

"Can anybody vouch for you?"

"No. I was alone. In bed by nine o'clock."

"Where was your mother?"

Parker lowered his voice and said: "She was out for the night."

"Why did you lie about knowing Kimmie Turner?" Jewels yelled, as his hand smacked the table with a gun-like crack. Parker jumped in the chair, then he sat up straight. His body was shaking all over, like a wet dog would shake from head to tail.

"I was confused. Just confused," he whined. Then Parker stood up quickly from the table and yelled out: "I want a lawyer. Bring me a lawyer!"

Jewels left the interrogation room, and he and Woodhouse joined me in the observation room.

"We have nothing on him," Woodhouse said, "but we could hold him until tomorrow, just to put the fear of prison in him."

"Maybe arrest him, charge him with Kimmie Turner's murder and get his fingerprints." I suggested. "Then drop the charge and let him go, before Milo Regis catches wind of the arrest."

Both detectives shook their heads in agreement.

Bryce Parker was arrested, fingerprinted and charged with Kimmie Turner's murder. Twenty minutes later the charge was dropped, due to insufficient evidence.

Parker was driven to his house in a taxi, carrying his wet pants in a brown paper bag.

Before I left the station, Woodhouse told me that the serial numbers had been burned off the pistol that was used to kill Kimmie Turner.

It was nearing six o'clock. I was sitting in my Buick outside the police station smoking a cigarette.

It started to rain, steady rain, no wind. I thought about Bryce Parker's description of the man who spent the night with Kimmie Turner. *Black cowboy boots and older than her* is a vague description, since so many older men in Los Angeles wear black cowboy boots.

I was tired and hungry. Drove to Abe's Deli, ordered a warm sandwich and a glass of water. My bruised jaw hurt when I chewed.

After leaving the deli, I went home and put Gene Ammons' album *Blue Gene* on the record player. I poured a shot of bourbon and threw it back. As the rain came down harder, wilder, Ammons' bluesy tenor saxophone felt like a buffer between me and the storm.

I walked to the window, looked down at the street and saw all the sorry bastards running for cover. Watched a homeless black man stuff himself into a tiny doorway, like a hermit crab taking over a shell. He pulled a soiled brown tarp over his body, as cover against the weather.

Thanks to the claptrap press releases by Commissioner McKenna's assistant, everyone assumed that they'd be next to take a bullet to the forehead. Los Angeles was under siege. An invisible homicidal maniac was causing high anxiety citywide.

The phone rang. It was Dave Wells.

"Joe. I need to confront the Spanish art dealer aboard his yacht. It's time. So, you're on your own with the two o'clock appointment tomorrow. And by the way, Max Lee is a Kung Fu Master."

"Okay, Dave. Thanks for the heads up, and be careful out there."

The phone rang again. "Joe. Jewels here. Commissioner McKenna's assistant released another bunk press statement. Said we are *closing in* on the killer, but still didn't mention that all the victims are connected to The Open Blouse."

"Of course, not," I said. "McKenna's protecting his good buddy Milo Regis' new business venture."

"I believe you're right," Jewels said. "One other thing. The autopsy showed blond head hairs and dried gobs of white stuff on Kimmie Turner's pubic hairs. They're thinking that the white stuff is saliva. We'll know for sure after the lab report."

"We could be dealing with a psychopathic sexual pervert," I said.

"You may be right again," Jewels said. "And at this point, we could assume that he's blond. Also, the pistol had the same setup as the others, one used round in an otherwise empty chamber."

After the phone call, I crawled into bed but couldn't sleep. My head was overloaded with chatter. But one clear thought surfaced above the racket:

Everybody is hungry for something: for fame, for money, for love, or blood. It's that simple.

16

When Max Lee walked into the office the next day, she had on a black leather jacket with a black hooded sweatshirt underneath. She wore tight, black jeans and black Doc Martens. Her midnight-black hair was parted slightly to the left and hung just past her shoulders. Standing about five-seven, she was sleek-looking like a jaguar. Beneath her open leather jacket, I saw a Ruger .38. It was black, like mine.

Despite her sexiness, Max Lee was tough looking, too. But her loud and fast-talking voice pulled me out of my thoughts over her stunning appearance.

"Mr. Stone. Max Lee. A huge fan, Sir, a huge, huge fan of your work. Let me tell you, Sir, this is such a pleasure for me to be standing in front of you. I'm honored, Mr. Stone, just for the consideration. You have no idea what this means to me, Sir, no idea. I was telling my father about this interview. He's the District Attorney for the City of Detroit, and…"

"Miss Lee," I interrupted. "Please, have a seat." I had to reel her in with authority, if only to relax her. "I was looking forward to meeting you as well. Please take some breaths." It felt condescending to talk to her like that, but I also needed a minute to compose myself, over my surprise that Max Lee was not a man.

She sat down quickly in a straight back chair in front of the desk, and leaning back, she stretched out her legs in a slow, smooth move. Her legs were long, shapely.

After a few seconds of observing her, I said: "I understand that, besides being a private investigator, you're also trained in martial arts. Congratulations."

"Thank you." She spoke softly this time. Her head was tilted down and turned slightly to the right, causing her hair to fall along the side of her face, as if protecting her from my gaze. Without moving her head, her eyes looked up at me. "I don't take compliments well," she said. "I was nervous about meeting you, Mr. Stone."

With her index finger she tucked the fallen hair behind her ear, and her face came into view again, and I was captivated by this unusual blend of femininity and tomboy, by her sexiness and toughness.

"Let me start over," she said, sitting up straight in the chair, and pulling her legs in. "Hello, Mr. Stone. My name is Maxine Lee." Her voice was steady, confident, with a sophisticated tone. She looked directly into my eyes.

"Please Maxine, call me Joe or Stone, but never Mr. Stone, and definitely not Sir."

"Yes, Mr. Sto… I mean, Joe. And call me Max," she said with an alluring smile.

I said: "Max. I'm hungry. Are you?" She shook her head yes. "Okay. Lunch is on me at Abe's Deli, just around the corner. It'll do us good to get out of the office, to get some fresh air."

When Max Lee and I walked down the street, every head turned to watch her. She looked like a striking character from a spy novel, and she had a bright-shining inner star with a powerful magnetic pull. People on the streets seemed star-struck as she passed by them.

At Abe's I ordered steak, fries and beer. Max ordered steak, extra fries, beer, a bowl of corn chowder, onion rings, salad, and then apple pie à la mode. She consumed all of it without having to sit back to catch her breath. It just disappeared between her beautiful lips.

I was also impressed with her intelligence, and with how articulate she was. She told me about her family background: District Attorney father, a British immigrant with a Ph.D. in criminal justice. A Japanese-American mother, a Professor of Business at the University of Detroit Mercy.

Given Max's streetwise demeanor and her inner-city toughness, it was hard for me to imagine that she was raised in an upper-class environment. Another thing that caught my attention was her humbleness. And this twenty-nine-year-old beauty with both brains and brawn wanted to work for me.

I agonized over bringing her on as an associate. She could be dangerously distracting. I had to think about it for a few days, needed to be objective.

"Max, listen, my process for bringing on a new associate is to give myself a few days with my thoughts on the matter."

"I understand, Joe."

"Thank you for understanding. You've been a private detective now for how many years?"

"Ten years, since I was nineteen. Took a summer job with a p.i. firm owned by my father's friend. Worked as his office assistant. Then he brought me into a case, an alleged infidelity. A woman had claimed her husband was sleeping with their neighbor. I saw straight through the wife's deception. The wife was trying to set up her husband for a fall, so she could divorce him and take his bankroll. The neighbor was in on it. She was paid to lie about having an affair with the man. I cracked the case, and then decided to become a full-time private detective."

"Congratulations. And your academic parents, how do they accept your choice of profession?"

"Dad is supportive. As hard-knuckled as he comes off with his fiery temper, he has plenty of understanding. Mother is different. It confuses her."

"The martial arts, when did that start?"

"Dad is a Kung Fu Master. He got me interested. He insisted I give it a try. I was nine-years-old then, and was hooked."

I nodded and said: "Tell me about your college studies."

"BA in Criminal Justice. Was bored with school. Wanted to work as a private detective. I dropped out of graduate school and Daddy got me in with a large p.i. firm. Spent a few years with them. Learned a lot fast." She stopped to order a cup of coffee, then changed the subject. "Crime Investigator Magazine and Detective Magazine write about you with admiration. When I read about your case-winning history, I was determined to work for you. That's why I moved to Los Angeles, several months ago."

I nodded and smiled, and we sat there staring at each other for what seemed like a long enjoyable minute.

The coffee came. Max took a sip, and her eyes watched me the whole time.

"I was insecure about approaching you," she said, "so I worked for other agencies. To get to a feel for Los Angeles. Then I met Dave Wells at a whisky bar. He told me that you were looking for an associate. Now, here we are. Thank you, Joe, for taking the time."

Max's enthusiasm was what I needed. She reached across the table and touched my hand, as a thank you gesture. It felt warm and inviting. The waitress interrupted us.

"Would you like anything else, Joe, or just the check?" I asked for the check and suggested to Max that we go back to the office, to continue our conversation. There were a few open cases I wanted her to look over, to get her perspective. I reached for my wallet, but Max stopped me with another touch of her hand, and my heart sped up this time, at the touch of her hand.

"Lunch is on me," she said. Her inescapable smile spread like a net that trapped me inside of it, and I wanted to stay there.

While Max was at the counter settling the tab, I waited outside. The midafternoon light had turned into a medieval dusk. Heavy dark clouds sat thick and motionless, like an oil spill across the sky. The air was chilly, and the rain had started again. It was soft, soundless, almost soothing.

I walked to the corner of Hollywood and Vine, stood under an awning and watched a stream of strangers floating by. Their rigid faces pushed through the cold air, like porcelain masks strained with anxiety. After all, there could be a homicidal monster walking next to them.

"Hey, buddy, ya gots a light?" His voice was wet and gurgling.

A short, stocky man was talking to me. He had the body of a bulldozer and a car wreck for a face. An unfiltered cigarette hung from his fat lips. His dark setback eyes were like open graves, and his thick, bushy eyebrows resembled mud smeared above his eyes. There was something familiar about him. Though I couldn't place it.

"Yeah, sure," I said.

I reached inside my coat pocket for a match, that's when the man grabbed my throat with one hand. It had the power of a gorilla's grip. He pulled me across the sidewalk with that hand, and, while squeezing my throat, he slammed me onto the hood of a car on my back. Both of his hands were now around my throat, tightening like hydraulic grips. His thumbs pushed into my windpipe, trying to crush it. I was gagging, pulling for air. I tried to break his hold, but his muscular arms were iron-like and unmovable. I repeatedly punched his face. He didn't flinch.

"Yous killed my brother. Yous dirty sons-a-bitch."

He squeezed my throat harder. A blackout was coming.

"Today's yer day ta die!" he yelled. His grip tightened more, and saliva spilled from one side of his mouth, while his fat, slug-like tongue hung out from the other side. He was breathing and slobbering like an irritated bull.

"Hey! Asshole." It was Max Lee. She was thirty feet away, speeding towards us. When she was twenty feet away, the thug reached behind his back with his right hand and pulled a pistol, while still choking me with a powerful left hand. When he took aim at Max, her Ruger appeared like a fast sleight of hand. BLAM! She plugged the asshole in his right shoulder while still moving towards him. He flinched, as if he had just gotten a flu shot, then his arm fell limp but his hand still held the gun. The man threw me to the ground with his left hand, grabbed the gun out of his right hand, and aimed it at Max again. BLAM! A .38 slug ripped through the man's chest, and he dropped and died like a raindrop hitting hot concrete. His eyes were frozen open.

The people on the street were lying face down in puddles or had crawled under cars. One woman ran down the street screaming and pulling her two children along.

High pitched sirens invaded the scene from all directions. A police car squealed up to the curb. The door flew open and a cop rushed out, yelling at Max to drop her weapon, to get on the ground. His pistol was aimed at her head.

I was on my hands and knees gasping for air, trying to pull oxygen into my lungs.

"Joe!" It was Harley Jewels with Brick Woodhouse.

When I was able to focus and look around, I saw Max lying stomach down, spread-eagle on the wet sidewalk. The cop's pistol was aimed at the back of her head. She was motionless. The dead man was next to her, lying on his back. His open eyes had filled with rainwater and they were spilling over, like he was crying about being dead.

"No. No!" I said to the cop, my voice strained. "She saved my life."

Max looked up at me with a faraway gaze, like she had slipped through a time gap and was no longer with us.

"Joe," Woodhouse asked. "What happened? Who is this?" He pointed down at Max.

After Jewels helped me to my feet and I helped Max up, I said: "This is Max Lee."

I was slumped over, hands on my knees, trying to get words out.

"Huh?" Jewels replied. "*The* Max Lee? The one who likes palm trees?"

"Yeah, that one," I said in a breathless, raspy voice. "As of right now she works for me."

My decision was final. Yet, I could see that Max's thoughts were not with us. Her face was pale grey, and her dark eyes seemed to be coated with a hazy film.

17

Max Lee sat at my desk. Jewels and Woodhouse stood near the closed office door. They tried not to get caught staring at her. But it was hard not to stare at Max, she was a stunning creature.

I sat in the pink-cushioned chair near the window. My enflamed throat felt like a blazing furnace.

All was silent in the room.

Max's face had lost its vibrancy, giving way to a twisted construction of anguish. She sat in the chair with her back straight and stiff, like a yardstick, her forearms were stretched across the desk, with her hands tightly clasped, white-knuckling each other. She stared straight ahead into nothing.

I got up from the cushioned chair and poured Max a bourbon. She grabbed it out of my hand, threw it back hard, then said with a deeply strained voice: "I… killed… a… man." The words came out slow, shaky, tenuous sounding, with the frankness of a determined confession.

"In self-defense." I could barely speak above a whisper.

"I should've been faster, should've used my feet."

"He drew and aimed at you. You had no choice."

"He was going to kill you, Joe."

"You saved my life, Max."

"I didn't have to kill him. I should've kicked that gun out of his hand, and knocked him out."

"He was going to kill both of us."

Max closed her eyes and sat in silence again.

The telephone rang. I nodded at Jewels to answer it. He walked over to the desk.

"How am I going to tell my father that I killed a man?" Max lowered her head, her hair hiding her self-inflicted shame, like a black mask over her eyes.

"You did what you had to do," I answered. "You had no choice. You wounded him but he kept coming. He aimed his gun at you."

She looked up at me, her dark eyes steady, and said: "Your face was blue, Joe. Death was in your eyes."

"You moved fast, instinctively."

"Who was he? Why was he determined to choke you to death?"

Jewels placed the phone receiver on its stand and said: "The dead thug on the street was Ronnie Rotello, from Chicago. Younger brother to Bullfrog Rotello. Ronnie Rotello was a known killer. A hitman for hire. His method was to choke his victims to death. He was never arrested for any of the nine murders that he was suspected of."

"But why you, Joe?" Max asked. "Why did he want to kill you?"

"See that bullet hole?" I pointed to the wall. "Ronnie's big brother, Bullfrog, came in here last week, threatened me with a gun, then he took a shot at Dave Wells." I took a few seconds to swallow some thick saliva, to get it past the burning in my throat. "I put a slug in his head."

"Jesus, Joe. Here, in the office? What's going on? What's all this violence about?"

"It's all connected, in one way or another, to The Open Blouse murders." I walked over to the filing cabinet, pulled the folder out and handed it to Max. "It's all in here. Take it home with you. Read it twice. And if you still want to work for me…"

The phone rang again. Jewels answered it and said to Woodhouse: "We need to get back to the station." Then Jewels turned to Max and said: "Miss Lee, there'll be no arrest. Several witnesses gave the same report. What you did was in self-defense. But the District Attorney's Office will call you in, to hear your side of the story. You'll need to sign an affidavit."

"Miss Lee, I'm Detective Brick Woodhouse. This here is my partner, Harley Jewels. We go way back with Joe. You'll be seeing us around quite a bit." Woodhouse nodded slowly while lowering his eyes to the floor, then he looked up at Max and said: "We're sorry to have this tragic incident as our introduction. But you did what you had to do. You acted quickly, and saved Joe's life."

Max was silent. Her head was slightly lowered, arms hanging down along the sides of the chair, not moving. If she heard what Woodhouse had said, then there was no indication from her.

"How many more Rotello brothers do I have to deal with?" I asked.

"There were only two," Jewels answered. "But Ronnie has a twenty-one-year-old son, Ronald Vincent Rotello, aka RV. He's in prison, here in California. Two years for assault and battery. He beat up some guy for just glancing at his girlfriend. The victim was in the hospital for a month. RV inherited the psycho gene. There's no doubt."

"And his mother?" I asked.

"In a loony bin," Jewels said. "A paranoid schizophrenic. RV was placed under the care of his mother's sister, when he was six years old. That care ended when he turned eighteen. I heard that the unmarried sister is a devout Catholic, lives like a saint, but she couldn't reel RV in. Not with a father like he had."

Max was holding The Open Blouse file, reading through it. A grimace contorted her face. If she had held any romantic notions about being a private investigator in the City of Angels, then they died today with the reality of multiple deaths, all connected to a complex murder investigation. A greyish gloom seemed to have engulfed her. The gloom was so heavy that I could almost feel the weight of its hopelessness pushing against me.

In Los Angeles, this line of business can be tough. The entire city is like a seedy carnival filled with fruit loops, nut cakes and jittery criminals. All of them wanting to be somebody, somebody important. But in my experience of having to deal with people like that, most of them fail and fade away.

The storm finally came full-force, hitting hard against the window pane. The sky had turned an endless black. The window thermometer showed the outside temperature: forty-degrees. It was one of the coldest Los Angeles afternoons I'd ever witnessed.

After Jewels and Woodhouse left, I sat in the pink-cushioned chair watching the rain come down.

"Joe..."

"Yes?"

"I need to go. Need to call my father."

"You can call him from here."

"I need to go."

"Where do you live?"

"Silver Lake."

"Need a ride?"

"I have a car."

Max stood up and left the office without another word.

The Open Blouse file sat alone on the desk, like a harbinger of pending disasters.

18

Sitting alone in the office with the lights off, more troubled thoughts piled up into a heavy stack over the killings of the past weeks. There was a moment of clarity that Max Lee had brought with her, then she became hopeless and bleak, and deeply burdened by the killing of a man.

The rainstorm's drama shook me out of my head. I got up from the chair, walked over to the water cooler, drew a glass of water and swallowed it fast. The water wasn't soothing. Flames tore through my parched throat like wildfire.

I returned to the chair and looked down at the boulevard. Next door, the neon sign buzzed and crackled and spilled its red-powered mist into my dark office. The soft light hung in the air like a motionless, atmospheric fire. I sank into the chair and slipped back into my troubled thoughts.

The phone startled me.

"Joe, Dave here."

"Hey, Dave."

"What in the hell is wrong with your voice? You sound like that dead bullfrog-thug."

"There was an incident. It's all right now."

"Okay. How about Max Lee, huh? I bet that knocked you back a few steps, thinking that she was a guy and all. What a knockout, huh? Tough as nails, too. You think she'll fit in?"

"Well, like I said, there was an incident..." I told Wells the story.

"Joe, are you alright, your throat and all?"

"Yeah, I'm good. Not sure about Max though. Not sure if she's coming back."

"Well, that's disturbing news. She would've been a good fit. Anyway, listen, I've uncovered the art thieves. The cops have them in custody. It wasn't the Spanish art dealer after all. It was his two-timing French assistant along with her fast-talking Turkish boyfriend."

"Good work, Dave."

"Thanks, Boss. I could use some downtime now. You know those three weeks you keep telling me to take off? Well, I'd like to start tomorrow, unless we've got something pressing."

"No, there's nothing that can't wait. Go ahead, Dave. You deserve a rest."

"Thanks, Joe. I'll drop my case report off early morning, before I leave. My advice to you is, go home, Joe. Get some sleep. And stay away from that twisted Open Blouse case. Let the homicide dicks turn it inside out, until they've cleaned it up."

"I can't let it go. I'm too close to it to walk away."

"I'm concerned about you, Joe. I have this gut feeling that if you don't let it go, then it's not going to end well."

"I'll be okay, Dave."

"Then I'll see you when I'm back in town."

"Where are you going?"

"Not sure, but definitely away from this loony toon city. Maybe north to Santa Barbara. While I was up there on the case, I met a hot number by the name of Kim Ness. You know, the pretentious, fashionable type. She told me to come back and pay her some proper respect." He chuckled. "Not sure if I can handle a dame with that much glitter, but I'll give it a try.

"Sounds inviting." I whispered through a bruised throat.

After the phone call, I got up from the chair, switched off the lights and headed home. The rain was coming down like the sky had opened its tear ducts. Cold air penetrated my overcoat. It moved through my clothes, and dug into my skin with its icy fingernails. My body shivered.

I thought about destiny. At some point along the line, a ticket was handed to me for this ill-fated journey, and there seemed to be no way to jump off the train, to escape the acidic-tasting grief of loss, or to avoid the distressing uncertainty that had come with The Open Blouse murders. Then there were the women, Mya Regis and Max Lee, who walked to their own beat. There was no standing on the sideline for these women. They had jumped into the game of life and played to win. But Mya Regis lost it all, paying with her own life, and Max Lee was whittled down to survival mode by the pull of a trigger.

I stood under an awning, and watched the downpour batter this grimy City of Angels. Watched the filth being washed into the sewers, like bile spilling from a sick mouth.

A light green Ford sedan was parked nearby, its windows steamed over from the inside. Occasionally, a hand would press against the glass, leaving abstract imprints. Then the back window opened, just enough for a man's hand to drop a condom into the street. I watched the rain push the remains of lust into the gutter. A minute later the car drove off with satisfied lovers, or maybe one of them was a hooker, counting her money.

Behind me came a low, hoarse voice: "Hey, buddy, ya gotta light?"

My shoulders stiffened, as I gripped the butt of my Ruger in my coat pocket, while turning to look at the man. It was too dark to see his face, his hat was pulled low over his eyes. The red neon made his tight mouth and hard-set jawline look angry and determined.

"Sure," I answered, handing him the matches. My hand was shaky, my nerves still on edge.

He lit his cigarette and handed the matchbook back. Then he nodded, pulled his hat lower and continued down the street, until the dim light and steady rain blurred his shape.

Standing there alone, I heard Dave Wells' voice in my head: *I have this gut feeling that it's not going to end well.*

I pulled up my coat collar, buried my hands in my pockets, and walked to my Buick. The rain came at me, aggressive and hard, like it was handing out punishment to a fool.

19

A week after the Ronnie Rotello incident, I was busy with solving a missing wife case. Found the missing wife with an ugly black eye and a new lover. They were living together in a cabin in the San Bernardino mountains, hiding from her brute husband. She said she was in love with the woman at the cabin. At least she was safe. I never told my wife-beating client about finding the two women living together, even refunded his money.

I also uncovered an attempted swindle of an old couple's bank account by some greedy relatives.

I cleaned the office, organized my files, and even had the bullet hole in the wall patched and painted, but there was no word from Max Lee.

Around six o'clock hunger set in. When I opened the office door to head over to Abe's Deli, the ringing phone demanded my attention.

"Joe Stone, Private Investigator."

"This is Jewels. Get to Regis' warehouse. Now!"

I bolted out the door, down the steps and hurried along the boulevard to my Electra.

When I arrived at the Garment District, a heavy-weight north wind was coming at me, hitting my car like a big-fisted thug throwing tight kidney punches. The Buick rocked and bucked.

In front of the warehouse, there were several patrol cars parked along Paloma Street, with a dozen uniforms standing around the cars looking cold.

A sudden uneasiness made my gut churn. On the ground in front of the warehouse, a body was covered with a white sheet. Around the stomach area, blood had formed into a giant strawberry. I killed the engine and sat stock-still. With the windshield wet from drizzle, it was hard to get a clear view of anything more than the strawberry.

The wind howled along the alley where Arnie Bender had been murdered. The scene turned into a nightmarish *déjà vu*, the wet air, the dark alley, the red brick building. An icy chill attacked my neck and burrowed into my bones, but a sudden knock on the window jolted me out of my freeze. It was Detective Woodhouse.

"Joe. This way!" he yelled through the slightly open driver's window.

I got out of the car and followed Woodhouse to an unmarked cop car. Detective Jewels stood outside the car. His fedora was pulled low and tight to his head, hands shoved deep in his coat pockets. His lean, five-foot-ten frame was pulled in, trying to keep warm. He had a deadpan expression.

"Milo Regis is dead," Jewels said in a matter-of-fact way. "The killer is in the back seat." He gestured with his head towards the car. "She specifically asked for you, Joe, and I'd like to know why."

"Her name is Alice Moore," Woodhouse said. "Cousin to Mrs. Amy Regis, formerly Amy Moore. Alice

Moore stuck Milo Regis with a twelve-inch kitchen knife. Sunk it to the hilt. Sliced the liver going in." Woodhouse whistled and shook his head. "Since the knife stayed in the body, it took Regis a while to bleed out, so he had plenty of time to confess to the killings of his wife Amy and her lover Moe Merrit. Regis begged for a priest to come, wanted absolution. He was a corpse before the padre arrived. Milo Regis is a dead sinner now."

"Several witnesses, same story," Jewels said. "Regis yelled at Alice Moore to stay away from his warehouse. He called her a retarded piece of crap. Regis shoved her. She fell backwards to the ground. He bent over her, arm cocked, ready to punch her face. She pulled the knife out of a bag. Regis lost his balance and fell on top of her. The blade flayed his liver like a piece of Grade A meat."

I nodded with a cold, approving smile. Don't know why I smiled it just came out.

"Go ahead, Joe, get in the car," Woodhouse said. "She wants to speak to you."

I opened the car door, bent down and looked inside. To my surprise, the bag lady's eyes met mine, and her round face lit up like a perfect moon. I smiled warmly, then noticed her hands cuffed behind her back.

"Harley, are the bracelets necessary?" Jewels agreed to have them removed.

I slid into the backseat next to her. A young cop came to the other side of the car and removed the handcuffs.

"Officer, please bring us two cups of black coffee." I handed him some cash.

"Yes, sir. Mr. Stone. Right away." He walked down the street to a café.

I looked at the bag lady and said: "Hello, Alice."

"I knew you'd come, Joe." She reached inside her coat pocket and pulled out a copy of Crime Investigator magazine. It had my picture on the cover with two smaller pictures of Arnie Bender and Dave Wells, inset at the bottom right corner. The article featured the high-profile abduction case that we solved together, involving fourteen-year-old Ana Dia, who went missing last summer.

"May I have your autograph, Joe?" A sparkling flash caught her eyes like a dazzling lightning streak. She handed the magazine to me.

"You knew all along who I was?"

"I read detective magazines. Helps to pass time on the streets."

I couldn't stop myself from smiling again.

"Will you take care of my three pigeons for me?"

"Of course."

Alice closed her eyes and began to talk freely.

"As cousins, Amy and I were close, more like sisters. She was the graceful swan and I was the ugly duckling. But we were inseparable. We spent our childhood together nearly every day. Then we went away to different colleges. It was the first time we had been apart for so long. When she came back to Los Angeles, Amy met that horrible man at a dinner party, and then married him a short time later."

The officer came with the coffees. We sat in silence for a minute and sipped our drinks. Then Alice looked at me and continued. "Milo Regis was a disturbed man. He physically hurt Amy so many times. She would telephone me and then cry over the phone, saying that he slapped her face."

"I'm sorry, Alice, sorry it had to end with Amy's death."

"Amy's okay now. She's away from that dangerous man, and she's resting." Alice held her coffee cup with both hands, inhaling the aroma from the rising steam. Her face transformed into smile-lines, then frowned as she spoke. "Many years ago, he yelled at me to stay away from Amy, and he forbade Amy from seeing me. Mya wasn't supposed to know that I was her cousin, too. Milo hated me and I never knew why."

Through the windshield, Alice and I watched Milo Regis' sheet-covered body being heaved into the ambulance. Under the wet blood-stained fabric, the outline of his hefty form looked like a despairing ghost, broken and defeated.

"I watched him every day," Alice continued. "Knowing that every week on this day, and at this hour, he would come to his office alone. I'd stand in front of his building, not saying anything, not looking at him. But he would chase me off, yelling and cussing and pushing me."

"Why didn't you tell me that this was going on, Alice?"

"I just did, Joe. Now you know everything." Her face was lighter now. She was smiling again.

We sat in silence for several seconds, while the wind slammed the car like a rioting mob.

I looked at Alice and said: "You'll have to go to jail."

"You'll visit me and meet my new friends?"

"Yes, Alice, I will."

She reached into a bag on the floor, pulled out her cardboard-covered portfolio and handed it to me.

"Will you take care of this for me?" she asked.

"Yes. Of course."

Jewels came over to the car, said it was time to take Alice to the station. I rode in the back seat with her, while she told me about her medical condition, and why she walked the streets.

At the Hollywood Police station, Alice Moore was led off to a cell. After the booking procedure for the murder of Milo Regis was completed, Jewels and Woodhouse took me back to the Garment District to get my car. Then we met up at a whisky joint on Vine Street.

Over glasses of Scotch on the rocks, we talked about The Open Blouse case. We agreed that another killer must be at large, because Milo Regis had said nothing about killing Scott Drum and Patty Walker.

Realizing we might have a second killer, then two possible suspects came to mind: Bryce Parker and Jill Sabin. Both had probable jealousy motives over the Drum-Walker relationship. But how did Mya Regis' and Kimmie Turner's murders fit into this speculation? Bryce Parker was pushed aside by Kimmie Turner, but who did Mya Regis jilt? Could Jill Sabin have been Mya's jealous lover?

"Joe," Jewels said. "There was something else Milo Regis requested before he checked out.

He said: Tell Joe Stone to find my daughter's killer."

I said through clenched teeth, hissing: "For his entire life Regis was a domineering bastard, doing whatever he wanted with disregard for anybody's feelings. He came off as tough as nails, until he got to the end of the line." I shook my head. "He treated me like I was a moron. Now he wants a favor from me, from his grave?"

"Yeah," Jewels said. "You should have heard him crying out for redemption. It was priceless."

Woodhouse said with a smirk: "Regis begged to be forgiven for murdering his wife and Moe Merrit." He paused for a second, waggled his head. "And his god said I ain't sending no padre to save this sinner."

We lifted our whisky glasses and toasted the poetic justice that was finally handed to Milo Regis.

"Look at what he did to Alice Moore," I said. "She was a university art teacher, a professor, until she became severely ill with an emotional condition. She told me about it in the car. Her doctors called it feeble-mindedness, caused by losing her relationship with Amy Regis."

"What happened there?" Jewels asked.

"Milo Regis demanded that his wife Amy cut contact with her cousin Alice Moore. The sudden separation was devastating. It mentally destroyed Alice, leaving her unable to function normally. She lost her university teaching position, her friends and her house. She's been walking the streets of Los Angeles by herself, for many years, while at night she would stay in shelters for women."

"How'd you meet her?" Jewels asked.

"We met while sitting on a park bench. Maybe a few weeks back," I replied.

"Okay, Joe," Jewels said. I think he rolled his eyes in disbelief. He didn't need to know that we had met in front of Milo Regis' warehouse.

After we left the bar, I stood outside in the parking lot leaning against my Buick. I thought about how long gentle Alice Moore had been walking the streets, and I was wondering if being in jail, like a wild bird in a cage, would cause her more psychological damage.

20

Milo Regis' murder received immediate international press. Three days later, I attended the burial, but it was not out of respect. Along with being a repulsive man, Regis had been a cold-blooded killer.

I stood behind the large crowd of mourners. It was a good vantage point for observing some of the city's corrupt politicians shedding bogus tears. Maybe I should've stood with them handing out soft tissues.

What grabbed my attention was seeing the former Open Blouse employee Jill Sabin. She stood by herself wearing large black sunglasses, a black head scarf, and a heavy black coat that reached down to her ankles. I don't think she noticed me, but she gradually moved farther away from where I was standing.

Police Commissioner Daniel McKenna gave the eulogy, praising Milo Regis as "an exceptional citizen of Los Angeles, who was forced into doing something terrible". He talked on and on in that foolish vein for a couple of long minutes, then concluded with: "All of us will feel the loss of this great man for the rest of our lives." McKenna forgot to add: *even though he murdered his wife and her lover.*

Milo Regis was laid to rest in a vault next to his wife Amy, and his daughter Mya. There was something unsettling, even sordid, knowing that each family member had been murdered, and by a different person.

Before leaving the graveyard, I looked around for Jill Sabin. She was nowhere in sight. I wanted to ask her again about her relationship with Mya Regis, about how close they had become. Maybe they had pajama parties. I needed to keep an eye on Sabin. She seemed to be a fidgety bird, who probably knew more about Mya's death than she was willing to tweet.

The day after the funeral, I was in my office thinking about Max Lee. Still hadn't heard from her. Around three-thirty Commissioner McKenna swung my door open and barged in. The door slammed against the wall. We hadn't spoken since McKenna's dirty dealings forced me to quit my police career. That was twelve years ago.

McKenna, a five-foot-eleven, muscular man with a head of healthy blond hair, looked ten years younger than his mid-fifties. His tight, pale Irish face resembled a high-strung guard dog and his narrow, edgy blue eyes assaulted me with a frigid glare. His nostrils flared when he spoke through clenched teeth.

"So, this is what you've boiled down to, a second-rate snooper in a cheap suit in a shithole office. You make me sick, Stone, with your boy scout ethics. You're nothing! Nothing but a two-bit lush." He stepped closer to my desk, with his fists doubled at his sides. "If I could have it my way, I'd run your trouble-making ass out of this great city."

"What do you want, Danny-boy?" I was smirking. "Make it quick. Or I'll get my prickly broom and sweep your dirty ass out of my clean office."

McKenna rushed my desk, his fists clenched tighter. His pale complexion had turned bright red and his thin sweaty lips were squeezed together like a tight, pink asshole. I stood up and leaned into him. Was close enough to smell onion rings, cigarettes, and whisky bubbling up from his gut.

"I saw you at the cemetery," he said with a growl that let loose like a windstorm. His foul breath forced its way into my nose. "Here's what you're going to do, Stone. You're going to stay away, far fucking away from The Open Blouse investigation. Not your case. Not your problem. It's a cop matter. If you don't back off, I'll fucking bury you." His growl got louder. He flashed his canines. "I'll bury you in the tar pits mysel..."

"Who poured you out of your slime bucket, McKenna?" I wanted to rile him, hoping he'd take a swing at me, so I could bust his lip and loosen a few of his pearly whites. "The last time I checked, I didn't see my name on your list of scumholes for hire. I don't take orders from you. Not anymore, you crooked bastard."

McKenna reached across the desk, grabbed a handful of my shirt collar, and pulled me into him. Being this close, his breath smelled of dog vomit. When he shouted, spit flew like slimy string out of his mouth. Had to move my head sideways to avoid getting hit with slime.

Sweating profusely, McKenna's face turned a darker shade of red, then purple. Blue hammering veins protruded along his neck, and he was shaking like a back-alley junkie.

"You've always been a punk, Stone." He raised his voice. "You think you're some goddamn super dick for finding that abducted girl last summer. But you're nothing!" He cocked his arm, was ready to throw a punch.

"Go ahead, Danny-boy, go ahead and land that punch, and I'll own your badge, your house, your wife, and that pretty cottage in Woodland Hills, where you keep that cute Jamaican number. I'll own her too. Go ahead, throw it, tough guy!" I was beginning to enjoy myself, watching McKenna boil over like a pot of rancid stew.

Using his hand that held my collar, he shoved me back with enough force that I hit the wall behind me. "You're headed for dark times, Stone!" he shouted, and stormed out of the office, slamming the door behind him.

I sat down at my desk, shaking my head and thinking: McKenna is a dirty cop, so what was his angle on The Open Blouse murders? Who is he trying to protect?

"What in the hell was McKenna doing here?" Jewels asked walking into the office. "We were driving by, saw him bolt out of your door like an Irish Setter on fire. He almost lost his balance."

"He looked drunk wobbling down the street," Woodhouse injected. "What went on?"

"He wanted me to smell his breath. Was worried about a date tonight."

Both detectives chuckled, then I told the story.

"He threatened to kill you?" Woodhouse asked. "Jesus H. Christ, Joe, why do so many psychos want to kill you?"

I shrugged my response.

"Listen, we'll stop back later," Jewels said. "Maybe in an hour or two. We're on the move."

Woodhouse agreed with a few nods. They had a male stiff lying at the bottom of Mulholland Falls.

A few minutes later the phone rang. Didn't feel like answering it. McKenna's threat concerned me. I was also concerned about Max Lee's disappearance, and her emotional state.

These days it seemed that misery knew how to dig into me.

The phone was relentless. I finally answered it.

"Joe Stone."

"Hi." Her voice jolted me, knocking me out of my troubled head.

"Where have you been?" I asked sternly. I was still rattled from McKenna's melodramatic performance.

"In Death Valley, at Stovepipe Wells, in a motel." Her voice was low and soothing.

"How are you?" My voice softened.

"Doing better. Dad flew in the night of the shooting. He suggested that we get out of L.A. for a while, so we could talk and think."

"Is there anything I can do for you? Are you coming back here?"

There were a few seconds of silence.

"Mom and Dad want me to move back to Detroit." Her tone was serious.

"And?"

"I'm not sure what I'm going to do. There are so many reasons for me not to go back."

There was more silence, then she said:

"About The Open Blouse. I've memorized the entire case."

"You read the file once. How could you have mem…?"

"I have the ability to remember things exactly as I see them, with all the details."

"That's a powerful gift Max."

"Thank you. I just needed to let you know that I'm okay."

"I am relieved to hear that."

"Thank you, Joe. My father just walked in, so good-bye for now." Her voice trailed off like a bedroom whisper.

I walked over to the window and sat in the pink-cushioned chair, and thought: This day has been surprising and troubling. Max's phone call put an end to my concern for her emotional welfare, but at the same time, Commissioner McKenna had my stomach festering. McKenna's a venomous beast who would crawl inside of you and eat your spleen, while Max Lee is the antidote.

I needed to get out of the office. Had recently read in the L.A. Times that Mya Regis left her whisky bar Five In The Afternoon to Sherry Miller, her general manager.

It was four thirty-five. Could be there in thirty minutes. Just in time for happy hour.

Maybe that's what I needed, a happy hour, or maybe several continuous happy hours.

21

"Joe, it's good to see you," Sherry Miller said. Her usual upbeat tone was subdued.

"Thank you, Sherry. I hear congratulations are in order."

"I wish it were under happier circumstances, but thank you." Her eyes looked downward, then they closed and tightened, like she was trying to squeeze the bad memory out of her head. She opened her eyes again and looked at me, and I could almost see the memories spreading through her eyes like handwriting telling a story. She shook her head, as if to erase the memories.

"Are you here as a customer or as an investigator?" Her voice came cold from the inside, driven by the thought of Mya's murder.

"As a customer," I replied with a warm smile.

Sherry escorted me to an outside table, took my order and walked slowly back to the bar, apparently absorbed in her painful recollection.

Sherry Miller was a good-looking woman, with a slight resemblance to Elizabeth Taylor. She had violet eyes and shoulder length raven hair that turned under at the ends. Heavyset and big boned, she dressed sexy in an elegant way, and carried her large body with poise. At the age of thirty-three, Sherry had been working five years for Mya Regis, as the bar's general manager. Over the years, Sherry and I had come to know each other through my many visits.

"Scotch with water and ice. On the house." She placed the drink on the table. Her hand trembled, the ice cubes rattled.

"Thank you, Sherry. Do you have a few minutes to sit down with me?"

She sat down quickly, almost falling into the chair, and started to talk. Her voice trembled.

"I don't know, Joe," she said looking at me. "I don't know what to say, what to think. I'm trying to sort it out. Mya was a gentle soul, so why was she murdered?"

Her eyes welled. I handed her a napkin, and slid my drink over to her. She took a noisy gulp.

"Can you tell me about Mya's friends? The ones she spent time with, here at the bar."

"Oh, sure. Mya had a few friends that she would meet here. All of them men. One of them would come here more than the others. But I don't think he was a friend."

"Was there anything that stood out about that man? His looks? His attire?"

"Well, he seemed older than Mya, but it was hard to tell with the low lighting. He was tall, blond, and wore tailored suits with black cowboy boots. He seemed tough, in a gangster sort of way, with a rugged face, and nervous bird-like energy." She paused to dab her eyes with a napkin, then took another gulp of whisky, swallowing hard. "He would always look around in a jumpy sort of way, as if expecting enemies to walk through the door. He came here at least twice a month. Sometimes more than that. Mya was always exasperated when she saw him walking in."

"Were you introduced to him?" I asked anxiously.

"No. They always sat in that secluded corner inside the bar, near the window." She pointed across the deck. "Mya left orders to not be disturbed when she was with him. I kept my distance."

"Did she leave with him or did they leave separately?"

"He always left by himself, after about ten minutes. Mya would stay seated at the table, staring out the window at the ocean. There was always tension between them. They never looked happy while conversing. He did most of the talking anyway. His mouth moved fast." Sherry shook her head from side to side, and continued: "Then he would leave in a rush. He always looked angry on his way out the door."

There was a moment of silence. Sherry looked down at the table. Her eyes pooled with more tears.

"There is one other thing, Joe," she said while looking up at me with damp eyes. "The night of Mya's death, she and *this* man were arguing in the parking lot. I saw them out there. Mya had just left the bar after having drinks with you that night, and he suddenly appeared, confronting her after you drove off. It was creepy in the way he came out of the shadows. He must have been watching the two of you, from somewhere in the parking lot. The man was yelling at her. Mya slapped his face. It was a hard slap, his head snapped to one side. I saw it through the window, but I couldn't hear what he was yelling about." Sherry paused and gasped, as if stepping into cold water. She was trembling. "After that, he got into his car and drove off in a rush. Mya came back inside crying, then she went to her office. I didn't disturb her. She came out about ten minutes later and left without saying goodbye to me. It was unusual for Mya not to say goodbye.

That was the last time I saw her alive." Tears fell from Sherry's eyes.

"Can you tell me about his car. The color? Make, model?"

"No, I couldn't see his car. It was dark. And it was parked farther away from where they argued.

I saw the headlights come on, then the car sped away." She paused to dab her eyes with the napkin and said: "I have to go. One of my new employees just arrived. We have a scheduled meeting."

Sherry rose slowly from the chair as if she was too tired to move. She stood there watching the ocean for several seconds. I also got up. She turned and looked at me, her eyes red and swollen.

"I hope to see more of you, Joe. Please, don't be a stranger." She kissed my cheek, then turned and walked towards her new employee. It was Jill Sabin. I decided to stay.

Ten minutes later Sherry Miller's office door opened and Jill Sabin walked into the bar. She was dressed in a tight, white silk blouse with tight black satin slacks, wearing shiny black flats, her work uniform. Sabin was stunningly attractive, and her resemblance to Patty Walker was uncanny. When she noticed me sitting on the deck, her glare gave me the freeze. I smiled warmly anyway, but she came over to my table with a sour expression.

"Are you stalking me?" Sabin snapped.

"Stalking you? I didn't know you worked here. I came to visit Sherry Miller. She and I are friends. Anyway, should I be following you?"

Sabin gave me another sour look, and, with a shrug of her shoulders, snapped at me again. "I have nothing to hide." The force in her words felt like a strong slap across my face.

"Okay then," I said raising my palms towards her as if surrendering. "The new living arrangement in Boyle Heights, how's that working out for you?"

"I didn't have to move after all. This job saved me," she said with a sharp comeback, as if I was the reason for her previous troubles.

"I'm happy for you," I replied sincerely, resting my hands on the table.

"Would you like another drink?" She wasn't friendly about asking me.

"Yes, please. Scotch on the rocks, no water."

She rushed off looking like a ruffled bird.

After she left with the order, I reached into my pocket and pulled out the black coat button. I placed it on the table and just stared at it, wishing that the damn thing could talk.

When Jill Sabin came back with my drink, she immediately noticed the button.

"Where did you get that?" Her eyes widened and her head tilted slightly to the left.

"Why do you ask?"

"I used to have a coat with buttons like that, but it was taken from The Open Blouse one night." She shrugged her shoulders. "I don't know if it was stolen by a customer or an employee."

"I found this button on the ground near my office. I like buttons, so I picked it up. I collect them. It's an eccentric hobby of mine."

She said: "I find it surprising that it looks exactly like the buttons from my missing coat." She looked puzzled. "Well, I need to do my work. Customers are waiting. Is there anything else you'd like from the menu?" Her tone was noticeably softer.

"No, thank you. I should be going."

Sabin nodded. But before she walked away, I said: "I saw you at Milo Regis' funeral. Did you know him?"

"I walk around cemeteries when I need to get away from people. I do it often."

"You were dressed in black."

"People should always wear black when they visit cemeteries, Mr. Stone." She rolled her eyes at me and walked away.

I left the bar, then sat in my Electra in the parking lot, and thought about the information Sherry had shared with me, and especially about the details the coat button had just revealed.

Through one of the large wall-sized windows, I could see Jill Sabin talking to customers while flashing her fabulous smile, a smile to set any man's blood on fire. For a second, she resembled Mya Regis in the way she tilted her head to the left, while listening to a customer talking.

It was nearing six pm. I started the car and headed back to the office, while thinking:

There hadn't been a club-related killing since Kimmie Turner's murder, two weeks ago. Though the killer was at large, the streets were crowded with people. Everyone appeared to be relaxed, but it was easy for me to see that it was just an appearance.

22

Before going to the office, I drove to The Open Blouse to have another look around.

Pulling up to the curb, I killed the engine and sat there staring at the building. The sky was clear with a full moon. The moonlight gave the structure an eerie sort of strength, like a dark flexed muscle. Since Milo Regis' death, the front picture window and door were boarded.

I lit a cigarette and thought about Bryce Parker. The large paper bag he had carried into the club contained something bulky. Parker claimed that the bag had some extra clothes in it, that he kept in his employee locker. He had also carried the same bag out of the club, but the bag was empty and rolled up tightly.

I took a few more drags from the cigarette, flicked the butt out the window and watched the red tip die a slow death in the damp road. I took my Ruger .38 and a flashlight from the glove compartment and headed to the back of the alley. The trash cans and dumpster were empty, and the rats were gone, and so was most of the stench.

The back of the alley was dark, making it nearly impossible to see anything. I switched on the flashlight, directing the beam along the stairs leading to Scott Drum's apartment.

"Hey! I ain't doin' nothin' but sleepin' here, Officer. I jus-needs a place to sleep." Lying under cardboard on the top landing was an old, broken-down white man.

"Okay..." I said, "but you'll have to move along for now."

When I walked halfway up the stairs, the stench from the man was so repellant that it pushed me back down a few steps.

"I'm movin', Officer. Slow, but movin'."

He gathered his cardboard and limped past me, and I had a flashback to that dilapidated wooden warehouse, to that repulsive odor my body had once produced.

After the old man was out of the way, I moved to the top landing and aimed the flashlight at the apartment door. It wasn't boarded, but a large notice with red letters on a white background was tacked to the door. It read: *Under Police Investigation. Do Not Enter.* I put on my gloves, then picked the lock and entered the living room.

The apartment was cold with a sickening odor of mildew and death. I closed and locked the door behind me, and stood there shining the light around the living room. Except for the layers of dust, nothing had changed since my first time here, the day Scott Drum and Patty Walker were murdered.

I moved stuff around, lifted things up and turned other things over. Spent several minutes doing this in the living room and in the kitchen, then moved into the bedroom.

The blood was still on the bed, crusted and black. The pungent stench of leftover decay, mixed with the room's musty odor, produced a strong, foul smell of organic rot. It left me feeling unclean inside and out. I moved away from the bed. There were clothes scattered over the floor. I kicked through them, stirred them up, and then pulled out the dresser drawers. Nothing of importance in them. I opened the closet door. There was a black coat lying on the floor. I picked it up, letting the coat open full-length. It was long and hooded and was missing a button. I took the button out of my coat pocket. It matched the others. If Parker didn't bring the coat to the club, then how did it end up in Scott Drum's closet after the initial police search? But I saw Parker enter through the club's front door. He didn't go anywhere near the alley, and there was no back-alley entry to the club.

I noticed two doors in the bedroom. One led to the bathroom. Opening the second door, there was a narrow staircase that took me down to another door at the bottom, which was unlocked. I opened it and found myself standing in the office of The Open Blouse. From there I walked into the bar. The room smelled of stale perfume mixed with the bitterness of burnt cigars.

I gave the club an adequate search. From there I went to the employee breakroom, where I picked a lock on a locker door that was tagged: Bryce Parker. No spare clothes were kept there. On my way back to the stairs, I grabbed two bottles of Johnny Walker Blue from behind the bar. Back in the bedroom, I grabbed the black coat and left the scene.

At the opening of the alley, the homeless man laid on his side under the cardboard, beneath the lemon tree. I gave him a bottle of Scotch. With a weak, raspy voice, he said: "Thank you, Officer. Now I can sleep real good."

After throwing the hooded coat into my car, I pulled a wool blanket out of the trunk and covered the homeless man with it, and told him to go back to the stairs and sleep. Then I drove to the office.

There was a note from the detectives stuck to the office door: *The dead man in the hills took more of our time than we figured on. Call us when you get back, to let us know you're okay.*

It was late evening but I called immediately. They were still at the station. I asked them to come over to my office.

Waiting for Jewels and Woodhouse, I sat in the pink-cushioned chair and looked down on Hollywood Boulevard. It was glowing with red, green and blue neon. Some people were amusing themselves in whisky bars. Others were smoking reefer in the shadows on the streets. Hookers stood on the corners, insufficiently dressed and shivering. There were a few clean-cut couples walking arm-in-arm, while the homeless crawled into doorways, to bed down for a cold Los Angeles night.

23

"You did what?" Woodhouse yelled. "You broke into The Open Blouse and stole evidence? Jesus H. Christ, Joe. You are beyond crazy. What the hell were you..."

"I didn't break in, Brick. I picked the lock and walked in. There was nothing broken." I was sitting behind my desk, grinning. Woodhouse glared at me while shaking his head slowly, his lips pressed tightly together.

"Joe..." Jewels asked, "what were you thinking?"

"I should arrest you right now," Woodhouse yelled. "Should haul your ass in!"

Woodhouse plopped himself down in a wooden chair in front of the desk, aggressively smoking a cigarette. His face carried the tension of a poker game loser. Jewels paced the room back and forth, then he sat on the couch, then stood up and wore the floor down some more. His wiry body moved like that of a controlled puppet. He was all keyed up.

"The coat would not be admissible as evidence in any court," Jewels said with exasperation. "You should have left it there, and we could've gone back, found it ourselves."

Ignoring their concerns, I said: "Listen. You'll need to pull a search warrant for Bryce Parker's house. He might be connected to the killings. If his prints are on the buttons, you can grill him again. All you need to do is…"

"You're not listening, Joe," Woodhouse said, his voice still raised. "No judge in all of Los Angeles County would sign a warrant based on stolen evidence. Have you lost your mind?"

I ignored him and continued. "There's the scent of cologne on the coat and…"

"Okay–okay," Woodhouse interrupted. "Enough of this bullshit. Let's get back to the facts. You crossed a crime investigation line. You broke into the joint, you stole evidence. You've got three counts against you. How are we supposed to clean this up for you?"

"I'm glad you asked," I replied. "You're going to search The Open Blouse again, based on a tip from an anonymous caller."

Jewels started to interrupt but I raised my hand and said: "No, no. Just listen. I'll bring the coat back to the club. You'll find the coat, and have the buttons dusted for prints."

"Who does the coat belong to?" Jewels asked.

"Possibly Jill Sabin. Remember, she used to work at The Open Blouse, but she was fired. She recently told me that her coat was stolen from the club. Claims she wore it to work one night, but it disappeared. That was before the Drum-Walker killings. If we can prove that Parker had the coat in his possession, this could eliminate Jill Sabin as a possible suspect."

I told Jewels and Woodhouse about seeing somebody leaving the apartment on the night of the murders, wearing a coat like this one. Told them about finding a coat button near Patty Walker's body.

Woodhouse yelled again: "You removed more evidence from a homicide scene? Jesus H. Christ, Joe, I oughta throw the book at you with a rock tied to it. Stand up, I'm cuffing you right now!" He pulled out his handcuffs. His eyes were furious, his face was pinched. He walked towards me, swinging the handcuffs in circles like he was going to whip me with them.

"Okay, Brick, slow down a sec," Jewels said, his hand was raised high with a palm towards Woodhouse. "This may work. An anonymous tip will get us a search warrant, and we can sweep the club again. If Parker's prints are on the buttons, we can bring him in for a second time in connection with the murders."

Woodhouse nodded, but his lips were pulled in and clamped together, like a tightly sutured wound. It seemed to be his expression for letting us know that he wasn't fully on board.

I told Jewels and Woodhouse the story about running into Parker outside of The Open Blouse. Told them about the large paper bag that he carried. It was full going in, empty coming out, and that Parker lied to me about keeping clothes in his work locker.

I said: "That weasel is protecting somebody connected to the case. Or worse, he might be the shooter. Either way, you need to search his mother's house. My gut tells me it won't be wasted time."

Jewels nodded a few times, then Woodhouse put his handcuffs away, shaking his head in disagreement. His mouth still pinched like a prune.

"Okay. Bring the coat back to the club, and we'll call you when we have it," Jewels said. "Wait for the call and don't do anything else that resembles a crime." I nodded with another grin.

When they left, Woodhouse was grumbling all the way along the hallway and down the stairs.

An hour later Jewels called to say that they had the coat.

All went well. By two a.m. forensics had lifted prints from the buttons. They were Bryce Parker's. His prints were on file, since the dismissed charge against him for Kimmie Turner's murder. The detectives pulled a warrant for searching the house of Parker's mother.

Around four a.m. Jewels, Woodhouse and myself, along with six uniforms, stood on the front porch of Parker's house.

Located in Angelino Heights, a few miles west of downtown Los Angeles, the house was a run-down, two-story, yellow and white Queen Anne. It needed dry rot repair and a paint job.

Woodhouse knocked hard on the dilapidated front door.

"Los Angeles Police," he yelled. "We have a warrant to search your house. Open the door!"

Inside the house we heard heavy walking, then somebody running.

"Open the door. Now!" Woodhouse yelled again.

There was nothing. No more sounds. No movement.

Woodhouse was ready to kick in the door, but found that it was unlocked. Three uniforms went in first, followed by the detectives and myself. The other uniforms ran along the driveway to the back of the house.

The stench inside was overwhelming. It was a landfill of rank debris. In every room, there were takeout food containers with rotten scraps left in them, covered with ants. The walls and curtains were stained with black mold. The paper bag that held Parker's piss-wet pants sat on a worn-out stuffed chair. The damp bag was covered with mold. Both floors of the house were in the same squalid condition, and there was no evidence that Parker's mother lived there.

The uniforms completed their sweep of the house, inside and out. Bryce Parker was gone, but the back door was left wide open, suggesting that the running we heard was Parker high-tailing out of the neighborhood. Jewels radioed the station to put a lockdown on all public transportation and to have a judge issue a warrant for Bryce Parker's arrest.

One of the uniforms called out for both detectives to come upstairs. He found a metal box in what looked like Parker's bedroom closet. It was hidden in the back under a pile of clothes. Its contents were five Colt .32 Snub-nose revolvers. There was one loaded cartridge in the cylinder of each weapon.

On the dresser stood a bottle of cologne. Sniffing it, I could tell that it matched the scent from the coat that I found at Scott Drum's apartment. Jewels and Woodhouse had all the evidence needed to charge Bryce Parker with The Open Blouse murders.

Feeling nearly exhausted, I went home, took a hot shower, and then had some fried eggs with toast. Crawling into bed at seven-forty a.m., sleep came like a knockout punch.

24

At six-fifteen p.m. that same day, Harley Jewels and Brick Woodhouse were in my office. Jewels was pacing the floor like a nervous cat in a strange house. Woodhouse was sitting behind the desk thumbing a gun magazine. I sat in the pink-cushioned chair near the window. A fifth of Johnny Walker Blue stood tall on the windowsill, compliments of The Open Blouse. I poured three shots, delivered them to the boys, and sat down again. We toasted to the progress we had made, and savored the top-shelf whisky. We were convinced that Bryce Parker was the killer, which had placed Jill Sabin in the clear for now. More than convinced, we were excited about the revelation. It put us in a celebratory mood.

Jewels poured three more shots, and delivered them. He threw back his whisky quickly, then sat down in a chair in front of the desk. He stretched out his legs, tried to relax, then got up again, pacing the room.

Woodhouse looked over at me and said: "Damn it, Joe. You know I would have arrested you, if Harley hadn't stopped me." I tipped my glass in his direction.

"You would've been doing your job, Brick. You're a good cop. But we did what needed to be done, and in a situation like that, the end-result is all that matters."

Woodhouse tipped his glass in my direction. A smooth, easy grin slid across his mouth. His blue eyes widened and twinkled.

The phone rang. Woodhouse answered it. He was anxious to hear from forensics. After the call, he informed us that the metal box, pistols and bullets had been wiped clean of prints, and the serial numbers had been filed off the guns. And Parker's cologne bottle contained the same cologne found on the coat. Jewels and I grinned, our heads bobbing up and down like happy ducks on water.

I decided that this was a good time to tell them about the diamond earring. According to Bryce Parker, it belonged to Mya Regis. After pulling the earring out of my pocket, I told the story of finding it under Scott Drum's bed.

"No, Joe. No, no!" Woodhouse interrupted, raising his voice, pushing his palms towards me. "I don't want to know about it. Damn it! Don't want to know that you lifted it from the murder scene, and kept it from us."

"I'm just saying…" I said, "that it must have been a set up to make Mya Regis look like the killer. The jealous wife of her husband and his lover. Somebody put the earring under the bed to be found and…"

The office door flew wide open, banging against the wall.

"Which ones-yous assholes killed my father and my uncle?" It was RV, son of Ronnie Rotello, shot dead by Max Lee. Unlike his short, bulldozer of a father, RV was tall and skinny, and a bit stupid-sounding. His dark eyes were bloodshot, moist and jittery, and they were set back, like dirty cubbyholes, on his brainless-looking face.

Soaking wet, dripping all over my wood floor, RV stood in the doorway holding a black Bernardelli .32 automatic. He waved it around the room, as if the air needed fanning.

"Speaks up, or I kills all-yous." His high-pitched voice was loud and brassy, and his body shook violently, like he was having shock therapy. He was hopped up on something.

Behind the desk, I saw Woodhouse's hand pull slowly on a drawer. Woodhouse knew that I kept my Ruger there when it wasn't holstered. Jewels sat down in a chair against the wall, his feet nervously tapping the floor. I could see that he was ready to lunge at RV.

"Fer'da las-time. Which one-a-yous?" RV moved the pistol around the room, nervously aiming it at each of us back and forth.

I said: "Look at what you did to this nice floor. Go and get a mop, punk."

"What?" RV was distracted by my indignant response. He took his eyes off the others, while pointing the gun at me. "Er-you Stone?" His eyes opened wide, reflecting red from the neon light coming in from outside.

I looked at both detectives and gave them a nod to stand up. We all rose at the same time causing the punk to jump back a few steps.

That's when RV spotted the Ruger in Woodhouse's hand, but Woodhouse couldn't lift the pistol fast enough over the desk. BLAM! The impact threw Woodhouse back against the wall. He dropped to the floor behind the desk, moaning and cussing. Jewels rushed RV, but not fast enough. BLAM! Jewels dropped to the floor with a hand pressed to his bleeding stomach. He cussed and rolled around in serious pain. RV held the pistol on me this time, his trigger finger twitched like an agitated snake. His obsidian eyes caught the ceiling light and they seemed to throw flashes and sparks in my direction.

"Hey, asshole. Show's over." It was Max Lee. She had jammed her Ruger into the back of RV's head so hard that his face jerked forward and his head wobbled. With a panther's glare, Max's big, dark eyes peered out from under her black hood, and her wet leather jacket glistened under the ceiling light, giving her a menacing electrified presence.

RV spun around and tried to point his pistol at Max's head. With terrifying speed, Max landed a jackknife kick to his crotch. RV bent forward at the torso, hands hanging down, like he was about to tie his shoes. Then Max turned sideways, inflicting a quick upward elbow jab to his left eye. RV's head whiplashed back, and Max finished him with a palm jab up and under his jaw. The sound of cracking teeth and breaking bones made me cringe. RV staggered backwards, stopped and teetered for a few seconds, while blood and teeth spilled from his mouth, then the pistol slipped from his hand and he fell backwards, slamming into the floor with deadweight. His body lay still as a windless day.

I rushed to the phone, dialed the police, then looked at Max. Her eyes sparkled red from the neon lighting, as she stood over RV's body like a victorious boxer. The Ruger hung down along her side, calm and steady in her hand.

I helped the detectives up from the floor and seated them on the couch. Woodhouse was hit along the right shoulder. Jewels took a hit along the left side of his waist. The bullets had passed through in both cases, causing no dangerous bleeding, but there were holes in my walls again.

"You okay, Joe?" Max yelled.

"Yeah," I was breathing heavily. "You were in Death Valley. How'd you get here so…?"

"Been in L.A. for two days. Called you from my apartment." Her vocal intensity matched her reclaimed ferocity.

I looked over at the detectives. With a grimace Woodhouse said: "Oh, yeah, Joe. We forgot to tell you that RV escaped from prison."

Jewels snorted and added: "Pour us some of that fancy Scotch, Joe."

I poured four glasses of Johnny Walker Blue. We slammed them back fast, while staring at the bloodied body laid out across the floor.

Jewels and Woodhouse were sitting up grinning, like a couple of Cheshire cats, and their eyes were glossed over with a thin sheen of dopiness, while their heads bobbed around like tired drunks.

RV began to stir and moan. Blood bubbles formed around his nose and mouth, and his left eye was black and purple, and swollen to the size of a child's fist. Several of his teeth lay next to him on the floor in a pool of blood. The overhead light made them glint like spilled pearls on a crimson rug.

Sirens screamed along the boulevard with the intensity of angry alley cats. I could hear cops running up the stairs. Could feel the second floor of the building shake, as they ran along the hallway towards my office.

Jewels and Woodhouse were taken to L.A. General, and released a few hours later, all stitched up and bandaged. Lucky for them, the bullets had missed arteries and bones.

RV was arrested on three counts of attempted murder, two counts of shooting police officers and one count of killing a prison guard, during a violent escape from a transport vehicle. Handcuffed and taken away unconscious on a stretcher, RV looked like a scrawny dead rat caught by exterminators.

After about an hour of police commotion at the office, Max and I headed to Abe's Deli for dinner. I felt like we had survived a shipwreck in a violent sea. The rain had stopped but it was still cold. We ended up walking arm in arm, to stay warm.

At Abe's Max told me that she had decided to stay in Los Angeles, and that her father had returned to Detroit several hours ago. She said:

"The wide-open space of Death Valley was ideal for the catharsis I needed. My father was the right person to have at my side, while I sorted everything out in my head. He listened to my concerns without judgment."

I nodded and asked: "How did you know I'd be at the office tonight?"

"I hoped you'd be there."

"But you didn't call the office."

"I was hoping to surprise you."

"You came at the right time, again."

"It was meant to be."

"You could have shot RV."

"Didn't want to spill his idiot brains all over your fancy office," Max said with a wide grin.

I smiled and confessed: "Your speed was intimidating and exhilarating to watch. It terrified and impressed me at the same time"

"Like I said before, I'm fast."

"You seem to be okay with this one. I mean with the violence."

"Thanks to my Dad. He said that if I plan to stay in this business, then I needed to expect this kind of excitement now and then."

"It isn't always like this," I assured her.

"I know. Things will get better," she answered with a captivating smile, like there was a deeper, more personal meaning behind the phrase: *things will get better.*

Reaching across the table, I took her hand in mine. She didn't resist, even though a sense of shyness came over her.

After leaving the deli, we stood outside under the awning. The rain was coming down again like a vertical river, flooding L.A. before it reached the sea. Max and I seemed to be caught in a current of attraction and doubt. We stood there for a few seconds, not talking, not holding on to each other.

When I tried to take her into my arms, Max pulled back gently and said: "I can't, Joe. Not now."

I must have looked stupefied. She continued: "There's too much disorder in my life. Maybe I should tell you why I don't want to go back to Detroit. But it's probably best to keep you out of it." Her gaze dropped to the ground, and she stopped talking.

In silence, we walked to Max's black '58 Impala, parked in front of the deli. After she slid into the driver's seat, we both smiled faintly at each other, then she drove off. Looking at me through the window, Max's stiff half-smile seemed to project troubled thoughts.

25

Later that evening, sitting at the front window in my apartment, I looked down at the empty, wet street. The effect was disquieting, though I couldn't put my finger on why. Then it came to me: Jill Sabin should be informed that Bryce Parker was on the run, that he was the number one suspect in The Open Blouse murders, and potentially dangerous. Maybe even dangerous to her, since there was bad blood between them.

I looked at the table clock. It was nine thirty-four. I called Five In The Afternoon, and learned that it was Jill Sabin's night off, but Sherry Miller gave me Sabin's home number. I called her, letting the phone rang a dozen times. No answer. I called Max, gave her the rundown, and said I'd pick her up. I grabbed my hat and overcoat, and headed to the Buick.

It was a slow drive to Laurel Canyon Boulevard, because the storm seemed determined to sink the Buick. Max and I rode in silence, an awkward silence, a silence that wanted to be filled, but neither one of us knew how to fill it.

The rain on the windshield seemed to transform the oncoming headlights into blinding white flames. Somehow, it reminded me that I needed to pick up Millie and Arnie from the crematorium.

From the parking lot of Jill Sabin's apartment building, Max noticed that there were lights on in all the units except for Sabin's.

We knocked on the manager's door and asked about Jill. The manager was a middle-aged man with a thin pointed face and frizzy yellow hair. His alert copper-colored eyes were as round as pennies. He said that he hadn't seen her today. "It's kind of strange on her day off," he said. "She's usually in and out, even in stormy weather. She carries a camera."

The three of us took the elevator to Sabin's unit. Max knocked on the door. No answer. I asked the manager to unlock the door, then to walk out of sight. Drawing her Ruger, Max opened the door slightly. It was too dark to see inside. When she opened the door wider, we saw Jill Sabin lying on her side, on the floor. The outside streetlamp cast a line of yellow light over her face. Jill's eyes were wide open. She looked terrified. There was blood around her nose and mouth. Max stood at the threshold. Sabin gave a signal with her head, motioning towards the back of the door. Max nodded, and with the force of a bull, she kicked the door wide open.

"Damn it!" The curse was followed by a screech that sounded like a cat caught by a dog.

Max grabbed Bryce Parker from behind the door. He held a four-inch kitchen knife. She pulled him into the middle of the room and twisted Parker's wrist. He let out another screech, and the knife fell from his hand. Max threw Parker to the floor and cuffed him behind his back. His nose bled from the door cracking his face, and he continued to shriek, until Max gave him a sleeper hold. Yanking him from the floor, she slammed Parker into a chair, where he sat slumped, like an old rag doll. His nose was bent sideways, and it bled over his mouth and down to his shirt. His head hung limp, chin to his chest.

I helped Jill Sabin to the couch. She was shivering, her eyes were wet. I put a blanket around her and called the police. Then I turned back to Jill.

"Are you okay?" I asked. "Were you stabbed or cut? Is anything broken?"

"I'm not hurt badly," she said, her voice tremulous. "He slapped my face and I fell to the floor. Then you knocked on the door, and he ran to the kitchen for the knife." She shook her head, adding: "It happened so fast."

Max gave Jill a glass of water and sat next to her, holding Jill in her arms.

While we waited for the police, I noticed that Jill Sabin's walls were decorated with framed black and white photographs. All of them, abstract and surreal. Their style resembled Alice Moore's drawings I saw in the park the other day.

"Whose photographs are these? I asked looking around the room. "I mean, who took them?"

"I did," Sabin answered. Her bottom lip trembled. Her shoulders drooped.

"You're an artist?"

"I have a degree from Whittier School of Art." The terror in her eyes replaced itself with exhaustion.

When the police and the medics arrived, Parker was still unconscious in the chair. The medics attended to Jill Sabin first, then she was taken to L.A. General. Jill had bruises to her face but nothing serious. She was released a few hours later.

Bryce Parker, broken down and as pliable as modeling clay, was hauled to the station. He was arrested for the murders of Scott Drum, Patty Walker, Arnie Bender and Kimmie Turner.

It felt like the beginning of retribution. But it was too early to call the case closed because on the night Mya Regis was murdered, Parker was at The Open Blouse inquest.

It was a gratifying night anyway. Bryce Parker was in custody. With the pistols found at his home, he'd be booked tonight and grilled for four of the murders. But Parker needed medical attention first. He had a broken nose and a bruised throat. The interrogation would have to wait until the morning.

I drove Max to her apartment. Together we walked to the front door. Under the dim porch light, dressed in black with her hood up, she looked menacing, like a criminal that slips along the shadowy edges of a dangerous street. I wanted to reach for her, pull her in close, wanting some of that *danger.* Instead, I gave her a kiss on the cheek. But Max moved in closer. I put my arms around her waist. The tight curves of her body had me feeling lightheaded. I nibbled on her neck. She cooed and gasped. We bit and licked, smelled and tasted. Then we kissed, our mouths filling with raw hunger. We were breaking down the barriers, softening the doubt, the resistance, the awkwardness. Suddenly, she put her palms against my chest, pushing me back gently. Her eyes were closed. She was breathing hard.

"Joe. I can't." She opened her eyes halfway, her lids heavy with lust, and her hands were grabbing my coat now, digging at it with her nails, wanting to pull me closer again. She resisted, saying: "I work for you. You're my boss." Her breath moist against my face.

"I could fire you." My voice was breathy, my heart raced, and I was churning inside like a storm looking to climax.

"It's more than that. Much more than us working together," she said. "I'm married."

Startled, I pulled back from her, and my body stiffened like rigor mortis had set in. Only my mouth was moving. "I'm sorry. I had no idea. Maybe I should leave, and…"

"No, no." She pulled me into her again and said: "I'm waiting for the divorce papers to be signed. My resentful husband has done everything he could to stop the process. He doesn't want the divorce. I'm the one who filed."

"How long have you been married?" I didn't know what else to say.

"One year. The first five months were warm and cozy. After that it was miserable."

"Maybe I should leave," I said again.

"Yes, you should go." Her eyes were pulling at mine. "No. I want you to stay. Yes. I want…"

She pulled me in closer, tighter. I inhaled a lavender scent coming from her hair, and tasted the salty perspiration on her neck. Her hand was under my shirt, nails digging into my stomach. My hand was under Max's shirt, moving to her lower back, sliding down to the moist warmth. I sunk my teeth into her neck. She gasped, trembled. I pulled back, so she could unlock the door, and we took our lust to the bedroom. Like boiling lava, we spilled over until dawn cooled us down to two naked embers, sleeping next to each other. I was on my back, while Max slept on her side, her body against mine, with her nose in my armpit, breathing lightly.

At seven a.m., with a sheet around me, I walked into the kitchen. Max was at the sink banging pots and pans around, washing dishes.

"Oh!" Max said. "A Greek god for breakfast."

She wore a white silk robe that fell to the middle of her thighs, form-fitting her curves.

I stood behind her, my hands untying the delicate belt, while my *Toga* fell to the floor. Before breakfast we took a sultry shower together, until the water ran cold.

Sitting at the kitchen table, Max said: "I am concerned about us being involved while I'm your employee." Her voice was impassive.

"I'll make you a partner. Joe Stone and Max Lee, Private Investigators." The words rushed out sounding hopeful.

She smiled and asked: "What about Dave Wells?" Max got up from her chair, walked over to me and straddled my body. She was wearing the silk robe again. I was in my toga.

I had forgotten about Wells. "Dave will be working for *us*," I said. My heart racing again. She smiled, putting her forehead to mine. Her hair fell over my face like blackbird wings in flight. Her breath was in my nose, warm. She lowered her body over mine, taking me in, and she gasped multiple times.

We ate our breakfast cold, then dressed, and drove to the Hollywood Police Station, where Bryce Parker was being held.

On the ride over, Max filled me in on her estranged husband.

Geano Vesuvio was a thirty-five-year-old Detroit criminal defender, defending mostly mobsters and racketeers, which had made him quite wealthy.

Max and Vesuvio first met at a black-tie awards ceremony for two PIs, who had cracked a twenty-year-old cold case.

"You should see me in a black, sleeveless silk gown," Max said to me with a wide smile.

Vesuvio told her at the ceremony that he hated "private snoopers". Max let him know that she was a private detective. Vesuvio suddenly loved PIs.

Max was impressed by Vesuvio's intelligence, and by his self-confidence.

Against the concerns of her parents, about Vesuvio's mob connections, Max and Geano were married a month later in a small, private ceremony. Max's parents unwillingly attended.

Early in their marriage, Max learned that Vesuvio was explosive, erupting multiple times per day when court cases didn't go well for him. She described him as a five-foot-eight, one-hundred-eighty-pound, tantrum-throwing toddler.

Five months into their marriage, Vesuvio began to stay out late. When he did come home, the sexual odor of other women drove Max into the guest room: "He didn't have the decency to shower."

Max said that Vesuvio was just like his Sicilian-born grandfather, *Geano Vesuvio.* He had his grandfather's arrogance, his womanizer trait, and the same tank-like physique. But unlike his uneducated grandfather, Vesuvio held a law degree from Harvard, and he was a shrewd litigator.

It wasn't just the affairs that troubled Max, it was Vesuvio's aggressive demands for her to quit the 'snooper bullshit' and to start producing babies. Max had rejected both demands.

The first time Max smelled another woman's sex on Vesuvio's face, she refused to sleep with him. Vesuvio attempted to slap Max around over that rejection, but Max crushed his nuts, broke his nose and left him lying in a pool of blood on their kitchen floor. She filed for divorce, then secretly moved to the West Coast. But Max said that she was troubled by the thought that Geano would eventually get the word that she was living in Los Angeles.

26

It was a bad idea to let Bryce Parker cool down overnight. He should've been questioned right after the arrest. But he needed medical attention for his injuries. He spent the night in the hospital, insensible on a pain-killer cocktail.

Jewels and Woodhouse wanted to be the ones to grill Parker, but had strict orders from their doctors to stay home, to let their wounds cool down for a few days.

When Max and I arrived at the Hollywood station, Parker was in the interrogation room with public defender Ben Keller. Keller had spent the past thirty minutes talking to his client. Parker had a tight smirk across his mouth, looking irritatingly smug in a reckless way.

I didn't expect to see Jewels and Woodhouse at the station, but to my surprise, there they were ready to boil Bryce Parker down to the slag that he was. I could see fire in their eyes.

Jewels used a cane to support himself, protecting the stitches in his side. Woodhouse had his arm in a sling. If they were in pain, it was not apparent.

Max and I watched from the observation room.

Parker exuded the confidence of a man who knows what others don't. He sat straight up. Wearing his grey jail clothes, his hands and arms were stretched across the wooden table, palms down. His arms were as still as fish in a cleaning sink.

When Jewels entered the interrogation room, Bryce Parker looked directly into Jewels' eyes with the hatred of a mistreated mutt. Parker's upper lip was pulled back over his teeth, like a cornered animal ready to snap. Jewels kept his cool, showing no reaction to Parker's weak threat.

Ben Keller said: "Detective Jewels, if you don't produce substantial evidence, showing me that Mr. Parker murdered Scott Drum, Patty Walker, Kimmie Turner and Arnie Bender, then this pretense of an interrogation is over. I'll have my client free to walk in less than an hour."

"I'd like to speak with your client alone," Jewels replied.

"My client's rights are to have counsel at his side. I am here at Mr. Parker's request."

Parker eyed Jewels with a wider smirk that came from somewhere bitter and dark.

Jewels got on the intercom, asking Detective Woodhouse to bring evidence Item-A into the room. Woodhouse brought in the metal box.

"What's this?" Keller asked suspiciously. "Why wasn't I informed about this evidence?" Keller seemed a bit frazzled.

"It was in your client's house," Jewels answered, while grinning in Parker's direction. "It contains the same type of weapons used in the murders. The same set up. One loaded round in each revolver with the serial numbers filed off." Staring at Parker now, Jewels added: "Ya wanna tell me why this box of pistols was in your possession, Parker?"

Parker's face lost the smirk. His voice was low, without emotion. "They're not mine."

"Mr. Parker," Keller said sternly. "Do *not* answer any questions." Parker leaned back in his chair, hands resting on his lap. He threw another dirty grin at Jewels with an added sneer. His upper lip twitched, and his eyes narrowed down on Jewels with cold insolence.

There was silence in the room while Ben Keller flipped through the paperwork that had arrived with the box. His finger traced along the sentences of each page like a typewriter carriage. Keller looked up over his glasses and said: "There are no fingerprints on this evidence. Nothing to show that this box, or these pistols, belong to my client. The evidence is circumstantial, Detective. You'll have to do better than that."

"The box was found in his house in his possession," Jewels replied. "How much more evidence do you need?"

"It wasn't directly in his possession," Ben Keller retorted. "He wasn't holding it. You found it buried in a closet. Anybody could have put it there."

Parker threw a sneering smile at Jewels with a dry snicker behind it.

Jewels' neck muscles tightened. He quickly snapped his head to the right, to release the pressure. Then, with heated intensity, he asked Parker: "What kind of friends do you keep that would set you up for murder?"

"I don't have friends," Parker answered sharply. Keller placed his hand on Parker's shoulder to warn him against speaking.

"Then what you're saying is a stranger has a key to your house, and they could come and go as they please?"

"Okay, Detective Jewels," Ben Keller injected. "Enough with the leading questions. Either produce a smoking gun, or we are done with this clumsy interrogation."

Jewels looked up at Woodhouse. Woodhouse nodded, then left the room.

"Parker, you've told everyone that you live with your mother," Jewels said. "Yet, our research shows that your mother died ten years ago, from a chronic lung illness. So why the deception? Why not just say that she is dead and get on with your life?"

Parker's eyes welled, causing his black and blue bruises to shimmer under the fluorescent lights. Then he tried to lunge at Jewels, but Keller grabbed him, pulled him back in his chair.

"Please, Detective Jewels," Keller said. "Let's not throw dirty punches. Keep the questions relevant to the case."

Woodhouse came back into the room with the black hooded coat, and placed it on the table in front of Parker. For the first time Parker's eyes looked worried. He was going to speak, but Keller held him back while he read the evidence report.

"Okay," Keller said. "You have a coat with my client's fingerprints on the buttons and his alleged cologne mixed into the fabric." Keller looked over the top of his glasses at Jewels and said: "And your point is?"

"The coat belongs to Jill Sabin. It was stolen from her. Why was Parker in possession of the coat? And why did he bring it back to Scott Drum's apartment, after the initial police search?"

"Did you see him do this?" Keller asked.

"No, but…"

"Did you find the coat in his possession?"

"No."

"Then this is an assumption, Detective Jewels, leaving you with nothing in this evidence that ties my client to the murders. His fingerprints on the buttons of a coat doesn't make him a killer."

Detective Woodhouse placed several photographs on the table. They showed Jill Sabin's bruised face from different angles. Another photograph showed the four-inch knife that Parker had in his hand, when Max restrained him.

"Then we'll charge him with forced entry into Jill Sabin's apartment, along with assault and battery, and attempted murder with a deadly weapon," Jewels said with confidence.

"There is no evidence showing that the kitchen knife was intended for the purpose of committing murder," Keller retorted. "And Mr. Parker said that Miss Sabin opened the door for him."

"She opened the door because Parker told her he was building maintenance," Jewels retorted.

"Do you have proof of this?" Keller asked. "Because Miss Sabin telling you, is simply her word against my client's word."

"Okay, Mr. Keller," Jewels replied with his take-charge voice. "Let's get down to some real business. What we have here is an assault and battery charge, and there's nothing circumstantial about that. Your client will remain in custody until we can arrange for a judge's hearing, which could take up to thirty-six hours."

Jewels nodded at Woodhouse, who placed his hand on Parker's shoulder. "Okay, Parker, stand up." Woodhouse ordered.

Parker pulled away from Woodhouse and yelled: "Keep your fat hand off me." Tears ran down his cheeks into his mouth, and his tongue raced in circles around his lips. He was hyperventilating.

"No worries, Mr. Parker," Keller said. "I'll petition for bail and have you out as soon as possible. Just sit tight."

This time Parker yelled at Keller: "I don't want to stay in jail. It won't be safe for me in there. I didn't kill those people. Get me out of here, now!"

"What'd you mean, it won't be safe in jail?" Jewels asked.

Parker yelled at Jewels: "He has connections, everywhere!"

"Who?" Jewels asked. "Who are you talking about?"

"Okay. That is enough," Ben Keller said. "Mr. Parker, keep your mouth shut. Detective Jewels, we are finished here."

Bryce Parker's body shook like a rattle in a baby's hand. He was rocking back and forth in the chair, wiping sweat from his forehead with his fingertips. Scared animal sounds crawled up from his throat. He seemed to be having a panic attack.

Max and I watched Parker fall apart. He was vulnerable, ready to crack. Tears finally broke. Snot mixed with blood ran from his broken nose. He tried to pull away from Woodhouse, who had a grip on Parker's bicep. He was working on getting Parker to stand up. With only one hand available, Woodhouse had a difficult time. Jewels got on the intercom and asked for assistance in bringing Parker to a cell. Two uniforms came in and grabbed Parker's arms and pulled him out of the chair. As he was escorted out the door, Parker's legs weakened, almost buckling at the knees. His chin hung low, and his shoulders slumped. Parker acted like he was being led to the gas chamber.

Ben Keller looked at Jewels and said: "He'll walk today, Harley. I'll call Judge Herman. He'll set bail for the assault and battery charges in a few hours."

"It's a mistake, Ben. This kid is unstable. He'll most likely run."

"I'm just doing my job, Harley. Doing what's expected of me."

Ben Keller collected his paperwork from the table, adjusted his glasses and left the room.

Harley Jewels picked up his cane, turned towards the door and hobbled out. Deep wrinkles creased his forehead and his lean face seemed long and drawn with concern that Parker would run.

27

Max and I left the Hollywood police station and drove to my Echo Park flat. Waiting for the phone call of Bryce Parker's release, we placed our twin black Rugers on my bedroom dresser, side by side. After our clothes fell to the floor and our bodies found the bed, Max floated above me like tropical air. I thrusted upwards, reaching for the air, and Max became an ocean of breaking waves in a climaxing storm.

Two hours later Brick Woodhouse called and said: "Parker walks in thirty minutes. Ben Keller finalized the papers. Parker made his one phone call. Bail was posted anonymously through Always Open Bail Bonds." Woodhouse sounded robotic, exhausted.

I sent Max back to the station to tail Parker, in case he didn't go home.

Pulling into Parker's neighborhood, I parked my Buick down the street from his dilapidated Queen Anne. This gave me a good vantage point for watching the front door. Through the living room windows, I noticed that the once white curtains were smeared black with mold. It made me wonder if it had something to do with the condition that killed Parker's mother.

There was a gentle rain but no wind, and a ghostly grey light descended from a dark grey sky.

I thought about Millie and Arnie Bender's ashes again. The crematorium had placed them into a single urn, like I had requested. Millie and Arnie had once said to me that if they were to die at the same time, then they'd like their ashes placed in one urn, and for me to release their ashes into the sea, along the Malibu coast. I remembered laughing about the possibility of them being dead at the same time.

I had delayed taking responsibility for picking up their ashes, maybe because pouring their remains into the ocean would be the defining gesture of gone forever.

A yellow cab crawled along the wet street like a glossy beetle. I slid down in my seat, watched it through the steering wheel. Max's black Impala followed two blocks behind the taxi, as if a hungry predator on the prowl. The cab rolled past me and parked in front of the Queen Anne. Max parked her car across the street from where I was parked. She looked over at me.

Bryce Parker got out of the cab and stood on the sidewalk in the rain. His hands were stuffed into his pants pockets. His chin low to his chest, eyes staring at the ground. He stood motionless.

I looked over at Max. She nodded. We got out of our cars and walked towards Parker, who just stood there looking down at the sidewalk. The rain dampened his banana-yellow hair and the shoulders of his flimsy blue windbreaker. Max walked towards Parker on the same side of the street. I walked along on the other side of the road, until I stood directly behind him. Max stood several feet in front of Parker. He looked up, noticed her, but he seemed exhausted. His shoulders were slumped. She walked closer to him. With her hood up, she had a hostile appearance, but Parker seemed unfazed by Max's presence.

"What do you want?" I heard Parker ask with a weary tone.

"Who is *he*, the man that you're afraid of?"

There was a long silence. Parker shivered, and his hair was soaked through. Water dripped down the back of his neck.

"It doesn't matter anymore," he said in a dull voice.

"Is he setting you up for the murders?"

"He can do whatever he wants to do."

I crossed the street and stood a few feet behind Parker. He didn't notice me at first.

"Is he the killer?" Max asked.

Parker was quiet.

"Parker, answer me," Max demanded. "Is he the killer?"

Parker turned around and faced me. His tired eyes were half closed, and his colorless face had no expression. He just looked sick. His nose was swollen and caked with dried blood, and the areas around both of his eyes were stained black, blue and purple, like carelessly applied mascara.

"What are you doing here? He'll kill you," Parker said with certainty.

"Who, Parker, who will kill me?" I asked.

"You need to stay away from me." He paused and looked straight into my eyes. "Do you think the suicide note in your office was a prank?" He lowered his head and puckered his lips. Then his mouth relaxed. He tilted his head to the right, then looked up at me and said: "Well it wasn't." His bloodshot eyes were directly on mine, watching for my reaction.

"How do you know about the note?" I asked, showing no emotion.

A sparkling black Cadillac rolled along the street, then slowed down. The license plates were rubbed with mud and unreadable. Parker looked at the car with concerned eyes. He turned quickly and walked away from me, moving fast into his house. Max drew her Ruger. I looked at the Caddy, but the daylight was too dim to see inside, and the back windows had shades pulled down. There could've been three men, two in the front seat, one in the back. It was hard to tell.

Max walked into the street behind the Caddy. I walked closer along the driver's side. The car rolled along slowly, staying ahead of us, taunting us. We walked faster, along both sides of the car, trying to get a look inside. Then the engine roared with a smooth growl, and the Caddy sped off, tires hissing over the wet road like a nest of reptiles.

Max asked: "What was that about?"

"I don't know. But my gut tells me it had something to do with Parker's anonymous bail buddy, maybe to see if Parker made it home without talking to anybody."

I walked onto the porch of Parker's house and knocked on the door. No answer. I knocked harder. Parker's voice came through the door: "Leave me alone. Just leave me alone." It had the distant sound of him standing in another room. I could hear him walking around, then heard him go up the stairs, slow and heavy footed, until there was silence.

Max and I met back at my apartment, where we slid under the bed covers. It was a good place to be on a cold, dreary day, under the covers, together.

28

The next afternoon I drove to the crematorium, while Max drove to Bryce Parker's house, to keep an eye on Parker for a few hours. It sounded like a good idea.

Leaving the crematorium, the urn sat on the front seat of my car. As I drove, everything around me seemed to move in slow motion: the people on the streets, the quiet traffic. Even the birds seemed to fly in slow motion. It made me uneasy. Or maybe it was the ashes of my friends riding along with me that left me feeling this way.

I lit a cigarette and rolled down the window, then drove to Millie and Arnie's favorite whisky joint, The Double Shot, on Sunset Boulevard at North Van Ness.

The bar was empty and the lights were low. I liked it that way.

"Hey, Joe. Long time, no see," the bartender said.

"Hi Tony. Good to see you." My tone was somber.

"What 'cha got there?" Pointing to the urn that I was holding.

"Millie and Arnie," I said mournfully.

"I'm sorry, Joe. I loved those two like they were family." His sable-colored eyes welled, becoming like black liquid, and his short, thick body seemed to freeze up. He stood there motionless, staring at the urn.

"Thank you, Tony. They loved you too. Loved your joint."

Tony looked at me and said: "I'm gonna hold a memorial for 'em, here at the bar. Two weeks from today. I hope you can make it, Joe."

I nodded, smiling weakly.

I sat on a stool and placed the urn on the bar, as if a begging bowl for the dead.

There was silence between Tony and me, maybe a moment of memory for our friends.

Then Tony asked: "The usual bourbon and water, Joe?"

"Today, I'll have Millie's usual," I said nearly whispering, looking at the urn. Tony nodded, then shuffled away with his big shoulders slumped, to the other end of the bar. His sadness looked heavy, like it was slowing him down. When he came back, he carried two of Millie's Scotch and ginger ale on the rocks. We toasted to our friends. After we finished Millie's drink, Tony brought us two of Arnie's favorite drink, a shot of bourbon with a water chaser. We threw those back, and for several seconds we were silent.

"The joint ain't the same wit' out 'em," Tony lamented. "Arnie's jokes, his laugh. Millie's classy style, her gorgeous looks, those sea-blue eyes." He sighed, moving his head from side to side. His face drew long and mournful. The blows from this reality seemed to have set in a little deeper. His voice trailed to a whisper.

I nodded in agreement, and pulled out some cash for the drinks. Tony declined the money.

"What'ch ya going do with their ashes?" he asked.

I told Tony about their Malibu request. His eyes welled again.

"Joe, ya gonna get the scum who killed Arnie, right?"

"Yeah, Tony, I'm going to get him."

Back at the office, I placed the urn in the pink-cushioned chair, where Millie Bender always sat.

I remembered the first time Millie saw my office. She said the grey walls were drab. Said the office felt cold, and in need of brightness. She suggested that I should have the walls painted white, and to have the large floor-to-ceiling window fixed, so it would open. Because it was the only window in the office.

Three days later, after working on a case of tailing somebody day and night, I went back to the office to set up my new Remington typewriter. To my surprise the office walls were freshly painted, and Millie had a big pink-cushioned chair delivered. She placed it next to the window that now opened. I liked the white walls and the polished oak woodwork and floor, but was not drawn to the vibrant pink of the large, theatrical-looking cushioned chair. 'The chair stays', Millie insisted. And the big pink-cushioned chair became a symbol of her bright disposition. That was in the beginning of our relationship, when we thought were in love.

After pushing paperwork around on my desk and making a few calls to clients, I headed north to Malibu. The urn was sitting in the passenger seat of my Buick. I drove slowly on Highway 1 thinking that this somber situation might change, if I drove slow enough. Then maybe Millie and Arnie would suddenly be sitting next to me again, alive and laughing.

Millie and Arnie had no family. I was their only family, and they were my only family. It was one of the reasons we were so close.

Pulling into Malibu, I parked along an empty stretch of beach, where the waves were rugged and determined. I sat in the car as stiff as an icepick. The urn and a long yellow rose sat next to me on the passenger seat. It was Millie's favorite type of rose. I attached one of Arnie's orange bow ties to its stem.

I sat there and stared out the windshield, frozen in my sorrow. The rain had stopped, but the late afternoon clouds were still dressed in funereal black. The wind seemed to sing a dirge and some quiet seagulls gathered in the sand, as if distant relatives to the deceased. I lit a cigarette, opened the window and slouched in the seat. I felt like going to sleep to avoid the inevitable. Instead, I turned on the radio. Billie Holiday was singing: *That's Life, I Guess.*

How simple death must be. To disengage from life, from scraping against the grain of this hostile existence, which leaves most people hungry for something else, for something peaceful.

The pungent smell of the sea came in through the open window, pumping a bit of life back into me. Pulling myself upright, I looked through the windshield and watched the ocean churn like a massive agitator. Thought about how it would wash the ashes, leaving Millie and Arnie clean and pure. My heart was pounding at my chest, as if it wanted to leave my body, to go with them.

I opened the car door, removed my shoes and socks, and rolled up my pant legs. Reaching across the seat, I picked up the urn and the yellow rose with the attached bow tie. Together the three of us walked to the waterline, like we had done so many times before.

An air patrol of a dozen pelicans flew over in slow motion, as if paying respect. A wave broke twenty feet in front of me, and the icy water rose to my knees, then pulled back, dragging hissing sand along with it.

It was time to let Millie and Arnie Bender go. I clutched the yellow rose with my teeth and placed both hands around the urn. The water came up to my knees again and I poured my two greatest friends into the sea, while thinking about a line from Rumi: *No dead person grieves for their death.*

Millie and Arnie floated on the water's surface for a few seconds, swirling and dancing together, until they were pulled out by the tide's back draw, to exist forever as salt and water. I watched lingering traces of their ashes holding back, refusing to leave, until a wave came through. It broke, pulled back, and they were gone. I laid the yellow rose with the orange bow tie on the water and watched them follow Millie and Arnie out to the horizon.

I stood there shivering out of my skin, with the air's icy grip squeezing the breath out of me. Then I went back to the car and just sat there with the engine running, heater blasting, watching the waves, hoping to see the rose and bowtie one more time. I didn't see them again.

I hadn't felt this empty inside since I was a teenager, after my father drowned in a boating accident and was taken by the sea.

I finally pulled enough energy together to drive back to my flat. I turned up the heater and was about to crawl into bed, when the phone rang.

"Hello?"

"How was it? I mean, with their ashes?" Her voice was soothing, like warm bath water.

"My head hurts," I replied. "The ashes swirled around in the water and clung to my shins, as if begging me to not leave them there." I was trailing off.

"I'm sorry, Joe, deeply sorry."

"It's good to hear your voice."

"I'm happy to hear that. Can I bring you dinner?"

"Thank you, but I'm going under the covers. I need to sleep, need to stop the aching memories for a while." I paused, and then said: "It needs to end, Max. These killings need to stop." I paused again to collect my thoughts: "I'll ask Jewels and Woodhouse to pick up Bryce Parker in the morning. To bring him in for questioning about the suicide note that was left in my office. Parker knows something about it." I let out a long breath and asked: "How'd the stakeout go?"

"No activity coming or going, nor any lights in Parker's house. I left after a few hours."

"You sound tired."

"I am, Joe."

"Get some rest. I'll see you in the morning."

Max's voice trailed off to a breathy "good night."

I collapsed on the bed, falling into a dead sleep. I don't remember dreaming. I only remembered Millie and Arnie on the surface of the water, the way they danced together one last time.

29

Around seven a.m. the next morning, the phone was ringing. I threw my legs over the side of the bed and stood up. Teetering from side to side, I shuffled into the living room. The relentless ringing jarred my skull, and my blurry eyes jolted with each ring. I reached for the phone and missed it, almost lost my balance. Got it the second time.

"Hello?" My voice was low, groggy.

"Mr. Stone. This is Elliot Mickle, the Public Defender assigned to Alice Moore. Sorry to wake you this early."

"Is she okay?" Suddenly I was alert.

"Yes, Alice is fine. She wants to see you."

"Yes, of course. When?"

"This morning at ten, if that suits your schedule."

"I'll be there. Are you sure Alice is alright?"

"Yes. I saw her last night. She is, well, as you know, Alice," he said fondly.

"Okay, Mr. Mickle. I'll be there at ten. Will you be there, too?"

"No. She wants to spend time with you alone."

I showered, shaved and put on a fresh shirt and suit, then grabbed a clean overcoat, a clean fedora, and called Max before heading out the door.

"Get in touch with Jewels and Woodhouse."

"What's going on, Joe?" She sounded sleepy.

"Alice wants to see me."

"Is she okay?"

"Yes, according to her attorney, Elliot Mickle." I added: "Go ahead and request that Bryce Parker be brought in. Tell the detectives that it's time for Parker to spill about the suicide note left in my office."

"Okay. Then what?"

"Ask the detectives to delay Parker until I get there. Maybe mid-afternoon. I need to hear what Parker knows about the note."

My head was prickly and dull at the same time. I needed fresh air and black coffee.

I drove to the office, parked in front of the building, and walked over to Abe's Deli. The brisk air injected some life into me.

I pulled myself together over two mugs of coffee and toast. Before driving to the jail, I walked back to the office, to pick up some art supplies I had bought for Alice. The phone was ringing when I entered.

"Joe Stone, Private Investigator."

"Mr. Stone. Elliot Mickle again."

"Mr. Mickle, you're beginning to worry me. Has anything happened to Alice since our last talk?"

"No, no Mr. Stone. I had forgot to mention that legally everything looks good for Alice. We have a sound case. Several witnesses have confirmed to the fact that Mr. Regis had slapped Alice in the face, which knocked her to the ground. He was about to beat her some more, when he lost his balance and fell onto the knife. We've already established that the knife was not a premeditated murder weapon. Alice carried it for preparing food she ate while on the streets. She pulled the knife out in unconscious self-defense."

"This is great news, Mr. Mickle. Thank you."

"Yes, of course, but it all depends on the judge we draw for the hearing. The arraignment date is not set. The courts are backed up."

"Okay. Thank you."

"Oh, and one more thing," Mickle said. "The DA is going for a premeditated murder charge. He wants to hang Alice."

"Of course," I answered. "He was probably on the Regis payroll."

"I don't know what that means," Mickle replied.

"No, of course not," I said. "I was thinking out loud."

Gathering the art supplies from my desk, I headed out the door. As always, I have a habit of arriving too early for everything. I parked on North Avenue 19, near the jail-house, and sat in the Buick smoking a cigarette, and watched the storm clouds gather into tight bundles.

A boney Mexican, maybe in his fifties, with an ashen face and long, stringy black hair that looked like licorice sticks, stumbled up to my car. He wore filthy, torn blue bib overalls over a tattered black sweatshirt. One strap of the overall was missing, and half of the bib flopped down like a goat's ear. His worn-down work boots had no laces, and he was sockless. He knocked on the window with a filthy hand and made the you-gotta-cigarette symbol, with two fingers tapping against his cracked lips. His teeth were missing and the whites of his eyes were urine yellow. He was shivering to the marrow. I got out of the car and gave him a few cigarettes. Then I pulled a wool blanket from the backseat and wrapped it around him. Before he staggered off, I handed him a pint of Scotch from the glove compartment. His toothless smile said it all.

While finishing my cigarette, I watched the man take cover in the doorway of a building down the street. That was when the water separated from the clouds, and the man buried himself beneath the blanket, in the company of cigarettes and Scotch.

Pulling up my coat collar, I grabbed my umbrella and got out of the car. I was walking fast towards the jailhouse, when I turned quickly, and ducked behind a parked delivery truck. Police Commissioner Daniel McKenna was running down the steps of the jailhouse. He got into his limousine and was driven away. He looked aggravated, but that was pretty much McKenna's daily expression. I had ducked out of not wanting to deal with another critical assessment of me from that corrupt cop. Because this time I'd probably knock the dirty bastard out, and happily pay the penalty.

Inside the jailhouse Police Captain Doug Roberts came down the hall. He was a good-looking older man with a lean body and a handsome face, and a head of creamy, silver hair. Captain Roberts was the homicide supervisor of the Hollywood precinct, and the boss to Detectives Jewels and Woodhouse.

"Hi Joe. I believe you're here to see Alice."

"Hi Doug. Yeah. I heard that she had asked to see me."

"I was just talking to her. She's quite a gal, that one. Quite a gal."

"Yeah, she holds a special place in my heart too. Um, one question. Who was Commissioner McKenna here to see?"

"Ah! Funny you should ask. He wanted to see Alice, but she refused his request."

"Is that so," I replied quizzically.

"How are you getting along these days with Millie and Arnie's deaths?"

"It's getting easier."

"That was a real shame, Joe, a real shame. I'm keeping the case open, until we nail the scum who killed Arnie."

"Thank you, Doug."

"Alright then, see you around, Joe. And get some rest, you look exhausted."

I walked over to the desk of the jail clerk. He was a tall, skinny, older man with a long, hooked nose that had nostrils the size of cave openings. His face was gaunt with dark, stone-like eyes that watched me closely. His head was nearly bald and his rutted skin was the color of grey putty. He had a small tight mouth that seemed to be glued shut.

When I placed my Ruger on the desk to check it in, one side of his stiff mouth twitched and pulled back. It could've been a grin. He nodded towards the sign-in log. His bony, liver-spotted hand held out a pen. I took the pen and signed the log. He turned around and opened the door behind him to a dark green windowless hallway. His head motioned for me to go in. Passing him, I smelled Bay Rum cologne, mixed in with the sweet corn-scent of bourbon.

The hallway was lit with bright fluorescent tubes, which led to a grey door marked *Visiting Room*. Another officer opened the second door for me. He was short and barrel-like with the same putty-grey complexion, only his skin was oily, and he had a round face with large crooked teeth and a wide, jack-o-lantern smile. He nodded when I passed through the door. Alice was already there.

The wall clock said nine-fifty-nine.

"Joe, you need food and rest."

"Thank you, Alice. It's always nice to see you, too."

"You look thin and tired, Joe."

Alice Moore looked youthful and rested. It was captivating to see her in clothes other than her tattered street garments. Even in grey jail clothes, her warm, round face exuded contentment. Her eyes sparkled like unique gems, and her hair was still frizzy and matted at the same time.

We sat at a wooden counter facing each other. There was a screen divider between us.

"The police captain visits me. He's a nice man."

"Yeah, Captain Doug Roberts, he's a good man. He'd make a decent police commissioner."

"He brought me flowers and a soft chair for my cell."

"He says you're quite a gal, Alice."

"He calls my cell an art gallery."

I smiled. Alice gave me a warm look.

"Everyone is so nice. And the food is hot and delicious. I wish my pigeons were here."

I nodded and slid the art supplies through the slot at the bottom of the screen. Alice's face blossomed like a Kansas sunflower.

"I have exercise classes every day," she said while looking around, as if talking to somebody else.

"That's nice, Alice. But please tell me why you wanted to see me."

"I'm happy to see that you're in love, Joe."

"Huh?"

"It's in your eyes. I can see her in there."

Without another word Alice got up from the chair, gathered the art supplies and headed for the door.

"Alice, where are you going?"

"Back to my soft chair."

"Why did you want to see me?" My voice raised in volume. "Alice, please!"

A short woman, with a wine barrel body and a crew-cut of light-brown hair, stood guard at the open door with a nice smile. Alice handed her the art supplies. The woman took the items and closed the door. Alice came back and sat down again.

"She left," Alice said.

"Who?" I asked. "Who left?"

"Joe, you should really eat more. I don't like seeing you this thin."

"Thank you. I will. Now, tell me what you…"

"What's her name?"

"Whose name?"

"Your girlfriend, Joe. Will she come to visit me?"

"Yes of course, she will," I replied with an irritated tone.

"She was so young when she left and she was alone. I was scared for her."

"Alice, what frightened you? Tell me the story."

"Amy was sad."

"Amy? Is this about Amy Regis?" I asked.

"When she came back a year later, she had changed. She seemed much older."

"Do you mean when Amy left for college?"

"She was only fifteen, Joe."

"Where did she go, Alice?"

"San Francisco was foggy in the summer. Maybe she could see the city from her bedroom window."

"Why did Amy go to San Francisco?" I asked. My patience was thinning.

"She was only fifteen. When she came back, she was sixteen. She changed inside. I could see it in Mya's young eyes, when I saw her and Amy on the streets."

"Mya Regis? *She* went away at fifteen? Tell me about it."

"I wasn't allowed to talk to Amy, and Amy was ordered by her ugly husband to stay away from me. And Mya wasn't allowed to know who I was."

Alice shook her head side to side, and looked down at the wooden counter where she was seated. And without another word she stood up and waddled towards the door. Before she left the room, she turned around and said:

"Amy and I met in secret once. She told me that Mya was sent away, because she was sick. I was scared for Mya. She was only a teenage girl, all by herself, so far away." Alice paused for a few seconds, then added: "San Francisco is foggy in the summer, Joe. Maybe Mya was cold."

"Please, tell me more, Alice. Think hard. Tell me everything you know about that time."

"Time? It's exercise time," Alice said. The barreled-bodied woman guard opened the door for her. Alice looked back and asked: "What's her name, Joe?"

"Who?" I was agitated by Alice leaving.

"Your girlfriend."

"Max. Her name is Max."

"How are my pigeons?"

Before I could answer, Alice was gone. The guard, whose jowl-sagging face resembled a junkyard mutt, smiled warmly at me. I smiled back. Then the door closed.

I decided to walk to a small breakfast joint on Humboldt Street. I looked across the street at the blanketed bundle in the doorway. The Mexican seemed to be tucked in, sleeping, or maybe passed out. There was no movement coming from under the blanket.

Opening my umbrella, I started to walk. The rain was pelting the concrete, sounding like an angry gang was attacking it.

Except for a few police officers running from their squad cars into the jailhouse, the streets were empty.

Inside the long, narrow cafe there was only one large window in the front. I sat next to the window in a worn-down, red-vinyl covered booth with a stained, white Formica table that was scarred with cigarette burns. I ordered a full breakfast and black coffee. After finishing my food, I sat back and stared through the window, wondering why Mya Regis was sent to San Francisco as a teenager, and what illness she might have had.

I looked down the narrow room for the waitress and caught her attention. She came over to my booth. Her short, dull grey hair, her bony frame and gaunt face, reminded me of a retired greyhound track dog. She smiled at me with a mouth full of dazzling teeth. She was kind of cute in a quirky way.

I ordered a second breakfast to go for the homeless man, and paid the bill.

While waiting for the food to arrive, my thoughts were on Alice Moore. About all the information packed inside of her head, and how it seemed impossible for her to string any of it together into coherent sentences. And what was Commissioner McKenna's interest in Alice?

I spent nearly an hour at the restaurant reading The L.A. Times, drinking coffee and waiting for the rain to let up. It finally tapered down to a drizzle. After leaving the café, I carried the breakfast in a paper bag under my umbrella and walked from Humboldt Street back to North Avenue 19.

When I got closer to the doorway that sheltered the homeless man, I saw two squad cars and an ambulance in front of the building. Their red lights flashed an edgy warning.

The Mexican man was on his back, in the doorway, exposed to the weather. The blanket and his boots were missing. In one hand, frozen tightly into his fist, was an empty barbiturate bottle. In the other was the pint of whisky, it was empty. The man's eyes were closed and he had a relaxed expression, as if he had made it on time to where he needed to be.

30

Around twelve-thirty I pulled up to the office, turned off the ignition, and sat there thinking about the dead homeless man. Had I known about the barbiturates, I wouldn't have given him the whisky. Maybe he'd still be alive. But for what, to crawl around the streets like a sick rodent?

Light rain played like a soft steel drum on the car's roof. It was rhythmic, upbeat, and in contrast to my troubled frame of mind.

The daylight was as dim as early evening, streetlights flickered on.

Sliding out of the driver's seat, I looked up at the office and saw a shadowy movement passing by the window. There were no inside lights on. I tiptoed halfway up the office stairs. The top and bottom lights in the stairwell were out, causing an eerie darkness. Drawing my Ruger, I pressed against the wall, sliding along, making it to the second floor. I scanned the hallway. The other three offices were dark. Moving along the corridor towards my office, I fingered the pistol's trigger with apprehension. Something solid dropped to the wood floor inside, hitting it hard, followed by footsteps. I removed my hat and overcoat, dropped them to the floor, then pressed my back to the wall. It was too dark inside the office to see movement through the jalousie glass. Pressing my ear to the door's wooden bottom, I heard a quick, dry cough. I looked through the keyhole. There was nothing visible in the dim light. There was another quick cough and more walking across the room. Heavy walking, maybe from a big man. The filing cabinet slid open. Was it Commissioner McKenna? Was he after The Open Blouse file? My breathing labored. I placed my hand on the doorknob and turned it. Damn that click sound!

The door flung open and a pistol barrel was jammed into the top of my head, nobody spoke.

I lowered my Ruger to the floor, while my eyes looked down at two black cowboy boots, made from shiny snakeskin.

"Dave?" I asked.

"Joe?"

"Yeah."

"What in the hell are you doing crawling around in the dark?"

We both laughed. I picked up the Ruger from the floor, holstered it, then stood up. Wells holstered his .357.

We shook hands and laughed again.

"What are you doing in the dark?" I asked.

"Looking for candles or a flashlight. The building lost power."

I walked over to the file cabinet, pulled the bottom drawer, and took out two candles. I sat behind my desk and lit the candles.

Dave Wells sat down in the wooden chair, and put his boots on top of the desk. He looked every bit the cowboy.

"Good to see ya, Joe." He was upbeat.

"Yeah, likewise, Dave. Are you here to stay, or are you dressed up fancy to go somewhere?" Wells wore a tailored grey suit. He looked youthful and vibrant.

"Just got back from Arizona. Nice weather. Dry and warm in the daytime. Chilly at night though, but as dry as an old coyote bone." His voice was spirited.

"Yeah, I've heard about that dry air," I replied. "I'm beginning to feel like a waterlogged tree at the bottom of a river. I've never seen so much rain in Los Angeles."

"Take a vacation, Boss. Get the hell out of this superficial town for a while." He stopped talking and reached down to pull a fifth of tequila, a lime and a salt shaker from a paper bag. He placed them on the desk and said: "Me and that gal Kim Ness from Santa Barbara, we were holed up in a fancy cabin in Sedona with plenty of tacos and beer."

I smiled in his direction, and pulled two glasses and a knife from a lower desk drawer. Wells dropped his feet to the floor, sat up straight, and poured the tequila. I sliced the lime. We clinked glasses, licked the salt from our hands, threw back the agave juice, then sucked on the lime wedges. Just then the lights came on. We cheered and blew out the candles.

"Kim Ness, huh? I thought she was too dolled up for your taste."

"Let's just say the floss and gloss and highbrow pretentiousness washed away in a desert hot spring. Kim is a downhome girl, not afraid to get her hands dirty or her shoes dusty. And she's such a drop-dead knockout." His lips formed a silent whistle, while his head wagged happily.

I congratulated him for having a gratifying vacation.

"So, are you back to work?" I asked.

"Here's the thing, Joe. It's time for me to get out of this cartoon city. I might move to Santa Barbara. I like the way that seaside town rolls. It's more my pace, and Kim is tied to her job there, as a hotel manager. It's not like I'm going to leave this week, but maybe in a month or two. I have a few important things here to finish up."

"Okay then," I replied. "It's good to have you back, for a while at least. First up, I need to send you to San Francisco."

"Why? When?" Wells asked in complete surprise, his voice an octave higher.

"Tonight," I answered matching his tone.

Wells' eyes opened wide in disbelief. His head oscillated a few times, as if he wanted to say no.

I gave him the information about Mya Regis being sent to San Francisco at the age of fifteen. Told him about Commissioner McKenna busting into my office, threating to kill me, and updated him on Bryce Parker's possible involvement with the killings, about the metal box, and the suicide note left in my office. Wells listened intently.

"In San Francisco, will I be looking through hospital records from about twenty-four years ago?" Wells asked. His eyebrows lifted, stressing the lines on his tanned forehead.

"Yeah, that's right," I said, adding: "There's a plane leaving L.A. in a few hours. I'll call ahead to San Francisco, and get you situated at the Warwick Hotel.

"Okay," Wells replied. "What do you think McKenna was up to when he busted into the office?"

"Possibly protecting somebody connected to the killings. And we're going to find out who that somebody is. McKenna's rotten to the core, and I'm aching to find the facts that will expose him."

I also told Wells about the trouble that Max was going through with her estranged husband.

Wells listened closely and said: "He sounds like an overbearing greaseball to me."

"The hallway floor is the new coatrack?" Max stood in the doorway, holding my hat and overcoat. She was looking slick in her black leather jacket and tight black jeans. Her Doc Martens were sparkling, like they were excited to be here.

"Max!" Wells said. "You're back." He stood up, facing her. "Good to see you again."

"Hello, Dave." They shook hands and exchanged small talk.

Max peeled off her jacket and sat down in the pink-cushioned chair near the window.

"Is Parker in a holding cell?" I asked Max.

"No," she answered. "The detectives and I went to his place. We were too late, Parker was gone. We searched that garbage hole of a house from crawl space to attic. We also searched the rat-infested garage in the backyard." She shuddered at the thought of it.

"Did any of the neighbors see anything?" Wells asked.

"Yeah. Two neighbors saw him get into an Angel's Cab Company taxi, early this morning. Both neighbors said it was around seven," Max answered, then added: "The detectives have an APB on him."

I nodded in approval.

"How's Alice doing?" Max asked.

I told her the story, then added that Wells would be going to San Francisco this evening, to follow up on what Alice Moore had said about Mya Regis.

"Max," I said. "I need you to tail Commissioner McKenna for a few days. You can start tomorrow morning. He's quick, smart and alert, so keep a good distance from him. Take photographs of everyone he talks to."

Max nodded a few times while biting her bottom lip. Her eyes were on mine with sexual intensity.

Wells got up from the chair, put his black Stetson on and said: "I'm going for some lunch. The tequila is for you, Joe. A treat from the Southwest."

I smiled, shook his hand and thanked him. He tilted his Stetson at Max. She made a cute face.

"Dave," I said. "Your boots look brand new."

"Yeah. These are black mamba from Africa. Bought them in Phoenix. My other pair was stolen from the locker room at the city pool, here in Los Angeles. Somebody jimmied the lock, walked off with them."

"No witnesses?"

"Nope. The boots just vanished like snakes in tall grass."

After Wells left, Max and I wrapped around each other with plenty of heat. We were too hot, and decided to leave the office. We ended up at my flat, where we slipped into bed and stayed there, through the evening and into the next morning. With the phone off the hook in the living room, the busy signal was screaming for an operator. I finally smothered it with a pillow.

A satisfying move, killing it that way.

31

The next morning, after Max left to tail Police Commissioner McKenna, I telephoned Angel's Cab Company, and learned from the dispatch operator that the pick-up at Parker's house was at six forty-three a.m. The rider was dropped off at Manhattan Beach near the pier. No specific address.

Then I spoke directly with the driver.

"I already told the cops what I know," the cabbie said. He sounded irritated.

"Yes, you have. But I'd like to hear it directly from the man who last saw the suspect."

"Okay, okay. The rider wore a white dress shirt with dark blue trousers and a thin blue windbreaker. No hat, even though it was a cold, drizzly day."

"What can you tell me about his emotional state or his physical behavior?"

"He was skittish. His eyes were uneasy looking and his teeth chattered, like nervous ice cubes in a glass."

"Anything else?"

"Yeah, he was white as bird shit. No color t'im at all."

"How about being tailed?"

"Nothing that I could see. If there'd been a tail, I'd-a seen it." Then he added proudly: "Nobody pulls that tailing bunk on me."

"So, the drop-off was at the pier and there was nobody around?"

"Yep, jus' like that," the cabbie answered. "Dropped him in the drizzle by 'im-self, then drove off and watched him in the rearview, jus' standin' there. He was shakin', and just starin' at the ocean. He had a loony look in his eyes."

"Did you feel threatened by him?"

"No. Nut'in like that," the cabbie said. "I don't think he noticed I was in the cab. Other than telling me where ta' go, we didn't talk."

"Did he pay the fare?"

"Naw. I jus' let 'im walk," the cabbie replied. "When they're that twisted up in the head, it's best ta' get 'em out of the cab and take the loss."

Stepping into the dreary morning light, I walked to a diner a few blocks from my apartment. Ordered hot food and black coffee. While having a second coffee, I put together a list of things that needed my attention. Calling Jewels and Woodhouse was near the top of the list. Hadn't heard from them in a few days now. I also needed to return calls to some clients. But the first thing on my list was to drive to Bryce Parker's house. I wanted to walk through it at my own pace.

I pulled into Angelino Heights around ten a.m., and entered the broken-down Queen Anne through the partially-open back door. The acidic stench of rot was near nauseating. Ants covered the left-out rotted food. There was a pile of raccoon scat in the kitchen, and a decomposing rat carcass in a corner. Its bulged-out eyes stared at me with frozen hopelessness, while maggots fed on its guts.

I found a tattered broom, and broke off the handle. Used it to lift-up things or to turn them over. After rummaging through the kitchen, I walked into the living room. It was obvious the police had searched this place: everything had been turned inside out and upside down. The pistols were all that the cops found. Maybe that was enough for them, but I was looking for information about Bryce Parker's mother, for anything that could tell me more about her son, and especially his father. After searching the living room and the dining room, I walked up the stairs.

A lone dresser in Parker's bedroom had the drawers pulled and dumped, except for one. It was hanging halfway out. When I slid the drawer out all the way, it dropped out of my hand and landed upside down on the floor. Taped to the bottom was a yellowing white envelope that contained a black and white photograph of Bryce Parker and possibly his mother. In the photo, Parker looked about ten years old. It was taken at Manhattan Beach near the pier. Parker was beaming with potential. And the woman was the good-looking classy type: stylish, sensual, with long black hair, wide-open dark eyes, nice lips, and high cheekbones. She looked at the camera with confidence. They sat on a blanket in the sand. Parker leaned into the woman, while looking up at her. Written in faded pencil on the back of the photograph were the words, *Grace and Bryce*. But who was behind the camera? Bryce Parker's father?

Seeing them together like that, brought back memories of a photograph of me with my mother, at Santa Monica Beach. I was around eight years old. My father had taken the photo.

Then I flashed back to the most frightening living nightmare of my life. My father was killed in a commercial fishing accident. I was fourteen at that time. He went overboard, his body was never recovered. With no husband to bury, my mother threw herself into the bottle. Mourning my father's death, she destroyed her liver with rye. The drinking reached a point where she couldn't function, and she lost her job. Shortly after that we lost our home in Santa Monica. We had to move into a crummy one-bedroom apartment, along the fringes of East Los Angeles. We lived on my father's meager life insurance.

The second living nightmare of my life was finding my mother dead on the kitchen floor of that crummy apartment. Pieces of her stomach were mixed in with her vomit. I had just turned eighteen when that happened. I had her cremated, then hired a boat to take me out to sea, where I gave her ashes to the ocean, near to where my father had vanished.

While turning things over in what looked like a woman's bedroom, I found a scrapbook buried under the rubble in the closet. It was old and tattered, and it contained a flyer from The Strip-A-Go-Go, on Sunset Strip. The photo on the flyer was of the same woman in the other photograph. She looked about nineteen years old. I pocketed the flyer, left the house and drove to the address of the strip club.

According to the owner of the beer joint that now occupied the building, The Strip-A-Go-Go had been closed for over twenty years. He said that a woman named Sally Point used to be the owner of that club. He also knew that after selling the club, Sally bought an apartment complex somewhere in Los Angeles.

I found Ms. Point's address in a phone directory.

She was living in an eleven-unit, single floor apartment complex, in East Hollywood. The stucco walls were painted tangerine, the trim was lime-green. It was festive looking. The complex was u-shaped, built around a garden court. It was luscious with tropical plants. There were plenty of colorful tables, chairs and benches for sitting around the garden. There were several pretty umbrellas too, closed-up tightly like sleeping birds.

Sally Point's apartment was number five, located directly in the center of the complex. The lime-green door was partially open.

"Hello? Ms. Point?" I yelled out after knocking on the doorframe.

"Yes?" The voice was enthusiastic, coming from a backroom. Then she floated up to the door.

Sally Point was a short, round woman who looked to be in her seventies, and she was heavy-set, with cropped orange hair. She wore a bright yellow multiflowered muumuu that hid most of her weight. She had a round yellowish face, accented by a bird-beak nose. Her grey-green eyes were too close together above a wide mouth with lips of no definition. They were painted red. When she smiled, her tiny yellowish teeth were stained with the red lipstick. Sally was loquacious, and she talked fast, too. It was not quite noon, and a copious supply of spirits sailed on her breath, like a pint of rye had tipped over in her mouth.

I asked her about the woman on the flyer. She said her name was Grace Parker. I asked her if she could tell me about Ms. Parker, anything at all.

"Oh, yes," Sally said excitedly. "Grace was the star of the club. They all came to watch Grace. Let me tell you, that young girl could dance and strip like nobody's business, if you know what I mean. She was one of a kind. Men lined up ten deep at her dressing room door, but Grace was classy and she had dignity. She wasn't a tramp, if you know what I mean. She was smart and sexy without pushing it around. After Grace quit the club was never the same, if you know what I…"

"Why did she leave?"

"She wás pregnant, and with the self-respect Grace had, she wasn't going to abort. She left the club to become a mother." Sally lowered her head and sighed. "She wanted to go to law school. She was a smart one, if you know what I mean."

"Can you tell me about the man, the possible father of her baby?"

"Grace kept her personal life private. There were men that she spent time with at the club, but she wasn't interested in a serious relationship. She had bigger plans."

"Did any of the men come around more than the others?" I asked.

Sally was contemplative. Her puffy chest swelled under the muumuu, as she labored to breathe. She looked down at the floor, slowly rocking back and forth on the couch. I studied her face. It was old and bloated, with the telltale look of a woman who had lived a good life. I liked Sally from the moment of meeting her.

"Yes, yes," she said softly, as if to herself. "Yes. There *was* one man. He wasn't a regular. I never got to know him." She nodded a few more times to herself.

"What do you remember about him?"

"He was young and tough looking. Gangster-tough. Dressed in tailored suits. He had the face of a bird, a raptor, a nervous raptor," she said with certainty, while shaking her orange head in agreement with herself.

"What color was his hair, Sally?"

"Blond. Well, almost yellow, banana-skin yellow, a full head of it," she answered quickly. "I saw them together once strolling arm in arm along Venice Beach. I ducked so they wouldn't see me, to give Grace her privacy, if you know what I mean."

"Sally, is there any chance of a name, or anything more? Was he tall?"

"Yes, he was tall. But he never stayed at the club for long, so I didn't get a chance to chat with him. He intentionally avoided me though. I never knew his name and wasn't going to ask Grace, if you know what I mean."

She lowered her head, then looked up at me with a serious expression and asked:

"Is Grace in trouble, Mr. Stone?" Her orange penciled in eyebrows rose-up quickly and her forehead creased into multiple furrows, then her eyes leveled on mine like search lights.

"Grace died, maybe ten years ago."

"Oh, poor child," she sighed. "And her baby?"

"She had a son. Bryce Parker. He appears to be missing. I am trying to locate him."

"I didn't know about her son," Sally said. "After Grace left the club, nobody heard from her again. It was like she never existed." Sally sighed again. "Does the boy look like her?"

"He's pale and blond."

"Probably like his father then," she said. "The blond one that I saw Grace with in Venice Beach."

I thanked Sally for the information. She offered me a glass of rye. I politely declined and took a rain check.

"Any time you want to sit and talk, Mr. Stone, my door is always open."

"Thank you, Sally, and please call me Joe."

"Do you drink rye, Joe?"

"No. Don't have the taste for it."

"Bourbon?" she asked playfully.

"Bourbon or Scotch," I said.

"It will be here for you, the next time you stop by," she said with a flirtatious tone. "You make an old gal like me perk up, Joe Stone. If you know what I mean."

Under the drizzly grey sky, I sat in the Buick outside Sally Point's apartment complex. For some reason, I was thinking about my father again. He was forty-three when he disappeared into the ocean. Mother was forty-eight when she killed herself with rye, five years later. She was a beautiful woman and a good mother, but I couldn't put her broken heart back together. Not even for me, her only child, could she find a reason to live. I wasn't enough.

I rolled down the window and lit a cigarette. The moist breeze latched onto my face and moved quickly through my hair. For some reason, it felt like a cold shake-down. Sitting there inhaling the chilled moisture, I began to feel that death had been busy keeping company with me. I counted all the recent deaths: Scott Drum, Patty Walker, Arnie Bender, Mya Regis, Millie Bender, Bullfrog Rotello, Kimmie Turner, Ronnie Rotello, and Milo Regis. To a certain degree each of them was linked to The Open Blouse. The thought of that place filled my head with uneasiness.

Turning on the ignition, I put the Electra in gear and drove towards the office. Through the open car window, the icy wind clung to my face, as if death itself was clinging to me for my warmth. The drizzle was more concentrated than it was a few minutes ago. I could barely make out the street signs. Maybe that was a metaphor for what I was unable to see about the case, about the connections that seemed to be as obscure as the street signs. What was I missing?

Back at the office there was paperwork to do, phone calls to make, and payments from new clients to prepare for bank deposits. I called the detectives and left a message for them to stop by my apartment after work for a drink. I called a few of my part-time associates and assigned them to some of the new cases.

After organizing my affairs, I headed to Abe's Deli for a late lunch, still thinking about The Open Blouse case, and what I was possibly missing. It had become a constant nagging thought.

Sitting near the window, watching the drizzle thicken even more, I wondered what my father would've looked like today, if he had survived the accident. I thought of my mother lying dead on the kitchen floor and…

"Joe!" It was an urgent whisper. It snapped me out of my head.

Max stood next to me. Her dark eyes pressed hard into mine, like she was holding on out of fear for her life. Her hair was wet. Her leather jacket was wet. She shivered uncontrollably. The weight of her desperation pushed down on me, as if I was a stepping stone for her survival.

"Max." Her name rushed out of my mouth.

When I stood up to take her into my arms, she tried to speak but her teeth just chattered loudly. She was incapable of talking. I held her close for a few seconds, then sat her down in the booth and called out for a mug of black coffee. We looked at each other in silence, while she shivered. She was too cold to talk.

The coffee arrived. Max held the mug with both hands, pressing the warmth of it against her cheek. I waited for her to speak. Her eyes stayed hard on mine. She trembled, then stopped, then trembled some more.

"I followed McKenna all morning," Max finally said. Her face was pale and drawn. "Followed him to Manhattan Beach." She took a deep breath, exhaled hard and loud. Her body shook so much that she had to put the mug down. It rattled on the table, while she held on to it. "Took photographs. Brought the film to Frank's Photo Shop. He processed the order fast."

She pulled two 5x7 black and whites from a manila envelope and slid them across the table. Her hands shook and her eyes seemed to be frozen open. They were as bleak as winter.

I looked at the photographs. One was of Commissioner McKenna with an extremely fat man, whose face was bloated and lumpy in a hideous manner. They were standing together near the pier, under a black umbrella that McKenna was holding. They leaned into each other, as if whispering.

The fat man wore a cashmere overcoat, unbuttoned and pulled open. His hands were in his pants pockets. He was dressed in an expensive looking suit with a vest. A dark homburg with a bowtie hatband covered his head. It accented the chubbiness of his face. He was a lot shorter than McKenna, and his body was shaped like an over-inflated ball, stressing at the seams. I had never seen him before.

In the second photo both men were facing the camera, as if their eyes were looking through the telephoto lens, straight into Max's eye. It was eerie, the way they seemed to look at her, but not see her.

"I wonder who the tubby poser is in the fancy clothes and pretty shoes," I said.

"Geano Vesuvio!" His name flew from Max's mouth like mud she needed to spit out.

32

After getting Max out of the deli, I drove us to her flat in Silver Lake. She sat motionless. Her complexion colorless. I checked the rearview for anything menacing. There was nothing tailing us.

As if speaking to herself, Max whispered: "He's put on weight, so much weight."

A black Cadillac that I had not seen before in this neighborhood was parked close to Max's flat.

I decide to drive past her apartment, and drove around the block. I came up alongside the Caddy and stopped. It was empty. I backed my car up. Got a sheet of paper from the glove compartment, wrote down the make, model, plate number, then threw the paper on the dashboard. Still suspicious about Max's apartment, I drove to my flat in Echo Park.

Pulling into Logan Street, I spotted an unfamiliar black Cadillac parked near my place, a few houses down. I stopped my car, got out and looked inside the Caddy. It was empty. Wrote the make, model and plate number on the same sheet of paper, then tossed it to the floor of my Buick, on the driver's side.

"He must've had my father tailed," Max said, as if detached from the present. "Must've had Dad followed around Detroit, then to Los Angeles, when he came here after the shooting."

Max seemed terrified, like a child who had committed a terrible wrong, and was waiting for the punishment.

"He'll hire local thugs," she whispered apprehensively, as if there was more that she wanted to say, but she went back inside herself and fell silent again.

I parked behind the Caddy, keeping an eye on my apartment. There was nothing unusual, except for the black Cadillac parked in front of me.

Pulling my Ruger from its holster, I checked the cylinder, then slid the pistol into my overcoat pocket.

"If I'm not back in five minutes, drive away and get the police." I gave her the car key. Max nodded, while she looked straight ahead into the wet-blurred windshield.

With my hat pulled low, I got out of the car and ran towards my flat. I lived upstairs. Below me lived John and Edith Morgan, a retired couple.

I walked onto the porch, knocked on their door. Had to knock again, then again. Edith finally opened the door.

"Hi, Joe! We were in the backroom watching television. You look wet. Are you locked out? Do you need the spare key?"

"Edith, listen to me." My clipped response confused her. Her eyes widened. Her jaw fell slack.

John came to the door with a smile, ready to chat. I made the hush sign with a forefinger to my lips.

In a stressed whisper I asked: "Have there been men looking for me?"

John shook his head of silver hair, letting me know that he understood. He whispered back: "Two men. Said they were FBI. Asked for you by name. Didn't seem like FBI to me. They were too dumb sounding and too gruff looking to be Federal Agents."

We stood in silence, looking at each other for several seconds. The empty space after his words was like an exhausting distance.

John said: "They wanted to talk to you about a case you're working on. After I told them that I didn't think you were home, they left and walked down the street."

"Which way did they go?"

"That way." He pointed.

"Joe," Edith whispered. "Are you in trouble?" Her eyes jittery, anxious.

"I'm going upstairs. If you hear loud noises, call the police."

Edith placed her hand over her mouth and gasped. John's tan complexion grew pale, his jaw dropped.

Opening the stairwell door, I crept in. Thin grey light came from a small square window at the middle of the stairs, but it was mostly dark. I took the Ruger in my hand, pulled the hammer back until it clicked. A sharp metallic sound reverberated throughout the hollow space.

Knowing there was a squeaky tread, I stepped over it and moved cautiously to the top landing. Pressing my ear to the door, I listened. There were no sounds coming from inside. Checking the door, it was locked. I took the key from my pocket and slipped it into the tumblers. The unlocking click reverberated thinly. The door creaked when I pushed it opened. My heart raced to my throat and stayed there, pounding like it was running out of time.

Crouching low, I shuffled into the apartment on my feet. The air was a mixture of cheap cologne and rank body odor. My pulse hammered inside my ears now, but what caught my attention quickly was the hard barrel of a cold pistol, against the back of my neck.

A raspy voice growled: "Lower the rod to the floor."

I did what the voice said.

"Get up on your knees, hands in the air, dickface."

I didn't move fast enough. The gun jammed harder into my neck, like it was looking for something to kill. I put my hands in the air.

"Good boy. Now stand up."

I stood up. He frisked me, but found nothing more. Then he shoved me hard with his free hand. I stumbled down the hallway towards the living room, trying to catch my balance.

At the next doorway, another thug turned on the light. He was long and lanky with a dumb-looking face that resembled a dusty potato, and his cheap-looking brown suit was too large for him, like it belonged to a fat man. While aiming a pistol at the front of my head, he grabbed a handful of my shoulder and pulled into the living room. He wasn't nice about it. I almost fell, but caught my balance again.

Dressed in a three-piece brown silk suit and squeezed into my lounge chair was Geano Vesuvio, looking at me with a self-satisfied grin. It was the kind of grin that made me want to keep slapping his face until his eyeballs rolled out of his ears. He sat straight up, strong and confident. One fat leg was crossed over the other fat leg, until he uncrossed them. Both of his pudgy hands, covered in gold rings and diamonds, were placed on the arms of the cushioned chair. It looked like he wanted to pull himself up but couldn't, so he stayed there in the chair, holding that smug grin. We locked eyes and glared at each other, my blood running cold at the sight of him. He was an unpleasant looking man with a flabby body and a large grotesque face, which looked more like a lumpy rubber mask than anything human. A bulbous nose, streaked with small purple veins, pushed out of his face like a chubby thumb had grown there. It added to his grotesque features. Vesuvio's tubbiness continued all the way down to his bloated feet, which were crammed into brown silk socks and polished brown wingtips. The shoes appeared to be too tight for his inflated feet. Fat poured out of the tops of the wingtips.

"Ah, Joe Stone," Vesuvio said, his grin widening with satisfaction. "The private dick, who fucked my wife with his not so private dick." His expression soured. He spat on the floor in front of me, and then wiped his mouth with the back of his hand and wiped that hand on the nice cloth of my lounge chair.

The two thugs behind me chuckled like a pair of twin idiots. I wasn't smiling.

Through clenched teeth Vesuvio asked: "What's-a matter, Joe, no sense of humor?"

I remained silent, thinking about the knife strapped to the inside of my left calf. The dumb thug had missed it when he frisked me.

"Okay, enough of the funny crap. Take off your hat and overcoat and sit down, Joe. Let's have a man-to-man talk."

I didn't move until the lanky thug standing by the door came over and landed a solid punch to my gut. My spine rattled like a bag of loose gravel. I gasped hard, bent over and almost puked, while trying to suck the breath back into my lungs. Beads of sweat formed on my brow. The thug pulled off my overcoat and shoved me into a chair, then he knocked the fedora off my head. It landed upside down on the floor, wobbling like it was wounded.

"Ah, that's-a better, Joe," Vesuvio said. "You look-a relaxed now. You wanna drink?"

Vesuvio nodded at the thug with the dusty potato face, who went to the bar and poured a single Scotch. I took the glass with a shaky hand, almost spilling it. Potato Face poured a whisky for his boss.

Vesuvio lifted the glass towards me and said: "To the asshole who fucked my wife." He threw back the whisky in one gulp, then added: "Drink up, Joe. It'll make-a you feel better."

I threw my drink back. It went down hard, like an axe handle shoved down my throat. Vesuvio nodded at Potato Face to pour me another.

"Okay. Now that we've developed a friendship, I'm-a gonna to tell you about the advice my loving grandfather gave-a me. He said sometimes it's-a best not to kill your enemy. Especially when they're weak and-a stupid, like you, Joe." His mocking grin stretched across his wet mouth. It was slimy, like a banana slug. "My grandfather said it's-a better to keep them alive, so they will suffer for the rest-a-their cheap lives…"

While Vesuvio continued to speak, I kept a peripheral view on the two thugs. They were distracted by items in my apartment. I was hoping that they'd be distracted enough for me to pull my knife, so I could slit Vesuvio's throat and bleed him like a pig.

Vesuvio went on with his grandfather's vulgar advice, speaking with a phony-sounding old-country accent.

"… and to do that, said-a-my grandfather, you need to take-a-something from them. Something that will cause them to hurt emotionally, because-a killing your enemy is-a-too easy and then poof, it's over!" He snapped his chubby fingers for emphasis. "What fun is that, right, Joe?"

My eyes were on his but I didn't answer the question.

"Ah! The silent type and good-looking, too. I'm not surprised my sinful wife fucked you."

He widened his idiotic grin. "So, you can stop-a worrying, Joe. I'm not gonna kill you. Like-a-my grandfather said, that would be too easy, and-a no fun at all."

"Your grandfather is a grease spot," I spurted. "He's repulsive and slimy, like you, Vesuvio."

The lanky thug stepped up to me and planted a hard-hitting backhand across my face. He wore a few big rings for emphasis. My cheek was ablaze from the whack and my brain felt like it had detached from my head. The whiskey glass fell out of my hand, spilled across the floor. Blood ran in a slow line from my nose to my lips, dripped to my chin, and bloodied my shirt. I caught some in my mouth. It tasted like rusted salt.

Vesuvio's grin disappeared. A hard expression mixed with the cruel lines of hatred spread over his repulsive face.

"Any more disrespect, Joe, will-a bring you hours of physical pain, but I can assure you I won't kill you." He brought the tight grin back, as he wiggled and shifted his greasy body deeper into my fancy lounge chair that he had now defiled.

"I heard my wife killed a man to save your life. That's-a-my girl. She's a rare gem. One that I'm going to keep for the rest-a-my life, because I don't give a damn about those divorce papers." He lit a cigarette, pulled a deep drag and blew smoke at me. Then he took another deep drag, exhaling more smoke towards my face. "I'm not-a letting her go, Joe. Nope. She and I are married until-a death do us part, because that's-a God's law." Losing the fake accent, he spoke with hissing breath, his top lip pulled tightly over his gum. "And you are going to hurt for the rest of your cheap, stinking life, knowing that I have her and you lost her." He hacked a dry cough, took another drag and continued to blow smoke in my direction, more as a statement than an exhale.

"Unfortunately, I'll have to punish Maxine for her adulterous crime, and it will hurt me as much as it'll hurt her. I'm going to beat the fear of God into her, and after that I'm going to beat all of the fight out of her." He gave me a creepy wink, while shifting his balloon-body in the chair again, grunting and snorting like a sow in heat.

I remained silent, still looking at his eyes, without giving the impression that my face and gut burned like hellfire.

"And you, Joe Stone, are going to wish you were dead, because you will suffer a fate worse than death. You'll drink yourself into a dirty hole, just like your drunken mother did. Yeah, I know about your sloshed piece-of-crap mother. I have friends in high places here in Los Angeles. They told me all about your pathetic mother. And you'll finish yourself off with bottles of rye, like she did, just to kill the pain of losing *my* adulterous wife. Why, Joe? Because you're a loser and I'm a winner. It's that simple." He raised his voice and slapped the arms of the chair for emphasis and declared: "I always win!"

The two thugs sniggered and snorted, like they were gagging on lumps of phlegm caught in their throats. They were standing behind me again. Vesuvio looked in their direction and nodded. One of them went out the door. I could hear him walking down the stairs, while the other thug pressed the barrel of his pistol to the back of my neck, to remind me of my manners.

"Joe," Vesuvio said jokingly. "You'll need to go to confession and tell the priest about how you coveted another man's wife." He broke into a sinister, bellowing laugh that felt like it shook the floor.

Clamping my teeth together, I hissed: "Confession is for the guilty. I have no guilt."

Vesuvio glared at me. His black metallic eyes were charged with hatred, as I added: "The only thing I'd confess to is killing you."

Vesuvio nodded at the thug standing behind me. He hard-slapped the side of my head. My brain slammed into my skull. Sparks flashed somewhere behind my eyes. I shook it off while the thug laughed at landing that slap.

We could hear footsteps coming up the stairwell. Maybe three or four people.

Vesuvio watched the hallway door with childlike anticipation, until his beady dark eyes widened into larger slits and his grin broadened to a big, sloppy smile. His overly large teeth added a clownish look to his freakish face. Then he laughed out loud and his rolls of body fat shook like a sack of slime. Vesuvio started to rock back and forth in the chair, huffing and puffing, until he had enough momentum to pull his massive weight to a standing position. He teetered a few times, then caught his balance.

"Joe," Vesuvio said, "a gentleman always stands up when a woman enters the room." His mouth stretched into a cocky, tight-lipped grin.

I stood up and turned around.

33

With her hands cuffed behind her back, and her legs chained together, with just enough play to hobble along, Max was presented as a defeated enemy. She had a gag over her mouth, but her eyes were fueled with the kind of rage she had when she killed Ronnie Rotello to save me.

When Max looked in my direction, rage flashed outward from her eyes with lightning bolt anger, but we were helpless. There were now four armed thugs in the room, plus Vesuvio.

"I dun like you wanted it, Boss," said a skinny thug whose pinched face looked like a sick mouse. "I told her to put the chains on, right there in the car, or I gunna blows yer head open. Just like you said to say, Boss."

Vesuvio nodded, maintaining the cocky grin. While he watched Max, his eyes were gleaming, and a strange humming vibrated from his throat. It sounded like a trapped locust. I guess he was excited.

The thug continued: "We gots the downstairs neighbors sittin' quiet."

Vesuvio nodded again, eyes still on Max, still humming, then his bulbous head moved slowly from side to side, like a bubble wobbling in a draft.

"Well, well. My cheating wife Maxine," he said in a steely voice. "And you probably thought you'd never see your loving husband again." He paused to sneer at me and said: "Oh! But this is awkward. Right, Joe?"

He belly-laughed hard and loud again, until his fat wiggled like a nervous jelly roll. Then he said: "Joe, you feeling embarrassed yet?" He gave me another creepy wink.

The four thugs chuckled and clucked and shuffled their feet, like chickens in a pen.

"Okay, you filthy sinners," Vesuvio growled. "Sit down. I'm-a-gonna tell yous-a story. One that my devout Catholic grandfather told-a to me."

He squeezed himself back into the lounge, then nodded to one of the thugs, who poured the boss a Scotch. Another thug, short and muscular, with a face like twisted steel, shoved Max and me into chairs. His cheap-looking suit was too small for him, and I could smell his reeking body. It gave off an offensive odor, more pungent than a skunk, as if a warning for people to stay back.

The room fell quiet while Vesuvio sipped his Scotch, his menacing eyes moving back and forth from Max to me, back and forth. When I turned my head to look at Max, a slap to the side of my face spun me around, until I was looking at Vesuvio again. Swells of fiery pain from the thug's rings rolled over my skin like a fast-moving fire. I shook it off until my eyes focused on Vesuvio.

He sat in the lounge, making slurping sounds with his whisky, then he guzzled the rest and extended his hand holding the empty glass. The skinny thug moved as quickly as a trained monkey wearing a fez, to refill the glass. He handed the whisky back to his boss. Vesuvio took a noisy gulp.

"Excellent Scotch, Joe. Now, who's ready for an old-fashioned story?" He pretended to ask politely, while pulling a crooked grin up the right side of his face.

I remained quiet. Max was still gagged.

"Nobody talking, eh?" He looked at me. "Joe, tell me about the talking, you and my *sinful* wife did while screwing each other." Around the room, the thugs snorted like congested hogs. "I imagine it was like this: oh, baby, deeper, right there, oh, baby, don't stop." The grin left his face, his expression soured. He hurled the whisky against the wall. Shattered glass flew like birdshot. The plaster splintered and booze ran to the floor. Chunks of glass glistened all around.

The thugs sniggered and shuffled their feet.

Vesuvio composed himself by adjusting his tie and vest. A bitter looking smirk cut across his face like an ugly scar, and his greased-back hair shimmered like oil, above his thick eyebrows. He nodded for more whisky.

"So, about the story I was going to tell you." He relaxed into the chair and proceeded to talk in a gravelly voice, emphasizing certain words with theatrical hand gestures.

"There was-a-this old man and-a young-a-woman. The young-a-woman, she was-a-given to the old man by a-her father." He dropped the old-country accent again, but the gravelly voice continued. "And they were happier than any couple in the village. And the old man's young wife was more beautiful than any of the women in village. The old man was also aware that another man had his eyes on his wife, and his wife had her eyes on this other man, who was young and fit. The old husband treated his wife kindly, but that wasn't enough for the young wife. She needed more, because her husband was not fulfilling her physical desires. After a month of marriage, the husband was told that his wife took walks into the woods, while he was taking care of the family business. The husband decided to investigate what he had heard. One day he followed his wife deep into the forest, until she came to a clearing, where the young man from the village was sitting on a blanket, waiting for her. The husband hid behind a tree and watched his wife and the man undress each other. And while the sinful lovers performed their filthy deeds, the husband stepped out from hiding and beat the naked man unconscious, and disfigured his face. The young man was never seen in the village again."

Vesuvio smirked while that image squirmed around in his toad brain. "From that moment on, the husband kept his wife locked in a cage in the barn. Sometime later, and by the guidance of his loving God, the husband impregnated his adulteress wife. After his child was born and weaned from its mother, the old husband tied his naked young wife behind a horse, and dragged her through the village then into the woods, to where she had committed her crime against God. The husband, who understood what God wanted, shot his half-dead wife in the head and left her body to rot. A short time later, the husband remarried and his new god-fearing wife gave him two more children. The old man lived happily in the Grace of God for the rest of his days."

After Vesuvio finished his disgusting story, one of the thugs handed him another whisky. Sitting there with his eyes on Max, Vesuvio stuck his short, fat tongue inside the glass and wiggled it around in a foolish manner, while making slurping sounds. The thugs found that funny. After Vesuvio threw back his whisky, he rocked back and forth to build momentum to rise from the chair. Once standing, he looked at me and said: "Joe, so what'd you think about the story? Makes sense, doesn't it? In the eyes of God, adultery is punishable by death." He exhaled a wheezing sound and continued,

"...and the coveting of another man's wife is also punishable by death, according to the laws of The Church. But, like I said, I'm not going to kill you, Joe."

Vesuvio pulled up his trousers, adjusted his vest, straightened his tie and extended his short, thick arms out from his sides. He looked like a fat scarecrow. The mouse-face thug slipped a suit jacket over his boss's massive body. Vesuvio brushed a hand through his greasy hair. I could smell the distinct musky, sweet scent of Vitalis. Then he wiped that greasy hand on the cloth arm of the lounge chair, and asked for his overcoat. He left a stain on my favorite chair. I wanted to rub his face in it.

"Joe, be sure to bundle up when you go outside. This storm looks like it could swallow any man who gets in its way." He gestured with his head at a thug behind me and ordered: "Put Maxine in my Cadillac, then drive us to the airport."

Max tried to resist, but to no avail. Two thugs escorted her roughly down the hallway towards the stairs, pulling and pushing her.

"Joe, unlike the old husband in the story, I'm not going to beat you. I'm just going to take what is rightfully mine." He was high on hope and desire. "Unfortunately," he said. "Maxine left me on our kitchen floor in a bloodied mess, before she ran into your filthy arms. So, I'll have to beat her when I get her on the plane. Then beat her again, just to be sure she understands where she belongs. I do have a cage waiting for her in Detroit. It'll keep her safe from sexual predators, like yourself. And after she bears my child, I'll kill her, as God wants me to do." Vesuvio's rubbery face bore a wide, wicked smile. Hissing through his teeth he added: "And you will hurt for the rest of your pathetic life, because you couldn't protect her." He sipped more whisky, and then said in a mock-friendly voice. "Here's what I'm going do for you, Joe Stone. I have friends with motion picture equipment. I'm gonna send you a movie of me gutting Maxine alive." His toad-like grin broadened from ear to ear. "You'll hear her scream, when I cut her open. You'll watch her bleed to death before your disbelieving eyes. It should be thrilling, to watch her bleed to death." His deep black eyes conveyed a degenerate thought, as he added: "I'll send along some buttered popcorn for that one. He chuckled and said: "I'm a generous man, Joe. Yes, a generous man."

Vesuvio lifted the whisky and nodded, as if toasting me. His vindictive smile had a cold, cruel edge. When the glass reached his mouth, I lunged at him with all my power, wrapping my hands around his thick, rubbery neck. With crushing force, he fell backwards into the lounge with me on top of him. The chair cracked, broke. Vesuvio squealed like an injured gerbil. With my thumbs pushing into his windpipe, his hot breath reeked of booze, fear, and garlic. From the impact, the whisky glass busted against his face. Blood spilled down his cheek to his double chin. It kept running down, turning his brown silk vest dark maroon. I pressed harder into his windpipe, until a flash bomb exploded inside my head, sending me into twilight. Ghostly contours of my parents floated by: their bodies translucent, eyes frozen open, faces dust-grey. Caught in a sudden twister, I spun through tubular darkness, where I couldn't see, taste, hear, or smell, or feel any pain.

34

"Joe! Wake up. Come on, wake up. Harley, get some ice. Joe, wake up."

I was lying on my stomach in front of the broken lounge chair. My head felt like a pry bar had split it apart. Through my dazed condition, I could hear voices.

"Here ya go, Brick," Jewels said.

Brick Woodhouse sat me up against the lounge, then placed the ice to the back of my head. My eyes opened but I couldn't lift my head up. I tried to speak but only drool spilled out of my mouth, onto to my shirt. My eyelids drooped and closed. I nodded off again.

"Joe, come on. Open your eyes. Look at me!" Woodhouse snapped. "Harley, a glass of water. Joe, wake up. Lift your head. Open your eyes."

I lifted my head, but my eyelids wouldn't collaborate. My head wobbled like a weather balloon floating through a fog. Jewels poured water into my mouth. I gagged and coughed up bile and pulled for air that seemed stuck in my throat. My eyes popped open. I guzzled more water, coughing and pulling again, until my breath broke through what felt like a straw's narrow opening. Gasping and gagging, I shook my head. That head motion made me feel even more queasy.

"Jesus H. Christ, Joe," Woodhouse said. "That's quite a lump you have."

He pressed the ice harder to the back of my head, which cooled the loud flames down to whispering embers. I tried to speak, but still couldn't. I wanted to nod off, but fought it, and stayed conscious.

Jewels was on the phone, while Woodhouse forced more water into my mouth. Then he poured some of it over my head. Chills ripped through my body like pins and needles. I shivered and swore. When I looked up at Woodhouse, there were two of him swaying from side to side, and the room swayed with him, and my eyes felt like they were venting fire.

"What happened, Joe?" Woodhouse asked.

When my eyes focused, I saw a trail of blood across the carpet that led to the hallway. Broken glass was scattered around the living room, glinting like eyes watching us.

Jewels got off the phone, knelt in front of me and asked: "Who did this, Joe?"

"Neighbors. Downstairs. Backroom." My breathing was labored and my speech choppy.

"I'll check on the neighbors," Jewels said.

Woodhouse pressed the ice harder to the back of my head, but the pressure made it feel worse.

I closed my eyes again. Flashing blue light pulsated rapidly inside my head. I reached back, pulled his hand away from my wound. My heart raced like a windstorm. I sucked in too much air, and gagged some more. Woodhouse dropped the ice on the lounge. He got up quickly, went to the bar and came back with a glass of Scotch. I gulped half of it and handed it back, while gasping and coughing.

Jewels came back into the room. His somber expression said it all.

"Joe, I'm sorry. Both of your neighbors are dead."

I snapped my head from side to side, trying to stop his words from entering my ears.

Then it came to me: "They have… Max… Black… Cadillacs… Airport…" I tried to get up, but fell back against the broken lounge. My head lowered in slow motion, like I was shutting down for the night.

"We found these plate numbers on the floor of your car," Jewels said. "We figured something was wrong. Your car doors were unlocked, one was ajar. It's a good thing you left a message for us to stop by today."

"APB… Now… Phone… Now." I tried to stand up. Woodhouse gave me a hand and helped me to the couch. I sat there like a bird with clipped wings, trying to work my breath away from the anxiousness that wanted to overtake me.

Jewels called-in the license plates, make of cars, their body colors.

Woodhouse asked: "Who has Max?"

"Geano… Vesuvio. Ex… husband," I replied in a semi-whisper. "Taking… her to… Detroit."

Woodhouse nodded at Jewels. Jewels repeated the information into the phone.

"Whose blood is on you?" Woodhouse asked.

"Vesu… vio's. Whisky glass… broke… against… his face. He's… very fat. Wears… pretty clothes."

Jewels repeated the information into the phone. He asked for the hospitals, train stations and airports to be covered with uniforms, and to watch for a fat man with an injured face, wearing expensive clothes, with possible blood stains.

"They have Max chained, gagged. Four goons and Vesuvio. Max took photos of McKenna and Vesuvio, together at Manhattan Beach." My body shivered, but I could more-or-less form full sentences now. "Max tailed McKenna for me. It shocked her to see Vesuvio in L.A. McKenna must've pulled a background check on Max, then contacted Vesuvio in Detroit." I stopped for a moment to collect my thoughts. "This is McKenna's dirty work. He set this up."

Woodhouse shook his head in agreement, and said: "Maybe so, Joe. This is the type of behavior McKenna's known for, but you can't be sure that he's involved with an abduction." I just stared at Woodhouse, my eyes were burning on the insides, the pain cutting deep.

With help from both detectives, I stood up from the couch. They held onto to me until I stopped teetering. Placing my hand to the back of my head, I had a hot lump the size of a walnut shell.

Sirens were screaming around the neighborhood.

"We've got to go," I said while holding the back of my head. The detectives insisted on taking me to the hospital. I refused, and gave them a fast rundown on Vesuvio's plans for Max.

Spotting my Ruger on the floor under the couch table, I bent over slowly, picked it up and holstered it.

The three of us walked down the stairs. Medics and police were going into the lower apartment, on Jewels' order. I stopped for a moment, looked inside the flat, and shook my head again. More police were running up the stairs to my apartment. Jewels stopped and gave orders to some detectives. Then the three of us headed to the airport, in their car.

The police radio was busy with chatter about the situation, but there were no sightings of black Cadillacs with those plate numbers.

Riding in the middle of the backseat, leaning forward, I watched the cars ahead of us. Traffic was light. Nighttime was closing in. The headlights from the oncoming cars exploded like fire bombs in my eyes. My head jerked sideways.

Harley Jewels drove as fast as the road conditions allowed. Said we'd be at LAX in twenty minutes, if traffic near Westchester was light. It didn't feel fast enough though.

Woodhouse got on the radio, gave our location and asked for an escort. We needed more flashing red lights and sirens to keep our path clear. Within a minute, two squad cars joined us, one in the front and one in the back.

A report came over the radio that one of the Cadillacs was pulled over on the 110, a few miles ahead us. Two of the thugs were apprehended. A third thug tried to shoot his way out. He was gunned down. There was no sign of Vesuvio or Max, nor the fourth thug.

When we reached the police stop-scene on the 110, two handcuffed thugs were being led towards patrol cars, stumbling and slipping on the wet road, as they were shoved along. The third goon, the one with the twisted face and the bad hygiene, lay dead in the road. One arm was straight out in front of him, the other was at his side. It looked as if he was swimming through the puddle of blood, trying to get away. We raced past the scene, sirens blaring.

Woodhouse radioed for reports on flights with destinations to Detroit. While we waited for that information, we picked up speed. It was dark now and the airport was in sight. The lights of LAX shimmered like a mass gathering of fireflies.

Report of a private jet with a Detroit itinerary came through, with another report that the airport was shut down. All departing flights were grounded. All arriving flights were diverted. All passengers and visitors were moved to safety zones. LAX was in an emergency lockdown, with a report of a possible shooter holding a hostage in one of the terminals. Police had already boarded the private jet. It was fueled, ready for departure. Taken into custody, the pilot was grilled. He knew nothing. "I'm just the pilot. The plane company tells me where to fly, and I fly." He added that his client *was* Geano Vesuvio.

A few minutes later a new police report came in. The second Cadillac had been pulled over a few miles from the airport, heading south on the 101. The report said that the fourth thug was now in custody, and that he crawled on his knees begging for forgiveness. He spilled the dirt faster than an overflowing slop bucket. The mouse-face thug told the police that he had dropped Vesuvio and Max at Central Terminal. Said that Vesuvio's wound was bleeding badly, and added that Vesuvio was in severe pain, with a glass shard jammed into his face, under his left cheekbone. Said that Vesuvio had drugged Max with sedatives. He later said that it was Augustine Rotonda, the dead thug floating in his blood on the 110, who had needlessly killed the downstairs neighbors.

At Central Terminal our car came to a sliding halt. We jumped out and hit the sidewalk running. I wasn't as fast as Jewels and Woodhouse, kept losing my balance. Blue lights flashed behind my eyes, as if the seconds were ticking away in color. But I kept moving forward, like a determined bullet fired at its mark.

35

The terminal crawled with cops, inside and out. A short, older sergeant, with a round body and a red droopy face, rushed over to fill us in: "Several rooms are not cleared, including a men's restroom, a maintenance room, and two storage rooms," he said slightly winded.

"Which way to the restroom?" I asked.

"This way," the sergeant said. He moved swiftly along the corridor. The three of us followed him, almost running to keep up. My gut told me that Vesuvio had possibly ducked into a bathroom to treat his injury.

Four uniforms stood near the bathroom. Two on each side of that door, backs pressed to the wall. Two medics waited out of sight. The sergeant nodded at one of the cops. The cop pushed open the door. BLAM-BLAM! Two shots fired from inside the bathroom sent us diving to the floor. The young cop at the door took a slug to the shoulder. He twisted sideways, jerked backwards and fell hard, moaning and cussing and rolling around, holding his bleeding shoulder. Another cop dragged him out of the line of fire, leaving a smear of blood across the white marble tiles. The second shot had struck a wall-size window that splintered into cracks and lines. We all crawled out of view of the doorway.

The Sergeant commanded a rugged young cop to swing a ram, and knock the door off its hinges. The cop did it with two quick blows, then ducked along the wall. The door crashed to the floor, landing inside the bathroom. BLAM! Another shot from inside. It hit the tiled wall behind us. Pieces of tile flew like shrapnel. The piercing gun blast carried itself down the hallway until it disappeared, swallowed by the corridor.

It occurred to me that if Max was drugged, she'd be oblivious to what was happening, and the fight would've been taken out of her. On the other hand, Vesuvio should be in critical condition by now. The mouse-face thug said that the glass shard in Vesuvio's face went up and under his left cheekbone, with the top of the glass sticking out of his skin. He said that Vesuvio's left eye was swollen and partially closed. Since he was in severe pain, the thugs had robbed a Rexall drugstore along the way to the airport, taking first-aid supplies and painkillers.

Suddenly the aching in the back of my head was intense. Pain shot down my spine, knotting my gut muscles, and my eyes were blurred again. I shook my head trying to refocus my vision.

Then it hit me: here I was again, up against another homicidal maniac, but this one was ready to blow Max's head open if he felt cornered.

There's a difference between pain that is drawn out and pain that's inflicted quickly, with brute force. Not knowing Max's condition was the slowest of drawn-out pain.

"Hey, Joe. Joe!" It was Vesuvio. "I know you're out there, can smell your stinking fear." A loud villainous laugh erupted from inside the bathroom. "This is all your doing!" He laughed again. "You should've kept your nasty cock in your pants and not in my wife's beautiful cunt." More laughing trailed off to an eerie silence.

"Vesuvio. This is Detective Brick Woodhouse with the Los Angeles Police Department. Your back is to the wall. If you force us into it, we'll gas you out."

"Go to hell you moron copper," Vesuvio yelled. "Toss one cannister and Maxine's brains will be an abstract painting on the pretty wall." More sinister laughing. "I'm in charge here. I've got my gun to her head. I'm in goddamn charge here. Is that clear enough?"

"Okay," Woodhouse replied sarcastically. "You're in charge. Okay, boss."

"You bet your fat ass, I'm in charge," Vesuvio yelled. "I'll be telling *you* what to do, and you're going to do it and like it." His booming voice reverberated and bounced off the bathroom tiles and gushed through the door opening like a dynamite blast.

Detective Woodhouse yelled back: "What do you want, Vesuvio?" There was no answer, just more eerie silence after Woodhouse's voice faded along the corridors. Woodhouse yelled again: "Let's talk Vesuvio. Tell us what you want." Vesuvio didn't respond.

A police helicopter was hovering low to the roof, causing a loud metallic rumbling. Then it landed on the roof with booms and thuds, causing the terminal's support beams to shake with thunderous force, making communication for all of us impossible. I rolled onto my back and could see the steel rafters of the terminal, vibrating from the heavy pressure. My heart raced like it was working overtime, trying to pump all the blood out of itself. A knot formed at the back of my head, and pain gripped my shoulders with great pressure. I shook my head, trying to avoid the discomfort. It didn't work.

To my right, Jewels was on his stomach, yelling into his radio, his jaw moving rapidly. I think he was ordering the helicopter to clear the area. Because as fast as the chopper had landed, it lifted off the roof. The dull whop-whop of its rotors rose into the sky, then trailed away like a swarm of locusts changing direction. There was dead silence again, and for some unexplained reason my thoughts flashed back to my father. Could he have been saved from drowning? It was too much for me to think about. He was dead and Max was alive. She must be. Max was the only leverage Vesuvio had.

The air around me turned thick and hot. I was sweating profusely. I felt like hell. I could feel my internal drums beating everywhere. Beating in my head, my ears, my chest, in the pulse of my neck.

I reached inside my coat and pulled my Ruger from its holster. It felt reassuring in my hand. I lifted the pistol, spun the cylinder. It had five rounds. All I needed was one to drop Vesuvio, just one. I was sure of it.

The whop-whop sound had returned. Looking up, I could see the helicopter through the smaller plate glass windows, that were along the wall near the ceiling. Its spotlight made the rain-splattered glass glisten and flicker, causing the raindrops to sparkle, like fisheyes caught in light beams. Each time the chopper came close to the building, the blades slapped the panes with gale-force pressure, spreading the rainwater flat against the glass. The glass looked like it was melting.

Looking around, I noticed that Jewels, Woodhouse and the uniforms were standing again, holding their arms forward from their bodies, gripping their pistols with both hands. Their guns were aimed at the bathroom opening. Still lying on my back, I stretched my neck and tilted my head towards the bathroom. Everything was upside down, including Max.

She was standing in the doorway. She was still chained at the ankles, and her hands were still cuffed behind her back. Her eyelids were closed, then they'd open, then close again slowly, repeating that motion over and over. I flipped onto my stomach and stood up. I saw no reason for raising my Ruger, the cops had the new development covered from all angles.

Max's face glistened with perspiration and her nose was caked with dried snot. Parts of her sweaty hair fell over her face, sticking to the skin along her cheeks, making charcoal-like drawings of thick and thin lines. Her Doc Martens were scuffed at the toes and her leather jacket was ripped at the collar. She stared forward, most likely not seeing me at all, though I was in her line of sight. Her eyes were distant looking, like the glass eyes of an old-time doll. Her head would suddenly drop and she'd jolt and lift it up again, with an eerie sort of grin. She looked as drugged as a sick junkie.

Vesuvio stood behind Max with one of his arms around her stomach, holding a switchblade in that hand. He nervously twirled the pearl handle in his palm. A pistol was taped to his other hand and his index finger was taped to the trigger. The tape was white, like medical binding. The barrel of the gun was jammed into the back of Max's neck.

With a diabolical smirk, Vesuvio tried to appear in better shape than he was, standing slightly to the side of Max. He was no longer wearing his suitcoat and vest, and the knot of his tie hung to the middle of his stomach like something dead. His unbuttoned silk shirt was covered with blood and his tee shirt was drenched in sweat. He had a dry cough, and kept sniffing snot back into his nose, making a sickening sticky sound while doing it.

Vesuvio's left eye, swollen purple to the size of a baby's fist, was closed tighter than a pinched balloon. Yellow slime oozed from the corner of that infected eye. His wound had been dressed, but the dressing had come loose from the top. It was covered in dried blood and the dressing hung down, flapped over, like a lazy ear. The top edge of the glass shard was visible, sticking out of his cheek. It glistened under the ceiling lights like a holiday ornament. Hanging from his neck on a thin gold chain, a small golden crucifix sparkled brightly in contrast to the bloodied tee shirt.

Vesuvio moved his head farther away from Max's body, to survey the room with his good right eye. He wasn't looking at anybody directly. He just looked one way, then the other, slowly. When he noticed me, he moved his head out a little farther to get a better look. The way Vesuvio tilted his head, was like a fighting cock sizing up his enemy. With his teeth clamped together, his jaw was set hard, and his top lip was pulled tightly over his upper teeth. In his good eye, I saw the rapid movement of his thoughts, felt his vengeance directed at me.

Even though Vesuvio's open eye flared with malice, I could also see that he was exhausted and was suffering severely. The wound dripped blood and yellowish goo faster now, and his good eye must have been burning from sweat dripping into it. He blinked rapidly, as if trying to clear the salty stinging, and his head snapped violently from side to side.

There he stood, a Mafioso goon, royalty while in his Detroit hood, but out of place and cornered in Los Angeles, like a chess king running out of moves.

Vesuvio's good eye was glaring at me, and I could sense urgency in his labored breathing, the urgency to kill me.

36

Detective Jewels ordered the uniforms to lower their weapons. He didn't need any quick trigger fingers. From twenty feet away, Jewels kept his pistol aimed at the left side of Vesuvio's head. Woodhouse had his bead on the right side. Both detectives were expert shooters, and always in control of their weapons.

I glared at Vesuvio and he glared at me, while we held our pistols like gunslingers at a showdown. Only, my barrel was facing the floor and his was jammed into Max's skull.

"Joe, my drinking buddy," Vesuvio said through a wicked grin. "Did 'ja bring that good Scotch so we can celebrate our friendship?"

"I'm going to kill you, Vesuvio," I said firmly. "Then I'll celebrate your death."

Vesuvio broke into a booming belly laugh, causing Max to flop around like a boneless animal. Her head drooped slightly, then snapped back up. Her expression was as blank as a nail head.

"Joe, Joe, Joe." My name crackled from the bottom of Vesuvio's raspy throat. As he spoke, I could see strings of spit attached from his tongue to the roof of his mouth. "If not for you *stealing* my wife, we'd be good friends. Right, Joe?" He belly-laughed more, jolting Max's head again. Then he yelled out his next words: "This world of misery we're now in is Joe Stone's creation. This is his dirty game and we're all suffering because of it, and God knows there will be one winner. I will be the goddam winner. I *always* win!" His maniacal, thundering voice reverberated throughout the corridor. It felt heavy and repressive like an explosion.

Woodhouse yelled: "You're done, Vesuvio. You're not going to make it out of…"

"Shut the fuck up, copper! And listen to me. I'm walking out of here with my wife." He stopped talking, and laughed again. Then his tone turned mirthless. "We're going to board the plane and you idiot cops are going to clear the path for me." He looked at Jewels and said: "Get on that radio and clear the area. Clear it!" He was yelling again. "Get that chopper out of here. Get those floodlights out of here. Clear the area all the way to the plane. Now!" His booming voice bounced around the walls, floor and ceiling, as if he had surrounded us.

Vesuvio's wound was now leaking a steady line of blood. His once olive complexion was pale and tinged with grey. He grimaced, obviously in severe pain.

Jewels stepped closer to Vesuvio, who reacted by jamming the gun harder against Max's head. For a second, Max's eyes popped wide open, then closed again, and her head drooped.

"Go ahead copper, be an asshole hero. Go ahead, do it!" Vesuvio's gun hand shook like an automatic martini mixer and his jaw quivered, sending ripples through his chin-fat. Jewels backed off a couple of steps, but kept his bead on Vesuvio's head. His trigger finger was relaxed and ready.

Along the top of the terminal windows, the hovering chopper aimed a spotlight into the surrounding area. The glaring beam moved steadily over the top part of the wall, where Vesuvio was standing with Max. The light moved in slow sweeping motion back and forth, up and down, like it was painting the walls, but it couldn't get the angle needed to shine directly on them.

Jewels was on the radio, yelling: "Get the chopper out of the area and ground it. Clear a path from the gate to the jet!"

Vesuvio also demanded that the pilot be seated in the cockpit, with the engines running. After he heard Jewels shout those orders into the radio, he turned his attention back to me.

"Joe," he chuckled. "I'm a man of my word." He chuckled again, then hissed through clenched teeth: "I'll send all the gifts I promised you." His gravelly voice trailed off like he was falling asleep standing there. He appeared to be running out of steam.

Vesuvio pressed his dry mouth to Max's ear and said: "Honey, tell Joe how much you love me."

Max's eyes opened wide again but they were dull looking. "Tell'em, Maxine, tell'em how much you love me. Go ahead, tell him!" He shouted the last words. Max's eyes opened wider and her head moved in a slow yes-motion, until it dropped, and her dark hair hid her face like a Gothic veil.

My breathing accelerated. I wanted to lunge at Vesuvio and finish the job that I had started, but it would've been too chancy.

"Because we're drinking buddies, Joe, I'm gonna throw Maxine's hands into your giftbox as a bonus. I'll have them stuffed and looking pretty." His good eye opened wide, but he didn't laugh this time. Instead, he spat on the ground towards me and said: "Yessir, thanks be to God, because you're gonna' suffer, Joe Stone. You are going to hurt so fucking deep that the pain will squeeze your heart out of your chest. You scumbag home-wrecker!"

With that bitter swell of anger, Vesuvio's good eye bulged out of his head, as if all the physical pain in his face was trying to escape through that one eye.

Jewels ordered the law enforcement outside to move out of sight. He reminded them to stand down. "No shots fired. We have a hostage situation." He told them again about the gun taped to the perpetrator's hand, the finger taped to the trigger. Jewels yelled into the walkie-talkie: "One shot at the perp might cause him to fire at the hostage."

Woodhouse ordered the uniforms around us to clear the area. Though I didn't look their way, I could hear them running down the corridor. Heard doors opening hard, slamming into the walls. There were men shouting to other men to clear out of the area. For a few seconds Central Terminal was as quiet as an empty morgue.

"Okay, rat turds, get the fuck out," Vesuvio barked. "If I see your faces between now and us getting on the plane, I'll sink this fucking knife into Maxine's shoulder." Then he chuckled. "That oughta wake her up." His good eye bulged out again, while his head snapped from side to side, waiting for us to leave.

Vesuvio's wound was bleeding steadily now, and sweat dripped faster into his good eye. He was blinking rapidly again. His clothes were soaked through with perspiration and blood, and his Vitalis-treated hair glistened like tar bubbles in an August heatwave. Yellowish brown goo oozed along the edge of the glass shard, bubbling up, ready to spill over. He was shivering and he appeared to be feverish. His good eye projected delirium.

Max lifted her head and stared at me with a remote look. Her face was flushed and she was sweating more than before. Strangely, her left eye closed and opened slowly. It was too slow for a blink. I hoped that it was a signal, something to show me that she was aware of the situation. Maybe she was coming down from the drug. My interpretation of the blink was that she did signal me, so I nodded. Max's head dropped slightly and came back up again. It looked like a slow nod. Then her head lowered to her chest and stayed there this time.

My thoughts went back to Vesuvio: there's no anti-venom for this rabid dog, other than a bullet to the head.

"Joe. Joe." It was Jewels in a calm voice, pulling me out of my thoughts. "We need to clear the area. Let's go."

Uncharacteristically quiet, Vesuvio said nothing. He just stood there, watching us through his bulbous good eye, which had become jittery, like it was being electrocuted. His head wobbled and his teeth chattered. The yellowish-brown goo had doubled in volume, and it was oozing out like boiling foam.

Jewels and Woodhouse walked backwards along the corridor, telling me to come along. The three of us continued to walk backwards, our pistols aimed at Vesuvio, until we turned the corner of the corridor. When we were out of his sight, I took off running at top speed, even though my injured head told me to stop moving. Jewels and Woodhouse were yelling at me, but I couldn't make out what they were saying. Their voices trailed in and out like in a faraway radio broadcast, then they faded altogether as I turned another corner, running towards the gate.

Propping myself against a window, I could see the gate door, part of the tarmac and part of the terminal. It had been cleared of all law enforcement. The police helicopter was grounded and out of sight. Under the yellow glare of the tarmac's floodlights, the entire scene looked like a modern ghost town of huge plate glass windows, concrete and steel. It looked eerie and foreboding.

I leaned far enough to the side of the window to look at the cockpit of the jet. I could see the pilot seated in the captain's chair. I could hear the engines humming. I leaned back against the window.

A short time later, the gate door opened. Vesuvio shuffled out backwards, still holding Max around her waist. His pistol still jammed into her head. He was turning the switchblade nervously in the other hand. He pulled Max along, both moving backwards. The right side of her leg chain had been released, making it easier to maneuver her. When Max's feet shuffled, the loose chain made a hissing sound, dragging over the tarmac. Her head was still slumped and her body was partially limp. Vesuvio pulled her along, stumbling at times. Occasionally, he would stop to catch his breath, then he'd turn his head quickly to look at the jet, to keep his bearings aligned with the short flight of stairs to the fuselage. He just about collapsed once, when his knees buckled slightly. Another time, the two of them almost fell over backwards. It was impressive how Vesuvio pulled out of that one in his condition. For the entire time he never lowered the pistol from Max's head, never stopped spinning the switchblade.

Behind the tall lighting system, the sky was black, but the lights cast a sinister yellow glow over everything on the tarmac, making the two figures look otherworldly, moving backwards as one.

When they finally reached the jet, Vesuvio tapped the bottom step with the back of his left foot, then lifted that foot to the step without looking behind him. He squeezed his arm tighter around Max's waist. The switchblade stopped turning. Leaning forward, he brought his right foot up. He reached the second step in the same manner, while heaving Max up to the first step. Midway on the stairs, he stopped to rest, breathing hard. If Max had come down at all from the drug, she'd probably dead-weight her body against his, making Vesuvio work harder.

I leaned tighter against the window, sliding off to the side for a better view. From my vantage point, I saw Jewels and Woodhouse hiding along the corridor that led to the gate door. They were on their knees, peeking out of one of the large plate windows.

Vesuvio finally reached the last of the five steps. With the next step he'd be standing on the top landing. His breathing was labored, and his upper body seemed to stiffen with each inhale, then he'd teeter front to back after the long, heavy exhales. The switchblade was turning again, the pistol still pressed into Max's head. On the last step, Vesuvio stopped for a longer break, as if this was as far as he could go. His stamina appeared to be nearly depleted. He turned his head to the right to get a look at the top landing with his good eye. He struggled to step up while pulling Max with him. His legs wobbled, almost buckled again, but he found the strength to get himself and Max onto the landing. Catching his breath, he worked up more energy for the last step into the fuselage.

Standing at the opening, Vesuvio turned to the right, using his good eye for entering the plane. When he turned, he lost his focus on Max, and his gun-hand shifted away from her with the barrel pointing to the sky. With his head sideways, he noticed me standing behind him with my Ruger aimed just above his right ear. Vesuvio quickly spun halfway around, desperate to shoot me. When he pointed his pistol at my face, my left hand grabbed Max by the shoulder of her jacket, yanking her into the plane. BLAM!

The left side of Vesuvio's head blew apart like an exploding pomegranate. At point-blank, with the impact of a .38 slug traveling through his skull, his head snapped to the left with such force that I heard his cervical spine crack. What remained of his head was lying motionless on his left shoulder, as if he was looking sideways for a better situation than this one. Standing alone, Vesuvio's massive body moved in a slow circle backwards from right to left. Then his body pitched violently forward, lifting off the steps into the air, and landing belly down on the tarmac. The left side of his face was pressed into the ground, spilling blood. For a few seconds the toe of his right shoe pushed into the tarmac, as if he was trying to gain traction to move forward. Then his left leg slid back and forth a couple of times, like a slow, sweeping broom cleaning up this ugly trash.

When Vesuvio's body stopped moving, I noticed that the greased hairs on the undamaged part of his head were still in place. The Vitalis had accomplished what the advertisements had promised.

37

Max was on the floor of the fuselage, lying on her back. I was on both knees pulling her into my arms, breathing in her pungent sweat. I looked out the open door. The tarmac was filled with squad cars, ambulances and fire trucks. Flashing red lights threw stroboscopic images against the terminal walls, of men in manic motion. Other men moved like angry ants flushed from their nest, some of them yelling orders. Sirens blared with uncontrolled emotions. Two helicopters hovered loudly, their floodlights sweeping the area. One light stayed on Vesuvio's body, as if he was a Vaudeville star.

Jewels and Woodhouse gesticulated madly to the cops around them. Their bodies flared red in the emergency lights. Jewels was on his walkie-talkie, his mouth working like a nervous bird. Woodhouse yelled for somebody to cut the pistol from Vesuvio's hand. Medics pulled gurneys out of ambulances. The blood that had pooled around Vesuvio's head was thinning down to pastel red, as it mixed with the rain puddles.

"I'm sorry this had to happen," the pilot said. He had shut down the engines and now stood behind me.

"Do you have water? I need water. A bolt cutter. Bring a bolt cutter!" I replied with urgency.

The pilot ran to a tool cabinet in the rear of the plane, and returned with the cutters and water.

I tried to slow-feed the water to Max, but she was passed out. The pilot cut the chain from her leg, and the chain linking the handcuffs. I pulled Max's arms to the front of her body, poured water in my hand and cleaned the dried mucus from around her nose.

Two medics entered the jet and took over caring for Max. I stood up and leaned against a wall, exhausted. The medics checked her pulse, then opened her eye lids, shining a small light into them. After they wrapped Max in blankets, I asked the medics if I could carry her out of the plane. They said yes.

I bent down, picked Max up in my arms, and carried her down the steps to the tarmac. The medics helped me to place her gently on a gurney. They wrapped her in more blankets, then rolled her off to an ambulance. I just stood there, rooted to the spot, staring at Vesuvio's mutilated head, while several photographers anxiously documented his final pose. Dozens of flashbulbs popped in a seamless explosion, as if a celebration was in play.

Another medic noticed the lump on the back of my head, and he escorted me into the ambulance with Max. She was hooked up to an I.V. Her eyes were closed but her expression was soft and untroubled. Jewels and Woodhouse came over to the ambulance. Before the medics shut the back door, they reached inside and shook my hand.

"That was a brilliant move, Joe. Checkmate to that king of assholes," Jewels said with a wide grin. His light blue eyes wild with excitement over the outcome of this once hopeless situation.

"We didn't know where you ran off to," Woodhouse added. "It looked like that piece of crap was going to make it into the air." Woodhouse shook my hand again. I tried to smile but was too exhausted. I just sat there and stared at him. He wrapped both of his warm hands around my cold hand. A medic asked the detectives to step back, so he could shut the door. I looked over at Vesuvio's body one more time, and saw that it was covered with a white sheet now. The thin material clung to his chubby frame, detailing every line of what was left of that ugly demon. He looked like a bloated ghost that had fallen from the sky.

My head was throbbing. A medic was holding ice over the lump. I closed my eyes and exhaled a weary breath. That's when I started to shake, a forceful shaking, triggered by too much adrenaline coursing through my body. The medic wrapped a blanket around me, as the ambulance sped off into the night, siren wailing like a wounded animal. I tightened the blanket around my body, but I couldn't stop shaking, nor could I stop looking at Max.

After the emergency room doctors had attended to my head, I sat in a corridor waiting area with a few other people. They had tight, worried expressions. There were constant announcements over the PA system, for certain doctors to report to certain ER stations. Doctors and hospital attendants rushed along the corridor. A middle-aged nurse passed by reading a clipboard. Two older doctors in scrubs walked by, engaged in serious conversation. A male orderly pushed an empty gurney through swinging double doors with a sign that read *Medical Personnel Only*.

Nobody looked at me.

A clinical odor filled my nose. The germicidal scent brought back memories of the times my mother was rushed to the emergency room. I remembered the near-death expression across her chalk-white face, the oxygen mask over her mouth and nose, the doctors rushing her into a treatment room to pump her stomach.

The ripe smell of my own body suddenly hit my nose, like a dead animal gassing off. I needed a hot shower, and bourbon for the nerves. I closed my eyes, leaned back, and gently pressed my head against the wall, to avoid the lump on my lower skull. Sitting there, I dozed off.

"Mr. Stone." There was a soft voice, as if heard in a dream. "Mr. Stone, hello."

I jolted awake. My eyes were fuzzy and my lips were stuck together. The taste in my mouth was foul, and my lips felt like sticky glue.

"Mr. Stone, I'm Doctor Richard Swanson, the attending physician to Maxine Lee."

Standing in front of me was a tall, skinny young man, who wore black horn-rimmed glasses that kept sliding down his long, bony nose. About every ten seconds, he'd use two fingers at the bridge of his glasses to push them back in place. Impeccably dressed in a starched white physician's coat, he carried pens in a pocket protector, arranged from tallest to shortest, right to left. His expression was kind, his eyes caring.

"Ah, yes. Um, ah, you caught me dozing," I replied and then sat up straight. My eyes were blurred. I shook my head to clear them.

"Yes, you must be exhausted," he said. "I watched some of the news coming from the airport. It must have been horrifying. I cannot imagine how you are feeling. Would you like a glass of water?"

He ordered water from a nurse, who walked by. I moved to stand up, but he insisted that I stay seated. The nurse returned with the water. I guzzled it down and looked up at the doctor with searching eyes, leaning into him for the report.

"Miss Lee is doing well. Her vitals are good considering what she had been through. We have her on an I.V.

treatment for dehydration." He adjusted his glasses. "There are no broken bones or concussions. There are minor cuts and bruises, along with small abrasions here and there, but nothing that needs sutures." He adjusted his glasses again. "And there are no internal injuries." He smiled after reporting that fact.

"Can I see her?" I asked with desperation.

"Well, given how late it is, and since Miss Lee needs uninterrupted sleep, I'll have to say no at this time. A blood test showed that she was given chlordiazepoxide. We found needle bruising for two entry points in her neck. The drug needs to work itself out of her system. It would be best to let her sleep it off for a day."

I nodded in agreement and looked down at the floor. That's when I noticed how filthy my shoes were.

"My suggestion," Doctor Swanson said, "is to go home, take a hot shower and get some sleep. I'll call you in the morning, to let you know when you can visit her." A soft, pleasant smile stretched over his mouth when he added: "She was lucky to have you there, Mr. Stone."

Doctor Swanson extended his hand. We shook hands and smiled. He then turned and walked away through the double swinging doors with the sign that read *Medical Personnel Only*.

I stood up slowly, was looking for a phonebooth to call a taxi, when a memory flashed by me. It was of the moment on the tarmac, before the medics closed the ambulance door. Inside the terminal, at one of the large windows, I had seen Police Commissioner Daniel McKenna standing by himself, his mouth agape, with what looked like shocking disappointment.

38

Four days had passed since Vesuvio's final eruption, and the newshounds had shifted to another headline.

Max and her parents were staying at a cabin in Borrego Springs, in the desert. When her parents were in L.A., I didn't get a chance to meet them. We were never at the hospital at the same time. When I visited Max in the hospital, she told me that her mother was insisting she move back to Detroit, to leave the "homicidal atmosphere" of Los Angeles behind.

Reflecting on that turbulent day at the airport, I was thinking that Geano Vesuvio had made three critical mistakes. His first was coming to Los Angeles, thinking that he could abduct Max without resistance. His second mistake was not killing me when he had the chance. Vesuvio's final blunder was losing control over Max, when he turned to point his gun at me. Considering his costly mistakes, it made sense that Geano Vesuvio had lost the game. Still bothering me though, was the image of Commissioner McKenna at the terminal window, with the troubled look of a high-strung loser. What was McKenna's role in this fatal tragedy?

I turned my attention back to The Open Blouse investigation. Bryce Parker was still on the lam.

I was in the office thinking about where his hideout could be, when the phone rang.

"Joe Stone, Private Investigator."

"Mr. Stone, my name is Kim Ness." There was a lovely sigh after those words. "Maybe Dave Wells mentioned my name to you?"

"Um, yes, he has. Ah, Kim Ness from Santa Barbara. The hotel manager."

"Yes, that is correct, except, I am a co-owner and not the manager. Dave didn't get that right."

"Ms. Ness, what can I do for you?"

"I need to speak with you," she said in a low voice, as if somebody might be eavesdropping.

"I'm listening."

"Well, actually, I need to show you something."

I could tell by the sound of her voice that she had cupped the phone, wanting to be private.

"Something about what?" I lowered and softened my voice. Talking with her made me feel that way.

"I would prefer not to discuss this matter over the phone. Can we meet somewhere other than your office? I do not want us to be interrupted."

"Are you in Los Angeles?"

"Yes."

"There's a café..." I gave her the address and the time, and asked: "How will I recognize you?"

"You will have no problem identifying me. I'll be wearing a light green dress with matching heels." Her low voice trailed off seamlessly to a dial tone.

At Star-Struck Café in Echo Park, I waited for Kim Ness. She was already twenty minutes late. I was about to leave when the cafe door opened. I had no problem identifying her.

The tailored, light green silk dress emphasized her substantial curves. The dress had long sleeves with white silk gloves at the ends of those sleeves. The dress stopped just above the knees, accenting the lines of elegant muscles along her calves. She wore seamless nylons and shiny green high heels. On the front of the dress, five decorative green buttons slid from side to side when she walked. Her walk was all hip motion, and it spilled over the cafe like hot syrup over French toast. Some older women were watching her with sour expressions. Their penciled in eyebrows had arched way up. Without moving their heads, their critical eyes followed the green dress with its persuasive hip motion, headed in my direction.

Ms. Ness sauntered up to my table like warm breeze through an open window. I stood up from my chair. Her subtle perfume made me rise in more ways than one. I felt like ordering French toast. She leaned into me lightly, as if I was there to hold her up. I politely stepped back. Against my five-eleven, she seemed to be about five-foot-six, without her heels, and she looked to be in her late twenties, maybe early thirties. It was hard to tell.

"Mr. Stone?" she asked with the same whispering phone voice, still leaning into me.

"Ms. Ness. Please, have a seat," I whispered. The whispering was contagious.

I extended my hand. She held it delicately for support, while the green dress slid into the chair with regal poise. She neither smiled nor frowned. Her other hand held a 5x7 manila envelope.

After taking my seat, I stared at her eyes, mesmerized by their color and shape. They were wide-open round eyes with lime-green irises. Parted in the middle, her blond hair fell just below the shoulders and turned under at the ends. She had high cheek bones with an aquiline nose, and her red lipstick glistened like Maraschino cherries. I suddenly felt hungry for cherries.

Her silk-gloved hands slid the envelope across the table without hesitation, while she looked around the café suspiciously. When I picked up the envelope, her anxious eyes widened even more, until the lime-green color intensified like neon lighting.

When I removed the contents of the envelope, Ms. Ness began to fidget. She looked around the café again. First over one shoulder, then the other. I scanned the café and saw nothing of concern.

I placed the photographs in a pile and looked at the top picture, then at Ms. Ness. She sucked in a quick breath, as if a dagger was pointed at her. I picked up the photographs and held them like a card shark, so other people couldn't see what I had. After viewing the collection, I stacked the photographs back into a pile, slid them inside the envelope. Though I was concerned over what I had seen, I displayed no emotion, not wanting to add to her anxiety.

"Where did you get these?" I asked, still whispering.

"From Dave Wells' jacket pocket." She leaned into me from across the table this time, tightening the space between us. "They were in the new jacket he bought, when we were in Sedona. He left it behind at my place. The jacket had dust on it and some dirt spots. I emptied the pockets before sending it to my cleaner."

I nodded, then shifted my thoughts to the many homicide scenes Dave Wells had photographed for the LAPD.

Ms. Ness continued: "After pulling the envelope out of the inside pocket, I placed it on a table. As the day went on, my curiosity got the upper hand." She quickly looked down, as if ashamed, then slowly looked up at me again. "You can imagine how disturbed I was. The shock of it. The horror. It physically made me sick. Then I felt angry, then confused, then frightened. Mr. Stone, please tell me, what is going on here?"

"You are aware of the kind of work Dave does for the…?"

"Yes! But is this a customary practice to carry these disturbing pictures around in your pocket?

I mean, for what?" Tears welled in her green eyes, creating the appearance of lime juice. She removed a white silk handkerchief from her white leather clutch. "What have I gotten myself into? I am terrified, Mr. Stone." She paused to collect her thoughts. "Should I be frightened? I should be, right?"

I nodded in agreement, not knowing what else to say. There was a moment of silence between us, while she patted her eyes with the handkerchief.

"Can I keep these?" I asked.

"No! I must put them back in the jacket after it comes back from the cleaners. I cannot let Dave know that I saw them. I mean, what would I say to him, if he knew?" She paused to dab her nose. "He's coming back to Santa Barbara tonight to stay with me, before he returns to Los Angeles." She paused, exhaled a sharp *ha* sound, and spoke quickly: "I am breaking it off with him, I have to. I cannot sleep with Dave again after seeing these photographs. I am so confused, Mr. Stone. That's why I came to see you. Can you help me?"

"I'll call Dave in San Francisco, to let him know that I need him here in L.A. first thing in the morning, so he won't be able to stay with you. You can phone him and break it off. If he asks for the jacket, tell him you'll mail it to my office."

"Oh, Mr. Stone, thank you!" Her expression turned quickly to that of a young girl receiving a long-awaited gift. She sat up straight with confidence.

"I will need copies made of these photos. Take them to this address." I wrote it down and slid the paper across the table. "I'll call the shop and let them know to expect you. The duplication process takes about two hours. When you pick up the originals, leave the copies at the shop."

"Yes. Okay. Thank you, Mr. Stone." This was the first time she had smiled. It looked like a storm had lifted and sunlight flooded her face. Her complexion was pastel rose.

"Should I call a taxi for you?" I asked.

"That is kind of you, but I have a limousine waiting."

I nodded and said: "You did the right thing, Ms. Ness. Let me assure you of that." She smiled again, and out of curiosity I asked: "Are you related to Eliot Ness?"

"Yes. He was my father's cousin."

I smiled and said: "I wish that I had met him."

"I am sure he would have liked you," she replied.

We stood up and shook hands.

The entire café watched Ms. Ness leaving. At a nearby table there was a teenage girl who had been staring at Ms. Ness with admiration for her style. She gave me a wink. Her father was pretending to read the newspaper, while peeking over the top, watching the tail end of Kim Ness oscillate out the door.

I stepped into a phone booth, dialed Frank's Photography Shop, and gave Frank a heads-up on Kim Ness. I also told him not to mention this order to Dave Wells. He assured me that our business would be handled discreetly.

I returned to the table, ordered another coffee and took my time drinking it, while I thought about Dave Wells and his collection of disturbing photographs.

After leaving the café, I drove to Frank's shop on Hollywood Boulevard. When I arrived, Frank said: "That good-looking dame was already here to drop off the photographs. She left a tailwind of heat that made me loosen my tie." He winked at me.

I smiled.

Then I asked Frank to write a bogus return address on the envelope that would contain the copies of the photographs, and to address it directly to me at my office, and have it mailed from the Bel Air post office.

With the originals still in Dave's jacket pocket, he would not suspect that Kim Ness had seen his perverse collection of forensic photographs. Or maybe in some deranged way, he wanted her to find them.

39

Back at the office, I left a message at the San Francisco hotel, for Dave Wells to return to Los Angeles that night, and to meet me at the office in the morning. I left Max's phone number, too

I was staying at her place until my flat was put back together. I didn't like the changes, after the thugs had redecorated it.

At three p.m. I went for a sandwich and a beer at Abe's Deli. Spent an hour eating and chatting with some regulars. At times, blue sparks flew around inside my head like glowing satellites, but the severe pain was gone, and the lump had shrunk considerably.

Walking back to the office, the clouds were glossy black, as if lacquered with ebony glaze. A dense drizzle dampened my overcoat and hat. A string of cars traveled slowly along Vine Street, their wipers pushing back the drizzle, their headlights blurred by the moisture. Except for a few bums littering the doorways, the wet sidewalks were lifeless. Pulling my hat down, I tucked into my overcoat and lowered my head against the dampness. My thoughts shifted to Mya

Regis, to her cold body lying in that dark vault. Thought about the last look Mya gave me at Five In The Afternoon, when we had drinks together, and made plans together. A sudden anxiousness came over me, recalling Dave Wells' warning: *You need to let this go, Joe. I'm telling you to let it go.* But I couldn't let it go without closure, without knowing why Mya was murdered. Or why Arnie Bender was murdered. More of Wells' words sounded in my head: *This isn't going to end well, Joe.*

I stopped at a liquor store and bought Mya's choice in whisky: a fifth of Famous Grouse Scotch Blend. It was expensive and sophisticated, like Mya. She was the type of redhead that could make a priest rip the Roman collar from his neck.

In a phone call earlier that week from San Francisco, Wells mentioned that he had uncovered something significant about Mya Regis. He preferred not to talk about it over the phone, and only said that this information would complicate The Open Blouse investigation. Dave Wells was a wizard when it came to producing case evidence, but the content of his photographs in the envelope troubled me and had frightened Kim Ness. The photo copies from Frank's shop wouldn't arrive at the office for a few days, so I had the time to figure out a strategy for confronting Wells. I needed to play this smart, to find out first about what he discovered in San Francisco. Then I would bring up the photographs. We were good enough friends to talk this through.

Back in the office, I placed the bottle of Scotch on the desk. It was four-thirty p.m. I removed my hat and overcoat and sat down in the pink-cushioned chair. Blue lightning flashed from the back of my skull to my eyes, and there was more tension in my neck. I thought about my murdered neighbors, John and Edith Morgan. They were always looking out for me. Their two children would never understand the circumstance of their deaths. Eventually they would contact me, seeking answers. My thoughts shifted to Max. For as much as I was pulled in by the erotic magnetism of other women, it was Max I wanted. There was a lot of classy competition out there, but then I'd look at Max, from her ink-black hair down to the soles of her black Doc Martens, and I knew that no other woman could measure up to her. I got up from the pink-cushioned chair and walked over to the desk to open the Scotch. The phone rang.

"Joe Stone, Private In…"

"Hi."

"I was just thinking about you." My heart sped up.

"Warm and cozy?"

"With a side of nudity."

"Mmmm," she replied. "How's my apartment been treating you?"

"Comfortably lonely. Your scent is everywhere."

"That's good. I brought along one of your shirts for sleeping in."

"We should sleep in it together." Max giggled. Then I asked: "Are you feeling rested?"

"A bit edgy. Confused at times. Other times relaxed." She lowered her voice and said: "A long night of sleeping with you is what I need."

"When you get back to L.A., we'll lock ourselves in your apartment. No phone. No T.V. No newspapers."

There was a breathy whisper from her end: "I'd like that."

"How are your parents?"

"They're still determined to move me back to Detroit. I told them it's not going to happen." She paused, sighed and said: "I'm the inheritor to Vesuvio's estate, because I was still married to him when he died. My father's office assistant called, here at the cabin. Said that I need to sign the papers in front of Vesuvio's attorney. This is one of the reasons why I'm calling."

"Estate?" I asked.

"His mansion in Detroit, a villa in Tuscany, a beach house in Miami." She sighed again. "His bank accounts, his investment holdings, rental properties." Another sigh. "Joe, I don't want to do this. I just want to give it all away. It's dirty money."

"Think of it this way, you can buy a new car."

"But I love my '58 Impala!"

"If ever a car owner and their car looked alike, then it's you and your black '58 Impala."

Max giggled again.

"I will have to go back," she said. "After we leave Borrego Springs, we're heading to Detroit." She sounded frustrated.

"For how long?"

"A few days. Maybe more. My parents are inviting you to come with us. They want to thank you in person. They were sorry they didn't get to meet you."

"Max, I can't. I'm tied up here with pressing issues. Tell your parents we'll visit them in Detroit this spring."

After we hung up, I put on my damp hat and overcoat, grabbed the fifth of Scotch, and drove to Max's flat in Silver Lake. Streetlight reflections covered the wet roads with a thin yellowish film, which quivered like cold skin when the wind blew.

The living room of Max's apartment had a bay window with a view of the lake, but the lake was dark, nearly invisible. Occasionally, a car would pass by, and its headlights would attach themselves to the nervous water, while the wind lifted the lake into small agitated waves. I sat in a lounge chair watching the darkness outside and inhaling Max's lingering scent, coming from the chair's fabric. The phone rang.

"Hello?"

"Joe. Dave Wells here."

"Hi Dave." My tone was flat.

"Look, Boss, I'm heading to Santa Barbara after I leave San Francisco." He sounded irritated. "Kim Ness and I have dinner plans for tonight. Besides, I left my new jacket at Kim's house. I need to pick it up."

"I need you here, Dave. First thing in the morning." I was stern. "Have Ms. Ness mail the jacket to you, if it's that important."

"But Boss, if you could see Kim Ness, you'd understand. I could leave Santa Barbara early morning, be at the office by midmorning." He was anxious, insistent.

"Dave," I said. "I need you here well rested, ready to go, early morning. We need to get on that new car heist case. With Max recuperating and you out of town, I'm..."

"How is Max doing?"

"Much better. But she'll be away for several more days, and..."

"Okay," Wells said. "I'll fly back to Los Angeles tonight. I'll be at the office at eight tomorrow morning. You can count on it."

After the phone call, I slouched into the lounge chair, brooding.

Staring through the window into the darkness, I thought about Dave Wells' collection of illicit photographs, and how they might implicate him.

40

When I arrived at the office at seven-thirty, Dave Wells was pounding away at the Remington. He was working on the Mya Regis report. Wells was dressed in a tailored dark grey suit, and wearing a thin black tie over a light grey button-down shirt. Black snakeskin cowboy boots added a tough look. His pearl handled .357, with charcoal blue screws, sat on my desk, next to his black leather gloves.

Because of the steady typewriter noise, Wells didn't hear me come in. I closed the door hard enough to make it bang. He turned around quickly but wasn't startled.

"Morning, Boss," Wells said with an upbeat tone. "The Regis report is finished."

He stood up, pulled out the last page from the carriage, and handed all the pages to me. He said he'd been working on it since six forty-five.

"Dave, thanks for being here." We shook hands. "And so early, too."

"You were right. I needed a good night's rest." He nodded and winked.

I stood in the center of the room, going over the six-page report. Wells sat in the pink-cushioned chair, with the window half open, looking down at the street.

After reading the first page, I looked over at Wells. His head turned away from the window and he looked directly at me, with a solemn expression. I walked behind my desk, continued reading while standing. Then looked at Wells again. When he saw the disbelief in my expression, he tightened his lips, widened his eyes and arched his eyebrows.

"You doubled checked this information?"

"Three times," he replied. "And you'll see that I had a conversation with one of the nuns, who cared for Mya during her recovery. The nun was in her sixties at that time. She is sick and arthritic now. Her memory comes and goes."

I sat at the desk and finished reading the report. Wells lounged in the chair, lifted his boots onto the low windowsill, lit a cigarette.

Last night's rain had tapered off to a drizzle. The wind had settled down to a refreshing breeze. It blew lightly into the office, as if to clear the room of the ill feelings I had about Wells and his photographs.

"You're sure about this?" I asked again, needing more confirmation to clear any doubt.

Wells nodded, while exhaling smoke. He picked tobacco from his tongue and blew it off his finger. Grey daylight came through the window, giving Wells the look of an actor in a murder mystery, sitting there in the theatrical-looking pink-cushioned chair, with his gangster-like appearance.

My thoughts raced with too much information, then my mind tightened, like it wanted to snap. Wells looked at me and saw my unsettled expression. I gave Dave a forced smile. It felt plastic and cold.

Wells pulled a final drag from his cigarette, flicked the butt out the window, then exhaled the smoke long and hard towards the ceiling. He stood up and walked up to the desk.

"While you're mentally processing that information, I'll go to Abe's and get us some food."

I watched him grab his hat, gloves, overcoat, and his .357. It glistened while sliding into its shoulder holster, as if it were excited about going on a mission. I nodded, not really listening to what Wells had said. When the door closed, I realized then that he had left the office.

In a phone call last week, Wells had mentioned that his report would complicate The Open Blouse investigation. From what I had read, the report was an invitation to dig into some dirty cracks and corners, to ask some dirty questions, maybe get some dirty answers. I leaned back in the chair, troubled over what Mya had endured at a young age. This whole thing stunk like a sulfur pit. The nun remembered a man who came to see Mya, but Mya refused to meet with the man, after she peeked through a curtain and saw him standing there. The nun described the man as having blond hair, good looks, a sharp dresser, quite tall, and possibly in his early thirties. He claimed to be Mya's uncle, but refused to give his name. The man never showed up again. Mr. and Mrs. Regis were in the dark over who the man was. When questioned by her parents about the stranger, the nun said that Mya had stared out the window, said nothing. When her father asked if that man was "the one", the nun said that Mya remained silent, still looking out the window.

It occurred to me, that the man who had visited Mya in San Francisco could be the same man Sherry Miller had described as the one who argued with Mya, in the parking lot of Five In The Afternoon. Was this also the same man Sally Point saw walking with Grace Parker, along Venice Beach, twenty-eight years ago? I needed to speak with Sally Point again, as soon as possible. If I could jog Sally's memory just a little more, it might open a deep closet of information, pertaining to the "well-dressed blond stranger". Wells' report also stated that, after a year in San Francisco, Mya Regis returned to Los Angeles at the age of sixteen. I doubt that she had felt the sweet part of turning sixteen.

The office door opened. Detectives Harley Jewels and Brick Woodhouse walked in with three coffees and plates of food. We shook hands and tossed around some small talk. We hadn't seen each other since the LAX incident. They were busy working on Bryce Parker's disappearance. I handed Dave Wells' report to Jewels, who sat down on the couch to read it. Woodhouse sat next to him, receiving each page after Jewels completed one. When Jewels finished the report, his face tightened and his nostrils flared, and he shook his head from side to side in disgust. When Woodhouse finished reading it, he just sat there with a severe expression on his face. His bright blue eyes seemed to turn dark and cold. Looking towards the open window, he asked: "Any idea who this sick bastard is?" Then he turned and looked at me. His anger was fierce. I just stared at Woodhouse, as if I had a promising clue to share. But all I had was a gut feeling over who the deviant could be. I said no.

Dave Wells came back with two plates of food and two coffees. He put the food on the desk then shook hands with the detectives. We all sat around drinking coffee and eating. When Wells finished his plate, he went back to the pink-cushioned chair, lit a cigarette, blew the smoke out the window and said: "Wish I could've seen Vesuvio's face, when he saw you standing there, your Ruger to his head." He chuckled and added: "It must have been priceless."

"Yeah. Something like that," I growled, not wanting to discuss it any further.

The three of us sat in silence. Jewels and Woodhouse had their feet on the coffee table. Wells had his feet on the windowsill. My legs were stretched out, my feet resting on the overturned wastepaper basket. I was facing Wells.

We were all wearing our overcoats, the room was chilly from having the window open. The boulevard rumbled with noise. A block away, a jackhammer sounded like a fifty-pound woodpecker. A fire truck sped by blasting its warning.

Woodhouse congratulated Wells on his fine sleuthing. Wells nodded, smiled.

Jewels said: "Dave, you did some fine work here." Wells smiled at Jewels.

The room was silent again, as we fell back into our own thoughts. My thoughts shifted to what Kim Ness had brought to my attention. While both detectives were busy reading parts of the report again, I said to Wells:

"Dave, what are your thoughts on crime scene photographers who keep photo collections of homicide victims?"

"Huh?" His monosyllabic reply was quick, his voice at a near-whisper. "Uh, what do you mean?" Wells pulled his legs from the sill and sat up straight. My question had startled him, making his body pull into itself. Then he leaned back, like he was trying to hide inside the chair.

"I was thumbing through a photography magazine, while visiting Max in the hospital. There was an article on forensic photographers, who keep such collections."

Wells sat motionless. He looked as confused as a golf ball driven off course. Then he stood up, formed his lips into a tight circle and exhaled a thick line of smoke, while staring out the window. A sturdy breeze caught the side of his face, making him shiver. Police sirens raced along the boulevard. He shivered again.

Jewels and Woodhouse were still occupied with the report. They passed pages back and forth, pointing out certain sections to each other, and were not paying attention to what I was saying.

After Wells turned to look at me, his body was motionless, though rigid in posture.

"Do you know guys like that, Dave?"

"Um, like what?" he replied. He turned away from me, facing the window. His broad shoulders blocking most of it.

"Photographers who keep homicide photos, where they've posed next to the victims, smiling at the camera."

"Never met one myself." He turned to look at me. His eyes had a steely hardness, and his cheek muscles twitched steadily. Jewels and Woodhouse were still absorbed in the report. They were deaf to my questions, and oblivious to the tension between Wells and me.

"The magazine article was about photographers who keep photo albums for the horror of it, to jolt their friends."

"It sounds morbid," Wells growled.

He turned to face the window again, pulling a deep drag on his cig. The tendons along his neck were as taut as cello strings. He was steadily tapping the floor with his right foot, possibly in beat to some anxious thoughts. He took another quick drag and let out a noisy exhale, then he turned to look at me. His face was pinched around his mouth, and his eyes had narrowed down to a resentful glare.

"What are you going to do with the information in this report?" Woodhouse asked.

"I'll take it to Alice Moore," I replied still looking at Wells. "She might remember more details from that time."

"And you expect straight answers from her?" Jewels asked with a chuckle.

With a blank expression, I turned around and looked at the detectives, shrugging my shoulders. They grinned and went back to the report. Looking at Wells I said: "Some of the photographers pose with the victims, like hunters with trophy-kills. Others take pictures of themselves lying next to murdered females, while touching certain body parts."

"That's disgusting," Wells snapped.

"I agree, Dave." My mouth was dry. I drank some coffee and continued. "The article didn't give any photographers names, or how they get away with taking such photographs. Something about protecting their rights and…"

"What rights?" he asked with the same sharp edge.

"I'm not clear on that one myself," I answered calmly. "It seems wrong to me, no matter how many rights are pinned to it."

Wells turned his back to me again. He savagely flicked his cigarette outside, then closed and locked the window.

Jewels stood up and handed me the Mya Regis report, while Woodhouse walked towards the door and opened it.

"Dave," I said. "Are you ready to talk with our new client about his stolen '39 Porsche?"

"Yeah. I'll head over there now." He put his black leather gloves on, grabbed his Stetson and his overcoat, then holstered his .357. He nodded at everyone and left the office.

"What was that about?" Woodhouse asked. "He seemed annoyed."

"I read a disturbing article in a photo magazine and wanted Wells' opinion."

"He looked confused," Jewels added.

"Dave has a lot on his mind," I replied. "He's been thinking about leaving Los Angeles to go back to Montana, or maybe Santa Barbara."

"He'll be missed," Jewels said. "Wells is one of the good ones."

Woodhouse nodded in agreement, his lips protruding and tightening for emphasis.

The detectives left the office. While they walked down the hallway, I could hear them talking about Bryce Parker.

I wasn't sure when to tell Jewels and Woodhouse about Wells' perverted activity. Legally I was bound to tell them, but my concern was, that they might arrest him immediately.

The room felt damp, from when the window was open. A chill found my spine, my blood felt cold and heavy. Finally, the office heater kicked on.

I finished my coffee, grabbed my hat, and headed out the door to the jailhouse. I had a pressing need to draw additional information out of Alice Moore.

41

"Is that the one used to kill that fat wop?" asked the same bony jail clerk with the putty grey skin. His relaxed Southern accent elongated his vowels. His knobby index finger was tapping the butt of my Ruger, lying on the desk. His stone-like eyes bore hard on mine.

I didn't respond to his bigotry.

After I signed the login sheet, his tight mouth slid into a tiny thin line along the side of his face. That must have been a big smile for him.

I walked along the green windowless hallway under the fluorescent tubes, towards the grey door marked *Visiting Room*. The heavy-set female guard from my last visit was at the door. When I stood next to her, she said: "Mr. Stone, thank you for saving that woman at the airport."

I nodded and smiled while she opened the door for me.

"Joe, why do you always look tired?" Alice had a content expression. Her time in jail was like a vacation. She was well rested and looked orderly, even though her hair was still wiry and matted. "You should get arrested, spend some time in here with me. It would do you good, Joe."

I smiled, sat down and slid my cold hands under the screened partition that separated us. She took them into her warm hands, until I pulled my hands back, to take the drawing paper out of my bag. When I slid the paper towards Alice, her eyes twinkled like a starry sky. The ceiling lights registered brightly in her blue-grey irises, creating sparkling gold flecks.

"I give art classes every day," she said. "My students call me Professor."

"That's nice to hear Alice, and you're looking younger than ever."

"Do you want to take art classes, Joe?"

"Yes, one of these days, from you."

Alice looked up at the wall clock. Her expression turned serious. She stood up quickly, gathered the pads of paper, and headed for the door.

"Alice, where are you going?" I snapped at her.

The guard opened the door, took the paper from Alice, and then walked her back to the chair.

"I don't want to be late," she said looking up at the wall clock again.

The guard answered in a gentle tone: "You have plenty of time Alice. Enjoy your visit with Mr. Stone."

I nodded at the guard. She smiled warmly and left the room.

"Will they write about you again in the magazines?" Alice asked.

"Don't know. I hope not."

"Always the hero, Joe," she said proudly. "Would you autograph the cover for me?"

"Yes, Alice. But tell me more about Mya Regis' time in San Francisco." My voice was soft, almost begging, without seeming desperate.

Alice's eyes widened, then narrowed down, like she was gathering the past in front of her. "There's so much to tell, Joe. But some memories are…" She stopped and looked up at the clock again.

"Are what, Alice? Tell me what memories are, especially to you."

"Time consuming," she said softly. "I have an art class to teach." She sat there adjusting her grey jail clothes, head bent down, eyes looking at her hands. They were folded together on the wooden counter. When she looked up again, penetrating pain furrowed her face, carving deep lines around her eyes. She seemed to have been pulled back to the past. She lifted one hand and waved it through the air, as if chasing the bad memories out of her head.

"What did your cousin Amy Regis say about Mya's condition?" I asked softly, wanting to coax her into a conversation.

"She knew who was responsible." Alice was looking down again, avoiding my eyes. "But that ugly husband of hers never knew. Before Mya started to show, her parents took her out of Los Angeles."

"Who was the man responsible?"

"There were two of them." Her voice soft, small, almost distant-sounding, like she wanted to leave that information buried in the past.

"Two men were responsible?"

Alice was quiet again, looking at her folded hands, as if they held the answers. Tears pooled at the bottom of her reddening eyes. I didn't want this, didn't want to upset her. Alice forced the words out, whispering slowly through a quivering bottom lip.

"It was the beginning of the following summer, when Mya came back..." I leaned in to listen. With her damp eyes, Alice looked up at me. "Amy said that Mya stayed in her bedroom and wouldn't talk to anybody. When school started that fall, Mya went back to her school routine, like nothing had changed." Alice's eyes welled as if small oncoming storms, and tears finally broke.

I couldn't do this to her.

As if powered by a similar force, we stood up at the same time.

Without saying goodbye, Alice turned and waddled off through the door that the guard held open for her.

I stood there and watched Alice disappear through the opening, as if she had slid into a protective crack, where memories couldn't find her. The door closed, and I stood alone in the room. The air smelled stale and it was hot. I left the visiting room and walked outside. Light rain was falling, polishing the streets to a glossy finish. The air was fresh, the sidewalks deserted.

On the steps of the jailhouse, I lit a cigarette, took a drag and blew the smoke upward. A few cars drove by with steamed windows. For some reason the steamy windows made me feel empty inside.

I flicked the unfinished cigarette into a puddle. It hissed with resentment at being drowned in that water. I walked in the direction of the Buick, parked down the street. My thoughts were cluttered with Dave Wells' issue, with Max going back to Detroit, with Millie and Arnie Bender's deaths, and with this new information about Mya, that Alice gave to...

"Mr. Stone."

With his leather briefcase tucked close to his chest and holding a black umbrella, Public Defender Elliot Mickle walked up to me. His black hat and black overcoat were dry, unlike mine. We shook hands. I had met Eliot Mickle a few times before.

"What a coincidence seeing you at the jailhouse," Mickle said, his eyes smiling brightly.

"I don't believe in coincidences," I said under my breath.

"Huh?" he said with a perplexed expression. His eyes narrowed down on mine, as if to see if I was feeling okay.

"Mr. Mickle. Yes. It's good to see you. How's Alice's case coming along?"

"Let's stand under the awning." At that request he displayed a wide, confident smile.

We walked up the jailhouse steps and stood where it was dry. Mickle rummaged through his briefcase, pulled out a folder, opened it and handed me a document.

"This…" he said with noticeable pride, "is a signed release form for Alice. I had a meeting with Judge Steven Harris, who was appointed to her case." Mickle touched the stem of his glasses with his index finger and thumb, and continued. "We discussed Alice's case for about an hour. After going through the witness statements, Judge Harris concluded that Alice acted in self-defense and that the case would not go to a juried trial." Mickle nodded several times after that statement and added: "Judge Harris also concluded that Alice is not a threat to society, as the prosecution had insisted upon." He beamed with joy. "She will be released sometime this week. I have the paperwork going through the system to make that happen." He nodded over and over excitedly, and his beaming smile seemed to take up his entire face.

I didn't know what to say, was at a loss for words. I was beyond pleased that Alice Moore would not be tried for premeditated murder, like that narrow-minded D.A. had wanted.

Elliot Mickle shook my hand with intense physical strength packed with explosive enthusiasm. He nodded vigorously several more times while his pointed chin punctured the air. His smile was authentic, mine was tight and shallow. I was sidetracked by too many thoughts that gossiped inside my head, like multiple operators on a party line.

Sitting in my maroon Electra with the window down, I thought about Mya Regis. Even in the light of Dave Wells' report, nothing made sense to me, especially not Alice Moore's riddles. I needed to rework them in my head, until something clicked in place. Who were the "two of them" she mentioned in connection with Mya's condition? And when Dave Wells' photographs arrive at my office, what situation will I find myself in, after confronting Wells about his morbid preoccupation?

I started the Buick and drove to Hollywood Boulevard. Found parking in front of my office. Turning the engine off, I sat in the car and listened to the agitated inner voices, spinning my head like a dizzy dreidel.

42

Maybe it was the dark clouds that brought on this unsettled feeling, or maybe it was the burden of life's ruthless nature, blowing a little too hard through my head. My thoughts shifted to Sally Point, to the time when she owned the Strip-A-Go-Go, where Grace Parker had danced. Sally might be unintentionally holding on to more information about the nameless blond man, that Grace was involved with. I needed to meet with her again, to pry open her memory. My gut tells me that she could be a cornucopia of facts, waiting to spill.

Somewhere a car horn blasted. I tried to ignore it, but the horn kept nagging me, until I realized that a car had pulled alongside my Buick. A man's voice yelled something over a heavy wind that had kicked up. I rolled down my steamed-up window halfway.

"Hey, Joe!"

It was Detective Harley Jewels. He was in the passenger seat of the car next to me. Detective Brick Woodhouse was in the driver's seat, laying on the horn like a child with a noisy toy. I rolled the window down some more, and the jarring wind slapped my face, snapping me out of my brooding thoughts.

"Harley, what's going on?" I yelled above the wind.

"Manhattan Beach. A stiff on the pier. Follow us!" he yelled back.

I asked: "Parker?"

Jewels shrugged his shoulders and shook his head at that question. Maybe he didn't understand it. He rolled up his window and they sped off with me in their tailwind. We were headed for the 110 going south. I looked at my watch: eleven-twelve. Then I said out loud: "Bryce Parker. How else could it have ended for an ill-fated punk like you?"

The north wind continued as we drove, but the dark clouds seemed motionless and fully loaded, as if they'd reached their destination.

When we arrived at Manhattan Beach, about thirty minutes later, two squad cars and four uniforms had blocked the pier's entrance.

Despite the wind, the crime-gawkers had gathered. Many more were approaching along the walkways and along the beach, as if pulled by invisible guy lines. Some of them were wrapped in blankets, but most of them wore hefty coats with hoods. Some had binoculars, to get a closeup view of a stranger's tragic ending.

Two unmarked cop cars, three squad cars, and an ambulance were parked at the end of the pier. We parked our cars next to them, then wobbled through the muscle-bound wind, flexing its strength.

I could hear Art Pepper's *The Prisoner* blasting from one of the buildings near the beach. The music was atmospheric and poignant against the seagull cries and emergency sirens.

At the end of the pier was the Roundhouse Café, a circular building of classic Deco design. It had white stucco walls with terracotta roof tiles, tall arched windows and doors, with turquoise trim all around. Its upbeat appearance seemed ill-suited for a homicide scene.

Looking into the café, I saw that it was brightly lit. A young, black woman was sitting at a table with two uniforms, who were questioning her. She had a terrified expression. She was shivering and had her arms wrapped around herself, rocking her lean body back and forth. One officer got up from his chair and wrapped his coat around her. The young woman lowered her head and sobbed.

Her body jerking violently.

Jewels, Woodhouse and I walked along the right side of the café, where two detectives, a uniform, two medics and the coroner were huddled together, as if trying to keep each other warm. The gusty wind carried dense sea spray from the breaking waves. I pulled my hat down tight and tucked into my wool overcoat.

While Jewels and Woodhouse talked with the other detectives, I walked around to the backside of the cafe, curious to see what kind of ending Bryce Parker had met. What I came across stopped me in my tracks.

Her eyes were open, staring straight up. There was a wet hole dead-center forehead, glistening with dark red moisture. The stucco wall behind her head was smeared with blood and skull fragments. Some of it had slid down to the decking and pooled with the rainwater around her naked ass. Her mouth was slightly open. Her small teeth and thin lips were stained red, and the openings of her long, boney nose were caked with dried blood. The left cheekbone was cut and swollen. Possibly, somebody had punched her hard.

In a white silk sleeping gown, which outlined her thick body and sagging breasts, she sat propped up against the building with her short legs slightly apart. Her hands rested between her legs, where a chrome Colt .32 Snub-nose revolver lay in a puddle of rose-colored water. Her cropped orange hair was disarranged, and her head was turned up, tilted back against the wall, as if she was looking for something in the sky. Maybe her salvation was in view.

Bending-down, I closed her eyes and asked one of the medics to cover her with a sheet. They covered her immediately.

"Joe, there was no identification on her," Woodhouse said, standing next to me now. I was squatting in front of the dead woman, looking up at him.

"Sally Point," I said with a quick exhausted sigh. "Her name is Sally Point." I looked back at Sally. Under the white sheet, she seemed clean and whole, but she was bloodstained and broken.

"How are you connected to her?" Woodhouse asked.

"Sally was connected to The Open Blouse, in a distant way."

"How distant?"

I stood up, inhaled deeply, and a dull pain penetrated my chest. I exhaled a shaky breath and said: "Twenty-eight years ago, Sally Point was Grace Parker's boss. Grace danced at the Strip-A-Go-Go, which Sally Point owned. Grace Parker was Bryce Parker's mother."

Detective Jewels walked over to us. I told Jewels and Woodhouse about my visit with Sally, at her house.

"Okay," Woodhouse said above the wind. "You got an address for Sally Point?"

"Yeah," I shouted. "Let's go inside the café." The wind was growling now, showing its canines.

Jewels had to yell above it: "The coroner put the death between three and four a.m." Woodhouse and I nodded vigorously.

The three of us walked along the side of the building to the front, staggering and holding on to the iron railing.

Inside the café it was almost quiet, except for the officers talking in low voices to the young black woman. I gave Sally's address to Detective Woodhouse. He used the café's phone to call the station, for a homicide squad to be dispatched to Sally Point's apartment complex.

A uniform walked over to Jewels and said: "This was the woman's second week on the job."

Then he handed Jewels the notes from when he had questioned her. Jewels thumbed through the pages and walked over to the woman. She was sitting at the front of the café, staring out the window at the pier. Her eyes were red, swollen, wet, and her body shook uncontrollably. Her beautiful face was streaked with tears.

"Do you feel the need for hospital attention?" Jewels asked. His voice was soft and compassionate.

The woman shook her head no, still looking out the window. "I just wanna go home." Her voice was strained, exhausted. She hid her face in her hands and sobbed some more.

Jewels asked one of the officers to escort her to a squad car, to driver her home.

I looked out the window facing the beach. The crowd of gawkers had increased. Under the dark sky, it looked like a Gothic religious revival, as if the crowd had come here hoping for a revelation. When I turned towards the window facing the pier, I watched two medics lift the gurney with Sally Point's sheet-covered body into the ambulance. The sheet flapped like wings of a snowbird, as if Sally had flown into the ambulance on her own. A bare foot stuck out from under the sheet. The aggressive wind made it difficult for the medics to close the ambulance door. They were knocked around like wet paper bags. Eventually, they managed to close and lock it, and the ambulance drove off the pier to Manhattan Beach Boulevard, its flashing red light disappearing with a last flicker. No siren, no hurry.

I stared through the cafe window, feeling overdosed on loss, trying to make sense of it all. My life felt like a rope with knots in it, and this homicidal maniac was the force behind my tightest knot. He's tormenting me. Playing rough with me. Pulling me along as a spectator to his gruesome exhibitions, that he's obviously proud of.

The killer must have tailed me to Sally Point's apartment. Did he remember something that Sally could use against him, to expose him? But why did he bring her to the pier? Why did he stage this crowd-drawing spectacle? Was this display of Sally Point's grisly killing a metaphor with a complex meaning? Or did he simply do it this way to make his game theatrical, giving it a melodramatic edge?

Sally Point had lived a good life and retired into a good life, only to have a bloodsucker drain her of that life.

I looked at the beach again. The crowd just stood there in what seemed like a standing ovation, as if waiting for the players to bow.

"Joe. Let's move," Woodhouse barked. He was in a hurry.

43

We arrived at Sally Point's apartment complex just after two p.m. A few cop cars and a forensics station wagon were parked along the street. Away from the ocean, the wind subsided, but a thick drizzle had its own agenda. A dozen neighbors had gathered in front of the u-shaped apartment complex, holding umbrellas. They huddled together like a herd of nervous sheep. Uniforms were questioning them.

Inside the courtyard, cops went door-to-door, talking to the occupants of the other units. Another uniform was standing in front of Sally Point's door. He stepped to one side, letting us enter.

The living room showed signs of struggle, with overturned chairs, broken coffee table, some broken knickknacks, and plenty of blood on the light green carpet. A short, wiry photographer was popping flashes, squatting low, then standing tall for the right perspective. He moved around the room quickly, from corner to corner, like a trapped bird in a house. Then he'd stop, pop a few more flashes, only to move swiftly again.

While Jewels and Woodhouse were talking to another detective, I walked into the bedroom. There was blood on the white silk sheets, maybe from the punches to Sally's face. She must have resisted, because there were blankets scattered across the floor, all the way past the bedroom door. She must have been dragged into the living room, since there was a trail of blood that followed the blankets. Sally probably kicked and thrashed, causing the all-around disarray. She must have been punched again in the living room to quiet her: in one spot, there was a pool of blood on the carpet. Woodhouse walked over to me and said: "Both of her next-door tenants are out of town. A couple of other tenants woke up from the noise, thought raccoons were knocking trash cans around, so they went back to sleep. That was around two a.m."

I stared at the blood on the carpet. My neck and jaw tightened, as if something other than myself controlled the tension.

Jewels joined us in the middle of the living room. "The front door lock must have been picked. There was no sign of a break in," he said. "But there *is* one thing that will foster your curiosity. Follow me, gentlemen."

Jewels led us to the bedroom, to the side of the bed where Sally was dragged to the floor. There was mud crunched into the thick green carpet, slightly under the bed. It looked like the tip of a shoe print. The killer must have leaned hard on that foot. Maybe to pull Sally's heavy body out of the bed. The grimy mark was not round like a normal shoe print. It was sharply pointed, same as a cowboy boot. With only a toeprint, there was no way to estimate the boot size.

The forensics chief came over to us and showed us a suicide note, found on the bed:

I couldn't face old age any longer,
depression got the best of me.
Sally

The note was typed without a signature. I looked around the apartment, Sally didn't have a typewriter.

Back in the street, Jewels, Woodhouse and I talked to a uniform who reported that a neighbor on the other side of the street said he got up at two-fifteen a.m. for a drink of water. When he stepped onto his front porch for fresh air, he noticed a yellow taxi parked in front of the victim's apartment complex. He thought it was strange that the driver was sitting inside the car with the motor off.

"Cabbies usually keep the taxi running while waiting for their fare," the uniform said.

"Was it Angel's Cab Company?" I asked.

"Midtown Cab Company," the uniform said.

"Did the witness get the cab's vehicle number?" Woodhouse asked.

"No, Sir," the officer replied. "It was too dark to get a visual on the number."

"Did he notice anything else about the situation?" I asked.

The uniform flipped through his note pad and said: "Yes. A few minutes later he looked out the window again and saw a person in a long, dark coat, and wearing a fedora that was pulled low to their eyes. The person was bent down to get into the back of the cab. It looked like there was somebody else in the backseat slumped over. With only a streetlight for visibility, it was hard for the neighbor to make out any other details."

"About how tall was the person in the long coat?" Jewels asked.

"He was bent over, so the neighbor couldn't say, Sir."

Jewels called the Midtown Cab Company from Sally's apartment. They had no record of a fare in that area at that time.

The three of us left the crime scene and met up at Abe's Deli. Our conversation was about the cowboy boot print at Sally Point's apartment, and about the café employee's shocking discovery at Manhattan Beach Pier.

With his hands folded together on the table, Woodhouse said: "The press will run with another random murder story, selling misinformation."

"They'll push the city's panic pedal to the floor with this one," I added with certainty.

Jewels said: "We'll have to talk to the Midtown Cab Company drivers, whether they were on or off duty at that time. We need to question all of them." We all nodded in agreement.

Back at my office, I sat in the pink-cushioned chair. Jewels and Woodhouse sat on the couch.

I looked at my watch: six p.m. We continued discussing the case and talked about each of the seven victims and how they were connected to The Open Blouse, and to each other.

I said: "My gut feeling is that Kimmie Turner's murder, at Robert Rollin's mansion, was random."

"But the killer could've known that Kimmie Turner once worked at The Open Blouse," Jewels replied.

"Maybe he didn't know," I said. "They met at a whisky bar. Bryce Parker told you that."

"They had a date together," Woodhouse added. "The killer probably had no intention of murdering Miss Turner, until he did."

"My feeling is that Kimmie Turner was a bonus addition to his collection," I said. "He'll slap glue on the back of the news article and press it into his scrapbook. Arnie could have been murdered for that same reason. But what about Sally Point? How does she fit into this depraved sideshow?"

The detectives shrugged their shoulders and lowered their heads. They were tired, tired of guessing. We all were. It was a long day, and a longer investigation.

Then I thought: The Open Blouse case was like a baseball game played without rules. The pitcher was on the mound throwing ninety-mile-an-hour curveballs, and I was behind the plate, a catcher without a mitt.

After the detectives left the office, I got up, turned out the lights, then returned to the cushioned chair. The red neon glaze had transformed the room's darkness into a hazy bloodied wound, and I sat there thinking about Sally Point's murdered body.

44

A silvery morning light streamed through the office window, and it seemed to layer everything with a metallic sheen. It was eight forty-five a.m., two days after Sally Point's murder. I was sitting at my desk, going through the mail. There was still no envelope containing Dave Wells' collection of photographs.

I was reaching for my coffee, when the office door opened slowly, like a stage performance was about to happen. Harley Jewels and Brick Woodhouse swaggered into the room to their own clumsy rhythm. They were grinning, like a couple of juveniles at a girlie show.

Jewels took a seat in the pink-cushioned chair. Woodhouse spread himself across the couch, hung his feet off the couch's arm. He pulled his black fedora over his face so only his mouth was visible, which made his grin more pronounced. The two of them were unusually quiet, despite all the cocky grinning.

Sitting in the cushioned chair, the metallic sheen covered Jewels' body, turning him into a platinum statue. Then he stood up, lit a cigarette, took a hard drag, and opened the window. The exhaled smoke became a silver-blue circle that hung in front of his face, until the breeze swept it away. He sat down again, stretched out his legs, putting his feet on the low windowsill. The grin never left his face. I looked at Jewels, then at Woodhouse, then back at Jewels.

"Do I have to shake it out of you, Harley?" I asked with a smile. "Or are you going to let me in on the excitement?"

Woodhouse removed the hat from his face. He tried to smile, but it was more of a we-know-something-that-you-don't-know smirk. He looked over at Jewels, who looked back at Woodhouse. Now they were both smirking.

I lifted my eyebrows, shrugged my shoulders and said: "Okay, you got me. What gives?"

"Bryce Parker's been located," Jewels said flatly. He got up from his seat, pulled a wooden chair up to the desk, scraping the legs over the floor. He sat down and leaned into me on his forearms. The cigarette was smoking in his right hand, it was like a misty fog swirling in front of us.

"Sarge and Killer, two guys from that hellhole veterans camp in East L.A., made a possible ID from the mugshots," Jewels said in a confident voice. "They told us if it's him, then he doesn't look like the photos anymore."

"They said he's grown a scraggly beard…" Woodhouse added, while sitting up and leaning back against the couch, "and his hair is all twisted up in a mess. Parker wears a long army overcoat, an army beanie and combat boots, given to him by some of the vets."

"Let's sweep the camp," I said. My words rushed out like a direct order.

"We did that already," Woodhouse replied. "It's a big camp. We couldn't find him. Sarge and Killer wanted us to end the search as soon as possible. They said cops make the vets antsy."

The camp was along the fringes of East Los Angeles, near the river. It was an area for homeless veterans, for those who fought in the mud and blood on the front lines of war. They were shellshocked, angry, ready to snap. The military supplied the camp with big army tents, truckloads of rations, water, GI clothes, bedding, and wood for fires.

"Are they protecting him?" I asked.

"Most likely," Jewels replied, while holding his chin between his thumb and index finger. He looked over at Woodhouse, who nodded in agreement.

"These guys are a brotherhood," Woodhouse added. "Except for Sarge and Killer, the rest of the hundred and fifty-something men wouldn't talk to us." He shrugged his shoulders and said: "Can't blame 'em, though."

"Yet, they took Parker in," Jewels said, nodding his head slowly, then added: "A department artist made a sketch of Parker from the mugshot, adding a scraggly beard and a beanie."

Woodhouse got up from the couch and walked over to the desk. He reached into his coat pocket and pulled out the sketch. I grinned when I saw the new Bryce Parker.

"We also noticed cases of expensive bourbon, Scotch, vodka, rye and gin in the camp supply tent." Jewels said. "We know damn well that our tax dollars didn't supply these guys with top-shelf booze." Jewels pulled a drag from his cigarette, blew the smoke upward, then picked tobacco from his lip, flicked it off his finger, and added: "So we took the liberty of assessing the booze inventory at The Open Blouse." Jewels grinned while waiting for my response.

"Let me guess. It was all gone."

"Bingo!" Jewels blurted. "All of it. From the bar supply down to the storage area below. Every bit of it was missing. And the stock of Cuban cigars, too. It was all there when the joint was searched the first time *and* the second time."

"That must be Parker's contribution for hiding out in the camp," I added. Both detectives nodded in unison with smirks and dry snorts. I laughed out loud, which I rarely do, but the idea of Parker living down and out in the mud, with a scraggly beard, unkempt hair and wearing combat boots, was somehow humorous to me.

"How many of you swept the camp?" I asked.

"The two of us and four uniforms," Woodhouse answered.

"Not much of a sweep," I replied. "Who told you that Parker might be there?"

"A couple of rookie detectives," Jewels said. "They wanted to make a name for themselves, so they volunteered to stay on the Parker manhunt. Said they wouldn't stop until they cuffed him. They decided to go to the camp, on a lead they had, and ended up questioning Killer and Sarge."

"So why not do a full sweep? Bring thirty uniforms along with the two rookie bulls?" I asked.

"It's a matter of respect, Joe," Woodhouse said. "Those vets have had their lives shattered. Most of them have no profession, and all of them have nothing but tragic memories. The camp is their sanctuary. It protects their emotional scars from being picked at by our goal-driven society. They've bled enough, literally." He stopped talking. There was silence for a few seconds until Woodhouse added: "They've pissed and bled mud, and they deserve to be left alone."

"Then how do we flush Parker out of the camp?" I asked with an edge to my voice, while shrugging my shoulders.

"We could plant an undercover inside," Jewels suggested. "It'll be tricky to find the right cop for the job. To find somebody who was a mud rat, but dug his way out of the past. Somebody convincing enough to play that part again."

"Okay," I said. "Until then, I'm bringing in a few of my associates, to keep eyes on the place."

I paused and asked: "How many entrances to the camp?"

"Two, north and south ends," Jewels said. "And both gates are guarded at all times."

"Listen, Joe," Woodhouse added. "I want no funny business and no hero stuff. None of your boys are to go inside the camp. We did a sweep. Now these vets deserve to be left alone. Are we clear on that?"

"Yeah, sure," I replied with another shoulder shrug. "But Parker is wanted for further questioning in a multiple murder case."

I stood up quickly, like somebody had stuck a pin in my ass. That made Jewels jump up too. The three of us stood there looking down at the sketch of Parker, that was on my desk. On the surface, the new Parker looked as tough as a mercenary. It really was humorous, because I knew it was only the surface.

I broke the silence: "Parker knew about my suicide note, which suggests my life is on the line here. I want to know what he knows about it." I shook my head a few times and said: "I'm going to find Parker, and, if needed, I will knock the information out of him. I'm done with the interrogation room bullshit." There were no objections from the detectives.

We talked some more about the camp. About the possible dangers of stepping into that hornet's nest of emotionally-disturbed Korean combat soldiers, who were now in their thirties and forties.

It was eight-thirty when the detectives left the office.

In need of breakfast, I headed over to Abe's. At the deli, I placed the sketch of Bryce Parker on the table in front of me. Stared at it the whole time, while I ate fried eggs and toast, chased with mugs of black coffee, then read the Los Angeles Times. I left Abe's around ten.

A thick drizzle was turning the city into a silvery impressionistic painting. That *paint* was so wet, that it dripped off the canvas and ran along the gutters. I pulled my coat collar up, tucked my head down and headed to my car. The dense drizzle dripped from my hat in a steady stream. Before reaching my Buick, I stopped at a liquor store to purchase a fifth of Jack Daniels. The overnight low would be a ruthless twenty-eight degrees. Been forty years since Los Angeles had dipped into freezing digits.

The daylight grew dimmer, the air was colder. I should've gone to Max's flat. Instead, I drove through the drizzle towards East Los Angeles.

45

At a hundred yards away, I sat in my car, watching the camp through binoculars, only to be startled by a tap-tap-tap on my side window.

Two men, maybe in their early thirties, stood next to my car. They were dressed in army fatigues under army overcoats, and wore black combat boots. One of them made the roll-your-window-down hand motion. When he stepped back from the car, his unbuttoned overcoat drew apart, like a heavy curtain, and there was a glint coming from inside the coat. The glint caught my eye and stayed there. A chrome Colt .45 winked in my direction, like it was flirting with me. It was holstered to his side.

"I'm Sarge. This here is Killer." He cocked a dirt-stained thumb towards the other guy. "We're the camp commanders." Sarge's banged up face looked like it had passed through a woodchipper. His deep-set dark eyes were close together, under bushy eyebrows. He was about five-six with a barrel-shaped body, short arms, and gnarly bear paws for hands. His hairy knuckles were knotted.

"What 'cha doing here?" he growled.

His jaw was set off to the right, so he spoke from the corner of his sloppy mouth. He had a short, thick nose, and it was wet and runny like a neglected child's nose. I wanted to hand him a tissue.

"Bird-watching," I said.

Sarge had a half-smoked Cuban stuck between his teeth. It had a soggy end. Syrupy brown goo coated the edges of his lips. His big lips were spongy. When he spoke, the cigar flopped up and down in his mouth, like it was waving at me.

"Bird watching, eh?" His words seemed covered in saliva.

"Yep." My response was quick.

"Wha' birds ya' lookin' fer?" Killer demanded with an interrogative tone. There was a Southern twang to his barking, with a nasty edge of stupidity.

Killer had a buzz cut of blond hair. It made his profile look like a hammer head. The back of the head was flat, and the front had a long, hooked nose. It formed the hammer's claw. Killer stood about five-nine, lanky, wiry, with jitter eyes that bounced around like Mexican jumping beans.

"Nothing in particular. Just birds," I answered with a smile.

Killer's dry, cracked lips held a soggy unlit Cuban that stained his teeth brown. His pale face was scarred from acne. He had a high-pitched voice, as if a thin sheet of metal was shaking inside his mouth, when he talked. Killer holstered a black Colt .45. He pulled back his unbuttoned overcoat just enough for me to see the iron. It was a charming side piece, long as it stayed holstered.

"Jus' birds, eh?" Killer asked, then looked at Sarge.

"Yeah. I'm in love with the little tweeters, with their cute little feathers and beaks."

"You sound like a wise-ass copper to me," Sarge growled. "Are you a cop?"

"Nope. Just a leisurely birdwatcher."

"Ya got ID?" Killer barked.

I had to stop myself from chuckling over the irony of his comical-sounding voice combined with his menacing nickname.

"Why do you ask?"

"Because this here area is off limits to civilians," Sarge answered loudly. "Unless ya'll have official business here, and I'm pretty sure you don't."

"I'm an insurance investigator," I said with authority.

"Then yer a copper," Killer stated. "A plain-clothes copper."

"Nope. Just a plain-clothes insurance investigator."

"Not much difference between the two, far as we're concerned," Sarge replied, shaking his head up and down while glaring at me. I could feel the weight of his contempt, it felt crushing.

I nodded, while staring at him square in his squinty eyes, just to stand my ground.

"What's your name?" Sarge asked.

"Williams. Evan Williams."

Killer asked: "Wha' sort-a bird ya lookin' fer, Mr. Even Willems?" Killer's stupidity was like a foul odor spoiling the air.

"A blond kid named Parker." I took the drawing out of my pocket and held it up, so they could see it. "He's wanted for questioning about an insurance fraud case. I was told that he might be hiding out in your camp."

They studied the sketch in silence with only their eyes moving.

"Look," Sarge said. "We don't want no trouble with the outside. The cops were here. We let 'em look around, but that was enough." His voice became soft, which made him seem less threatening.

"Have you seen him?" I asked.

Killer turned his head, looked back at the camp, then turned and glared at me. His edgy light-blue eyes narrowed down to pencil-thin slits. They were leveled directly on my eyes. He chewed on the soggy cigar while brown juice dripped down his chin. Something felt dangerous about Killer. Maybe it was his right hand gripping the butt of his Colt .45. His hand twitched, like it needed to pull the gun out to play with it. I quickly looked back at Sarge, and slid my hand inside my overcoat, gripping the butt of my Ruger.

"Yeah. We seen-im," Sarge answered in a less aggressive tone. "Found him wandering around about thirty yards outside the camp. Told us he was homeless. He was cold and hungry. We took him in, fed and clothed him. Now he comes and goes as he pleases. He's no bother to us." Sarge paused for a moment, then looked at Killer, then back at me and said: "But his name ain't Parker."

"What's his name?" I asked.

"Stone. Calls 'imself Stone," Killer replied. "Jus' Stone."

I nodded and laughed, then shook my head.

Sarge let out a loud growl: "What's so funny?"

"Just an inside joke, Sarge. Nothing personal."

"Then ya better takes yer inside joke and gets yer ass ta'hell out of here," Killer barked. Only his high-pitched barking was more like a teacup chihuahua. "An-don't come back, 'less yer lookin' fer trouble."

Killer's edgy blue eyes were set forward, like a pair of defending weapons beneath sparse lines of blond eyebrows. He gave me a steely glare, and is upper lip twitched wildly. In return, I gave Killer my prettiest dental whites, then put the Buick in gear and drove off.

The temperature had dropped again as the cold front moved into position, ready to strike at Los Angeles with its freezing bite.

Driving away from the camp, I passed several dump trucks loaded with split wood. The trucks were headed towards the camp. I had noticed earlier that each tent had a metal chimney with white smoke billowing upwards. The chimneys were most likely attached to potbelly stoves. Our used-up soldiers would stay warm tonight. Our tax dollars owed them at least that much. And thanks to Bryce Parker, they also had a decent supply of top-shelf whisky and Cuban cigars. Not much more a man needs when living on the edge.

46

Before going to Max's flat, I headed back to the office. Wanted to check the mail to see if Dave Wells' photographs had arrived. There was nothing.

I called Frank's Photography Shop.

"They were mailed four days ago, Joe. Should've been there by now."

"How was the envelope addressed?" I asked.

"Let me talk to the kid who handled the envelope," Frank said. "He's in the backroom. Hold on a sec."

I could hear Frank calling out for Lenny.

"Lenny handled the mailing. Said he addressed it to Joe Stone and Associates. Dropped it in a mailbox in the hills four days ago, just like you requested."

"Okay. Look, Frank, do me a favor. Burn the copy negatives."

"Are you sure about that?"

"Yeah, I'm sure. Burn the test prints and test strips too. Nothing should remain of this order."

"Okay, Joe. I'll get right on it."

"Has Dave Wells been around your shop lately?"

"Nope. Haven't seen Dave in a couple of weeks."

"Nobody but you saw the photographs, Frank?"

"Just like you requested. Is Dave in trouble, Joe?"

"Something like that. Take care, Frank."

The problem was that Lenny hadn't addressed the envelope to me, personally. He addressed it to Joe Stone and Associates. I had told my associates that mail addressed as such was for all of us to open. I'm sure Dave Wells was in possession of the photographs by now.

I was about to leave the office, when I noticed a typed report lying near the Remington. It was Wells' account of the missing 1939 Porsche. He found the car. The report stated: The Porsche had been stolen by the owner's twenty-year-old son, to sell on the black market. The car was recovered. Case closed.

Lying beneath that report was Wells' letter of resignation. There was also a note, saying that I should leave his check under the typewriter, nothing more.

After making out the check, and lifting the Remington to slip the check underneath, I found several folded sheets of paper with a typed note attached. The note read:

Don't know why I withheld this other information from you. Maybe it was out of jealousy over Mya Regis suddenly wanting you, even though we were sleeping together before you came along. I know it wasn't your fault. But jealousy is a bitter ambition, it loves to hate. Problem is, I was jealous about so much more. Obviously, I have a twisted mind that needs straightening out. What I need to do first is to look evil in the eye, then find the balls to kill my inner demon. I could say that I regret what I did, but regret is wasted energy, it changes nothing. Hopefully you'll find a way to forgive me, but forgiveness will never undo what has already happened.

The note was signed with Wells' signature in blue ink, and I had no idea what he was talking about. *Jealousy? Regret? Dave Wells and Mya Regis sleeping together?* Why didn't I know about that? *Hopefully I'll find a way to forgive him.* Forgive him for what? This was all too cryptic. I needed to speak with Wells, to talk it through.

The several folded sheets of paper were copies of documents, that concluded the investigation of Mya Regis' time in San Francisco. After reading through the pages, I understood now what Alice Moore meant at our last meeting, when she said, 'there were two of them'. There was also a detailed account of a conversation between fifteen-year-old Mya and her therapist, about what had happened at her house while her parents hosted a drunken pool party. The report was disturbing. The complete story was there with the appalling details. The fact that Wells had withheld this information also disturbed me. After reading the report, I turned the lights off and left the office, feeling cold and hollow. I needed food too, so I stopped at a steak house and ate a long, slow lunch. Then I drove around the city for over an hour, trying to clear my head. It didn't work.

It was nearing five o'clock when I opened the door to Max's flat. The phone was ringing. I was reluctant to answer it, concerned that it was Jewels or Woodhouse. Didn't want to talk to anybody but Max. I let the phone ring itself out. It stopped after a dozen more times. I sat in the lounge chair near the picture window and poured a straight bourbon. Putting my bare feet on the windowsill, I stared at the outside darkness. The cold came through the glass pane, triggering a chill through my body. Several cars drove past the lake. I could see from their headlights that the lake was black and motionless. It was an icy night without wind or rain. I threw back the whisky and slid deeper into the chair. My brooding thoughts were on Dave Wells. What kind of twisted disorder had taken a hold on Wells? Why hadn't I noticed his relationship with Mya Regis? What did he mean by *kill his inner demon*? I was exhausted, but my mind kept probing on Wells, exhausting me even more. I needed to organize my thoughts, and Bryce Parker needed to be at the top of my list. Was he dangerous? Could he have killed Scott Drum and Patty Walker out of persistent jealousy, fueled by his need for revenge? There was no doubt that Parker had a screw missing from his emotional framework. But that left Arnie Bender, Mya Regis, Kimmie Turner and Sally Point. Why would Parker have killed them, and if he hadn't, could there be two killers?

More baffling thoughts piled up in my head, sounding like blaring car horns in a traffic jam.

Given how tired I was, the bourbon hit me just right. I stood up, stumbled towards the bedroom. Before I reached the bed, the phone rang again. I looked at the clock: eight-seventeen. Stumbling back into the living room, I picked up the receiver.

"Hello?"

"Hi."

"Hoping it was you," I said through a whispered slur, while slouching into the lounge chair again.

"I want to be in bed with you," she whispered back.

"Mmmm. When are you coming home?"

"In four days." There was a pause. "I need to get out of here."

"Make it sooner."

"I can't. There are a few more legalities that want my attention." There was a long sigh. "So much paperwork with so many lines to sign on."

"Bring the papers back here to sign them."

"Vesuvio's scumbag attorney needs to be present while I sign them." Another sigh. "He made inappropriate passes at me. If he throws another pass my way, I'll crush his nuts. I swear, I will."

I chuckled and asked: "How are you feeling otherwise?"

"Strange in ways I don't fully comprehend. I hurt, and the pain is both emotional and physical. Sometimes my head feels so tight from my aching thoughts. Other times my stomach burns from the ugliness of it all, of how bloodthirsty Vesuvio was, and how it ended in so much violence."

"I'm sorry that this had to happen," I said, and added. "When will you be back?"

"I'll call you when I have my itinerary."

"I'll be waiting." My voice trailed off to a sleepy drone.

"Joe, you sound tired."

"I'm exhausted. The killer murdered Sally Point."

"I saw it on the news. I'm sorry."

"He has killed everyone I've talked to about the case. He must be following me, staying one step ahead of me. And I can't identify him or them."

"Them? Are you saying that there might be two killers?"

"I don't know what I'm saying. Don't know what to think anymore."

"Could it be Parker? Have you found him?"

"The police have his location."

I told Max about Bryce Parker hiding in the veteran's camp, and why I thought Parker could be the killer. Told her about his jealousy motive, and possible revenge tactic. Then there was the suicide note left in my office, that Parker knew about. There was Jill Sabin's stolen coat that was found at the crime scene, with Parker's fingerprints on the buttons. My gut told me it was Parker wearing Sabin's coat, when I saw the silhouette in the window of Scott Drum's apartment, on the night of the double murders. There was also Parker's resistance to the fact that his mother had been dead for years. This showed how emotionally deranged he was.

Did Parker steal Dave Wells' black cowboy boots too, using them as a decoy? Did Kimmie Turner's last lover wear cowboy boots? Or was that a fabrication by Parker to throw the investigation off course? Parker felt jilted by Patty Walker, Kimmie Turner and Jill Sabin. But that left Arnie Bender's and Mya Regis' murders. What motive could Parker have had for those killings? What about Mya's earring that I found at Scott Drum's murder scene? Parker knew the earring was Mya's, when I showed it to him. But why would he have planted Mya's earring under Drum's bed? To implicate her? Then there was Sally Point's gruesome murder. The person in a hat and long coat, bending over to get into the taxi, in front of Sally's house, was that Parker? Did Sally Point, who knew Parker's mother, know more than what she had told me? Would that information have put Sally in danger? Or was I just goddamn wrong about everything?

My brain was flooded with all these questions surfacing in a wild stream, then jamming up and going nowhere, except into Max's ear.

"Joe. I'm coming back as soon as possible. We'll figure it out together. I can be there in two days."

I whispered something incoherent. I was fading.

"Joe, listen, if the killer is tailing you, then we'll go backwards to get inside his head. We'll look at everyone you've talked to, the ones still alive and…"

"That's it!" I said. "Everyone I've talked to, including…" Suddenly I was alert and sitting straight up in the lounge chair. "Max, I gotta go. Need to get to her before he does."

"Joe, wait…"

I left Max listening to the dial tone, then made another call. The phone rang a dozen times at her home with no one answering. I called her office. The phone rang and rang there, too. Then I called Jill Sabin.

"No, she wouldn't be at home tonight," Sabin said. "The bar is closed on Monday nights, but she goes there anyway, to do paper work. If she is there, then it's unlike her to not answer the phone."

I telephoned the Hollywood Police Station, knowing that Jewels and Woodhouse were pulling a nightshift. The desk sergeant told me they were busy with a male stiff in the red-light district, but he would forward my message to the detectives.

47

I stepped outside, walking fast to my Electra, parked down the block. The sidewalks were empty, and the leftover rain puddles were as hard as porcelain. It was a starry night, thirty degrees and dropping. The freezing air felt like the weight of a dead body pressing against me.

The cold vinyl seat covers made brittle snapping sounds when I slid behind the steering wheel. Turning on the ignition, the engine started coughing, and finally changed to a steady purr. A few minutes later, a thin warmth rose from the heater vents. I put the Electra in gear, and headed west, creeping along like a maroon iceberg.

It took less than twenty minutes to reach Santa Monica. I parked a block down from Five In The Afternoon, and walked at a steady pace the rest of the way. Approaching the building, I saw her car in the parking lot, but there were no other vehicles. If he was here, then his car was parked somewhere else.

Five In The Afternoon was a one-story brown shingled structure that sat on three-foot high iron stilts. It had a square brown composition roof, and picture windows on three sides. The window panes were floor to ceiling, wall to wall. The front window faced the ocean, with a large redwood deck in front of it.

The icy air was infused with the pungent scent of coastal sage and sea kelp. Walking closer to the building, the gritty sand crunched beneath my shoes like an animal chewing on bone. Except for a dim yellow light coming from a backroom, and a small light coming from the bar, it was mostly dark inside. I crept through the coastal sage scrub along the edge of the lot, staying low and moving closer to the large side window that faced the parking area. There was sudden movement out of the corner of my eye. Something passed along the rear of the building. I watched, waited. There was no other movement.

I took my hat off and stepped up on a rock, and peered through the side window. A dim yellow light was coming from the office in the back of the building. The office door was half open, which threw a rectangular plank of yellow light across the floor of the semi-dark barroom. Through the door opening, I saw a black skirt that ended at the knees with legs in black stockings. I could see hands in a lap. She was sitting in a chair on the side of a wooden desk. There was a green-shaded banker's lamp aimed at a Corona typewriter. I could see one of his arms and a black gloved hand fingering the keys. The arm was coming out of a sleeve from a tailored grey suit jacket. I saw a grey pant leg pulled over a black cowboy boot.

Stepping down from the rock, I edged along the building to the front deck. The waves rolled and roared, breaking along the beach like an invading enemy. Icy mist needled my face. Exhaling dense steam, I stepped up to the deck and edged along the front wall, until I came to the large sliding glass door that faced the ocean. I peeked inside, having a better view of the office now. The club's owner, Sherry

Miller, was sitting in the chair next to the desk. Her body was shaking, jolting. There was a pearl-handle, chrome Colt .32 Snub-nose revolver lying on the desk, between the two of them. It glinted from the light hovering above it. His gloved-hand reached over to stroke Sherry's cheek, causing his head to bend forward, just enough for me to see his blond hair. Sherry yanked herself away from his hand. She shook her head violently from side to side, then lowered it slowly. Black hair fell over her face, covering it like an executioner's hood.

I unholstered my Ruger and reached for the sliding door handle, pushing it slightly. It was unlocked. The door slid open a half-inch. I stepped back out of sight, waited, then took another look. He continued typing, while Sherry's hands laid together in her lap like trapped birds. She was looking down at them, as if wanting to set them free. Her body shivered.

With a quick move, he stood up, yanked the paper from the carriage and reached for the Colt on the desk. I stepped off the deck. There was movement again towards the back of the building. Probably Jewels and Woodhouse. They must have seen my Electra down the street and decided to park there, to avoid announcing their presence. With the detectives covering the back of the building, I walked to the front deck again, then slowly slid the door open halfway. It took several seconds for him to realize that the sound of the ocean had gotten louder inside the room. He stepped out of the office and looked in the direction of the sliding door, but I had stepped into the shadows and was out of sight, still peeking through the glass pane. He stepped back into the office, yanked Sherry out of the chair, pulled her into the barroom and shoved her to the floor, while keeping his eyes on the open door. Sherry fell hard hitting the floor with a thud. She laid there in a fetal position, whimpering. He was holding the Colt in his right hand and the typed note in his left hand, while looking down at Sherry. I walked inside, the Ruger in my right hand, arm stretched forward, aiming the pistol at his chest. I was thirty feet away, when he noticed me. I should have fired. Should have dropped him. Should have ended it right there. What was I waiting for?

"So, you figured it out, eh? Maybe you're not as stupid as people say you are."

I didn't respond to his jab. He sneered at me and yelled through clenched teeth: "If Vesuvio had killed you, like I paid him to do, then you wouldn't be here taking up my time." Like red marbles, his bloodshot eyes were pushing out of their sockets, as if trying to get away from his hot-headed anger. "You can't depend on a fucking greaseball to do anything right," he growled. His breathing came fast and hard, and he was glaring at me, his hatred transmitting through the air like an electric charge needing to ground. Then his mouth twisted terribly, like somebody with a mental illness, whose rage was out of their control.

In the dim shadowy light, I almost didn't recognize him.

Commissioner McKenna's attention turned back to Sherry. She was on her back now, looking up, spooked by the gun barrel now aimed at her forehead. She closed her eyes, begging him to stop. Suddenly she flipped her body over and crawled on hands and knees, trying to get away from the gun's threatening hollow eye. Then she fell to her stomach, sobbing and moaning.

"My experience tells me you only have one round in the cylinder," I said. "Then what?"

He turned and aimed his Colt at me. His arm was stretched out in a steady position, and his feet were spread apart in a solid gunman's stance. The office light brushed over his snakeskin boots, causing them to shimmer, as if hissing a warning for me to stay back.

"Jewels and Woodhouse will be coming through the backdoor," I said calmly. "You have no way out of this one, McKenna. I finally have you and I'm bringing you in."

We heard the back door open. It creaked, then dragged over the wooden floor. Heavy footsteps came our way.

Daniel McKenna's jaw was agape, distorting his features even more. Dried saliva had formed around his open mouth, and his head oscillated hawkishly, moving from me to the back hallway and back to me. Then, watching the hallway, his blood-veined eyes widened in disbelief.

48

Standing in the doorway, holding a black Colt .45 at his side, Bryce Parker was barely recognizable in the dim light. Under his scruffy blond whiskers, his face was smudged with mud. Wisps of his oily hair stuck out from underneath the army beanie, which was pulled low to his eyebrows. An unlit Cuban was in the right corner of his mouth. He chewed on it nervously.

Despite the long army overcoat, the black military boots, and holding a .45, Parker's eyes had a fearful look. I could see it in his feet, too. They were antsy, tapping at the floor, his body rocking from side to side.

Standing ten feet away from McKenna, Parker aimed the .45 at McKenna's chest.

"Son. What the hell are you doing?" McKenna barked furiously. "You were supposed to wait for me at the camp, while I finished up here." His wide forehead beaded with sweat.

With Parker's .45 and my .38 aimed at McKenna, he backed up against the wall. Sherry Miller screamed, again and again, like a trapped animal, then crawled on her hands and knees across the floor, to hide under a table. She gasped, whimpered, and pulled her body inward tightly, as if trying to hide from this shocking nightmare.

Parker remained silent, but his gun-hand shook like a hillbilly caught in a snow blizzard. He pulled the hammer back. The metallic click reverberated throughout the barroom. He spit the cigar out of his mouth. It hit the floor with a soggy thud.

"Son, listen!" McKenna pleaded in a shrill voice. "We can do this one together. Make it look like Stone was the killer all along."

"Shut up, *Dad*," Parker yelled. "I'm tired of your fucking orders, of your plans. I'm tired of you, of the way you treated mom. You miserable asshole!" Parker stiffened his arm, as if he was going to pull the trigger. His face was sweaty, and his mouth made sucking sounds, and his neck-pulse visibly hammered against his skin, like a fast-beating heart had formed there.

"You set *me* up to look like the killer. You planted guns in *my* house." Parker's eyes welled. "You made me the decoy, and used me for your own advantage." Threads of spit flew from his mouth, thick saliva dangled from his chin. He was extremely angry, and he appeared to be seriously unstable.

It was electrifying to watch Parker and McKenna face off. I wanted to sit down with a bourbon and enjoy the show, but I kept standing with my Ruger aimed at Commissioner McKenna and my eyes on Parker. Father and son? Grace Parker and Daniel McKenna produced Bryce Parker?

"Yeah, Stone. It was me. I drugged Scott Drum and Patty Walker," Parker confessed. "Drum called downstairs to the club for two drinks that night. That was my chance. And I put Mya's earring under Drum's bed, just like my dickhead father wanted me to do, after he killed Drum and

Walker. I stole the earring from Mya's house, like this piece of crap told me to do." Parker snapped his head from side to side. His neck muscles were dangerously taut, like stressed cables ready to snap. "Dad said we were only going to drug them, for the fun of it. I believed him, but he's the one who murdered them!" Parker's body vibrated like an over-worked pressure cooker ready to explode. "I was the one who carried Patty Walker's body out of the apartment, hiding her behind the dumpster, like Dad ordered me to do." Tears rolled down Parker's face. "She was already dead from Dad strangling her. He was the one who shot her in the head, after she was dead." Parker's gun hand shook so fast, it almost blurred in the air. "I stole Jill Sabin's coat, so I could leave it at Drum's apartment to incriminate Sabin, like Dad wanted me to do. But I didn't leave it there. It was cold that night, I needed to wear it. I ripped a button off the coat and left it behind the dumpster with Patty's body, as a clue to make Jill Sabin look guilty, too."

Parker stopped yelling and took two steps towards McKenna, raising the .45 from McKenna's chest to his face. "Dad wanted Mya Regis and Jill Sabin to be suspects." Parker was yelling again. "I brought the coat back to the apartment and put it in Drum's closet, to make it look like Jill Sabin had been there. It was the same day that you confronted me in the parking lot of the club and..."

"You're a weak little prick. Shut up!" McKenna yelled at Parker. McKenna was gnawing on his tongue, pulling the tension from his upper face down to his jaw. "He doesn't know what he's saying, Stone. He's delusional. He's..."

Parker made quick forward steps and stood three feet from Commissioner McKenna. With the .45 still aimed at his face, McKenna flinched. I saw his eyes suddenly fill with bright, neon-like terror.

"Shut up, Dad," Parker screamed. McKenna pressed his back flat against the wall, while rising to his tiptoes, as if that would get him farther away from the gun barrel. Parker went on: "I didn't kill anybody, but because of you, Dad, I'm the one the cops are after. They're after me, and not you!"

"Don't listen to him, Stone," McKenna yelled. "He's out of his mind, mentally ill. He's…"

"And you killed Sally Point!" Parker screamed. "Why? Why did you kill her? She couldn't have hurt you. She was a harmless old lady. Why'd you kill her?"

McKenna suddenly lost it. With his eyes ablaze, he cracked and spilled like a bottle of truth serum. "Yeah, yeah. I killed all of them. Too bad, yeah? Too fucking bad." He was yelling like a hot-headed drunk. "I hated Scott Drum. I had Mya first and I wanted her again. She was mine. But Drum was in the way with that bullshit marriage. And Mya wanted nothing to do with me, no matter how much I begged her." He shrugged his broad shoulders and said in a mocking tone. "And poor Patty Walker. Boo-hoo. She just happened to be there that night. Ha-ha. An unlucky innocent. Big deal. Nothing lost there." McKenna was cornered and coming apart like a concrete dam slowly cracking. He snapped his head from side to side, as if trying to disconnect it from his body.

I was anxious for him to confess to murdering Arnie Bender and Kimmie Turner, but Parker was fixated on the truth about Mya Regis.

"What do you mean you had Mya? What? What the hell does that mean?" Parker yelled.

McKenna stood there, his eyes turning dull. He was looking through us, as if into the future, and far away from this cornered situation he was in. He didn't answer Parker's question. Then he looked down at the Colt in his right hand, as if the gun was too heavy to hold. The typed note, in his other hand, dropped to the floor. It zigzagged downward fast, like it was trying to outrun danger. Standing there, McKenna was caught in his own private hell, with all the crooked years of his past caving in on him.

I said to Parker: "Your father raped Mya Regis when she was fifteen and made her pregnant. He was in his thirties and…"

"Shut up, Stone! You don't know jack-shit," McKenna yelled. "Shut the hell up!" He was back with us again. His eyes were on me, explosive, hateful. "I didn't rape her. I made love to her. I loved her! Then Scott Drum came along and stole Mya away from me."

McKenna's face had the appearance of elastic rage, stretching from his damp eyes down to his sweaty mouth. His top lip was curled tightly over his teeth, like a vicious growl. Body tremors overtook him, and his tongue made agitated snapping sounds against the roof of his mouth.

Parker stepped another foot closer to McKenna. He was holding the .45 with a crushing grip, as if to strangle the butt. His finger was tight against the trigger, close to pulling it. His eyes burned with blistering rage, and his face swelled with blood and fire. He was about to lose it.

"I have copies of the paperwork," I said in a fast-talking surge, hoping to distract Parker from his deadly focus on McKenna. "I've got documents of Mya's time in San Francisco, from her doctor, from her therapist, from her nurses. She gave birth to twins, McKenna. Patty Walker was one of your daughters, and you killed her."

McKenna's mouth popped open, as if the jaw hinges had ripped. He tried to speak, but only huffs and puffs exploded past his lips. Then his mouth closed and his lips squeezed into a tight circle, that moved rapidly in and out, like a fish on land sucking air. He pressed his back harder against the wall, as if trying to disappear inside of it, but he was as cornered as a forty-five-degree angle.

I thought about that moment, the moment when a criminal realizes that there is no way out of the corner, that they've backed themselves into. And that fear of being trapped can cause a guilty person to run their mouth like a word-marathon. McKenna knew that the situation had spun out of his control. He was talking faster, stumbling over his words. It was impossible to follow his blathering. The gist of it was that he was the victim.

When he finally stopped talking, I slammed him with more facts. Wished I hadn't. Parker didn't need to hear this right now. It came out anyway, uncontrolled.

"Jill Sabin is your other daughter," I said. "Sabin and Patty Walker were twins. You raped a child, McKenna. That's what Mya told her therapist. She said you went at her like a sick animal, and she just laid there terrified and crying, while you satisfied yourself. It's in the medical report."

That's when it registered with Parker. "Jill Sabin is my sister?" Parker yelled. "I fucked my sister?" Parker charged so fast towards McKenna, that I couldn't stop him. BLAM! The slug entered McKenna's face through his left eye with such impact that his head snapped backwards, with ungodly force. The slug exited the back of his skull, taking blood and brains with it. McKenna was dead while standing there, he just didn't know yet. Then he dropped to the floor faster than a flash of light. As quickly as he shot Daniel McKenna, Bryce Parker put the gun barrel in his mouth, aimed upward and pulled the trigger. The explosive impact of the .45 slug caused the top part of Parker's head and part of his forehead to instantly disappear, then he dropped straight down, hitting the floor with a crushing thud. His beanie flew upward, momentarily clinging to the ceiling, until gravity dropped it on what was left of Parker's face. The hot pistol barrel was still in his mouth. Smoke coming out of the barrel escaped through his lips in a drift of ghostly white, until it vanished altogether, as if his soul had visibly left his body.

Sherry Miller broke into electrifying body jolts and sobbing. It was like she had ripped apart, trying to crawl out of herself. I holstered my Ruger then crawled under the table and took her in my arms. My body shook from the emotional storm that had consumed her. After a long minute, I crawled out from under the table and coaxed Sherry to come along with me. I sat her down at a corner table facing the ocean, and wrapped her in my overcoat. Her panic subsided, but the sobs and shakes continued.

Sounding like attacking birds, screaming sirens rushed the parking lot. I could see Jewels and Woodhouse running towards the building. Within seconds, cops and medics crowded the barroom. Two medics bundled Sherry in a blanket and walked her to an ambulance.

"McKenna confessed to the killings," I said. "Parker pulled it out of him before he shot McKenna, then shot himself."

Jewels and Woodhouse listened intently.

Sitting at a table with the sheet-covered bodies lying on the floor behind us, I told the detectives that Sherry Miller was to be McKenna's next target, just a trigger-pull away. Jewels looked at the typed suicide note that he held in his hand. I mentioned how the phone call with Max Lee helped me to figure out the next possible victim.

"The only murders McKenna didn't own up to," I said, "were Arnie Bender's, Mya Regis' and Kimmie Turner's. Parker didn't give McKenna time for that confession. My suicide note, left in the office typewriter, didn't come up either. Parker was angry, confused, tired, and had lost sight of reality. He didn't have to die like that. He needed help, needed somebody who understood that he was a victim as well."

"What was McKenna's motive?" Woodhouse asked.

"Relentless jealousy," I answered. "He was sick with it. Poisoned by it." I spat those words out like I needed to get them away from me, and then added: "McKenna was consumed with revenge over what he had created in his mind, about Mya being exclusively his. He was obviously delusional.

We talked about McKenna raping Mya when she was fifteen, then wanting her for himself, only to realize that he couldn't have her. I told the detectives that McKenna had confessed to bringing Geano Vesuvio to Los Angeles, with the purpose of killing me and to abduct Max.

I leaned back in the chair and listened to the ocean. It was loud and forceful with an agitator-cleansing action. It felt cathartic, as if the great city of Los Angeles was being washed clean of rank filth. Unfortunately, too many good people had died for nothing.

49

After the Five In The Afternoon finale, I must have slept for eighteen hours, because I don't remember anything between then and now. Maybe it was the empty fifth of Jack Daniels on the coffee table, or maybe it was total exhaustion.

I woke up in Max's bed at eleven thirty. The sun was bright and the sky was blue. It was almost too bright and too blue. I walked into the living room, looked out the window. Silver Lake glistened like a blue glass eye, holding the sun's reflecting pupil. The cold front had passed, and it hadn't rained for a couple of days. Los Angeles was warming up, ready to dry out. I opened a window and spring air entered the room, with the fragrance of plum blossoms.

I got dressed and decided to stop by my flat, to see how the repairs were coming together. When I saw T.V. crews on Logan Street in front of my apartment, I turned the Buick around and drove to the office instead. The news-hounds clogged the front of that building, too. I drove past them to Abe's Deli and parked a block away. The short walk to the deli was refreshing, and the absence of a heavy wool overcoat felt liberating.

The streets were busy with people, most of them reading newspapers. One of the headlines read: POLICE COMMISSIONER DANIEL MCKENNA SHOT DEAD. On the front page of another paper was a photograph of me with the headline: SLEUTH JOE STONE DOES IT AGAIN! I didn't care to read more. Had never been interested in stories written about me, not in newspapers or in detective magazines. I pulled my hat down low and kept walking.

"Hey. You're Joe Stone, that Private Detective, right?" asked a well-dressed, middle-aged man with a pink bald head, as smooth as marble. He came towards me with a sexy twenty-something on his arm. He put his hand out to shake mine. His pale hand floated through the air like a dead fish on water.

"No, I'm not." I answered sternly and kept walking. The twenty-something looked at me, puckered her lips and blew a kiss in my direction. She was a dark redhead in a tight, powdered blue silk dress. The dress was short, her legs were long, and her ice-blue eyes wanted my attention. I didn't give it to her.

At Abe's, I took a back booth away from the windows. The waitress came over. She was a thirty-something wholesome blond with long, thick hair and dazzling hazel eyes. Her white and black uniform was tailored to her body like custom seat covers in a Mercedes.

"Hi, Joe." She was upbeat, chirping like a songbird. "What would you like today?" I liked that she didn't mention the news.

"Hi, Janie. Fried eggs, home fries and toast, please."

She nodded and winked, filled my coffee cup, then turned and sauntered down the aisle. I lifted the cup to my lips, and watched her body swaying through the rising steam. She did a quick look back, and gave me a blossom of a smile, one that could turn sand into pearls. Then she playfully tossed her blond hair, like a lion shaking its mane.

While waiting for the food, I stepped into a phone booth, placed a call to a security company. I asked for two guys to clear the front of my office building, which I owned, and for two more guys to clear my apartment area. I owned that building, too.

Sliding back into my booth, I nursed my coffee, and watched Janie flirt with two old men, who were sitting together.

Suddenly my thoughts turned dark, switching to all the losses. If I could have stopped Bryce Parker from shooting Commissioner McKenna, maybe McKenna would have confessed to the killings of Arnie Bender, Mya Regis and Kimmie Turner. How could jealousy make a man spin so lawlessly out of control?

"Joe!" It was Janie standing at the table with my order. "Hey, snap out of it, Good-looking." She was smiling, while bending over to place the food on the table. I jolted and sat up straight.

"Thank you, Janie."

"Anything else?" she asked with a wink.

"Ah, yeah. What's your last name?"

"Miller. Janie Miller," she said, while flashing her fabulous smile.

"Any relation to Sherry Miller, in Santa Monica."

"Not that I know of," she answered softly. "Hey, do you want to get a drink later? I get off at five thirty."

I told Janie about my relationship with Max. Otherwise, I would've said yes. She took the compliment with a smile and a wink, and walked away, and coming through the window, sunlight coasted around her tight curves.

Left Abe's Deli at one thirty and walked to the office. From the corner of Hollywood and Vine, I saw that the newspaper gang was still there, and the security guards had just arrived. The guards got busy with moving the reporters, pushing them down the sidewalk, and clearing room for me to walk into my building. The news-hounds yelled at me like show barkers at a two-bit carnival. They were loud and persistent.

"Joe! Do you wish *you* had killed that murdering Commissioner McKenna?"

"Joe. Hey, Joe. Give us the juicy details."

...and so on with their ridiculous questions.

The phone was ringing when I entered the office.

"Joe Stone Pri..."

"I saw it on the news. I've been worried. I couldn't reach you, and..."

"Max. I'm alright."

"It's over. Isn't it, Joe?" she said.

"Yes. Unresolved, but over." I paused then added with conviction: "It was a grim ending to what lust and jealousy can do to people."

"Yes. McKenna was so vindictive," Max said with a rush of words, and added: "I'm flying into Los Angeles tomorrow, landing at three thirty."

"I'll be there, waiting with open arms." She cooed like a lovebird.

After our conversation, I walked to the window and opened it wide. Looking out, I saw a familiar figure standing on the other side of the boulevard. The three devoted pigeons were pecking the ground at her feet. She was bundled in layers of stringy clothes, looking like an undone ball of yarn. Her hands were holding two canvas bags stuffed to the seams. She was looking up at me. I gave her the wait-a-sec sign with my index finger, then ran out of the office and down the stairs. When I reached the sidewalk, Alice Moore was nowhere in sight. I went back to the office and placed a call to Jill Sabin. She was happy to hear that I was safe, and that *the monster* was dead. I think she meant Bryce Parker and not Daniel McKenna.

I decided that it was time for Jill Sabin to know that Mya Regis was her mother, that Police Commissioner Daniel McKenna was her father, that Patty Walker was her twin, and that Alice Moore was her cousin. But I didn't want to tell her all of this over the phone. Eventually she would discover that Bryce Parker was her half-brother, and having had sex with him was going to be disturbing news for her to process.

When I put the receiver down, the phone rang.

"Joe Stone, Private Investigator."

"Mr. Stone, this is Douglas Goodman. I am the estate attorney for the late Ms. Mya Regis, and the executor to her last will and testament."

"Yes, Mr. Goodman. What can I do for you?"

"I was told that you are fast at finding people."

"Okay. How can I help you?"

"Ms. Regis left her house in Bel Air, a Malibu beach house, and a cabin in Lake Tahoe, along with her investments and bank holdings, to her cousin Ms. Alice Moore. The problem is, I have no idea on how to locate Ms. Moore. Is that something that you could assist me with?"

"Yes, Mr. Goodman. I'll have Alice Moore at your office, as soon as I locate her." I had to hold back from laughing, about Alice's sudden windfall.

"Oh, that is wonderful. Thank you, Mr. Stone, and congratulations for tracking down that killer Daniel McKenna."

After the phone call, I sat in the pink-cushioned chair and laughed. I couldn't stop laughing until the phone rang again. I answered the phone.

"Joe. Brick Woodhouse." His mechanical tone sounded urgent. "You need to get over here, right away."

After Woodhouse gave me the West Hollywood address, he said: "You had probably been here before."

Maybe it was the warm sunny weather and the shedding of winter overcoats, scarves and gloves that made this reality of death seem lighter. I had spent the past few months wading through rain-filled streets and cold-blooded murders, watching the bodies pile up, like fish in a processing plant, while killer-McKenna hound-dogged my every step. But somehow, I accepted the reality of this next tragedy without anguish or grief.

50

Driving along Santa Monica Boulevard got me to the West Hollywood street address in ten minutes. The short, two-block street was cordoned off at both ends by patrol cars and uniforms.

The neighborhood was upscale with adobe-style houses painted in bright colors, and landscaped with vibrant succulent gardens. Both sides of the street were lined with lofty Mediterranean date palms and lush banana trees. Polished European cars sparkled in the cobblestone driveways.

A dozen neighbors stood together in front of a pink stucco house trimmed in sage green. Some of them were middle-aged potbellied men, dressed in quality suits. But most of them were elegant looking women in fine short-hemmed fashionable dresses, accented with matching glossy heels.

The women leaned into each other, talking, while holding delicate manicured hands to their chests, as if gestures of shock. They were lousy actors. Los Angeles was filled with lousy actors.

Pulling up to the address, it was a single-story terracotta painted Hollywood bungalow, with off-white trim and red clay roof tiles. Yellow ice plants covered the front yard. Three cop cars and an ambulance were parked in front of the house. A cream colored 1940s panel truck, with brown fenders, was parked in the driveway. It had *LOCKSMITH* painted in old-time lettering on the paneled sides.

I parked the Buick behind the truck and slid out of the car. Jewels and Woodhouse walked out of the house and came over to me. Their shoulders were rounded and their expressions grave. It made them look older than their forty-one years. We shook hands, and just stood there ill at ease. We all felt the impact of this one. When they finally spoke to me, it was with whispered funeral voices.

"We thought you should be here," Jewels said.

"You could imagine our shock," Woodhouse added.

"A neighbor across the street called it in," Jewels said. "She was in her garden, when she heard what sounded like an explosion coming from inside the house. Said it was disturbingly loud."

I nodded, not knowing what to say. We stood there looking at each other, as if prolonging the walk into the house would change this situation for the better.

"Detectives," an older uniform called from the front door. "The locksmith's about to pick the last of the two deadbolts, on that hallway door."

"Be sure nobody goes into that room," Jewels ordered.

"Keep a man at the door. And don't open it," Woodhouse commanded. "Let the locksmith know not to open the door."

"Joe, you don't have to come in," Jewels said in a soft voice.

I was looking down, noticing how scuffed my brown shoes were, and thinking I should have them polished.

We all stood in silence again, hands in our pockets, not moving, just looking at each other.

It was nearing two-thirty, the temperature was sixty degrees. It felt tropical compared to the severe winter we had endured. The sky was deep blue with streaks of violet. It felt like a good day to handle troubling news, even though the warm air almost made the situation feel ordinary.

I lit a cigarette, took a few quick drags, then flicked the butt into the driveway. It bounced across the concrete, throwing sparks in a show of angry attitude.

Woodhouse led us to the front door and opened it. Together, the three of us walked silently into the house.

The body was slouched in a high-backed yellow-cushioned chair in the living room. The corpse was covered with a white sheet. I didn't need to look under it. Didn't want to see the damage a .357 slug does to a human head. The three of us just stood there and stared at the sheet-covered body in its death pose.

Dave Wells had pressed the barrel of his cowboy rod dead-center forehead, and pulled the trigger. The slug traveled out the back of his head through the stuffed chair and embedded itself in the wall frame. It hollowed out the plaster and cracked the stud. Some of the stuffing from the chair had been blown across the floor, splattered with blood and bone chips. The high-backed cushioned chair had absorbed most of the hideous discharge.

Wells' new black mamba cowboy boots were lined up perfectly along the side of the chair, like an indication that he was home to put his feet up, to take it easy. The boots had been freshly polished, as if a last rite had been performed.

As I stared at the covered body, my breathing was steady. Maybe I should have felt something more, something deeper, something painful, but in that moment, I had no emotional reaction, only a vague chilled numbness that had crawled up my spine as an indistinct sentimental response.

The sheet was white, except for where Dave's head was. The blood had soaked through the cloth, causing the fabric to cling to his face, creating a tight red mask. The wet cloth had sunk a little bit into his open mouth, and his tented prominent nose was like a crimson mountain on a relief map. Under the thin cloth, I could see the impression of his .357 Magnum, lying on his lap.

There are times when I wished that I weren't in this type of business. Wished that I didn't know so much, or didn't have to find out so much: stupid people seem happier to me than all the smart assholes in Los Angeles.

I had forgotten that Jewels was standing next to me.

"We couldn't find a suicide note," Jewels whispered. I nodded but didn't look at him. Wasn't ready to tell him that I had the note back at the office, that Wells had left it there, along with his resignation. Sure, the note was cryptic, but now I understood what "killing his inner demon" meant. Though it wasn't clear to me why Dave thought that he had a demon in need of killing.

"Joe, follow me, let's go and take a look at the inside that room," Jewels said in a deep, low voice. He turned and walked down a short hallway. At the end of the hallway was a diamond-shaped window with an opaque, reddish-brown glass pane. Hazy light filtered through the glass, like a sepia-colored dream was manifesting before my eyes, pulling me into the dream.

There were doors on both sides of the hallway. The door on the right side was closed. A tall middle-aged uniform stood sentry.

Jewels opened the door, glanced back at me, then walked into the room and disappeared. For some reason, it felt as if I'd never see him again. Maybe it was because my friend was lying dead in the living room that had me feeling hopeless, just for the moment.

Walking closer to the open door, I could see a red glow radiating from inside the room, and a familiar acidic odor was filling the air. I followed Jewels into the room. Woodhouse was already there, standing in the middle of the floor. It was just the three of us standing there in a noiseless, windowless chamber. My breathing became shallow as if it had lodged in my throat. With the red light all around me, I turned in circles, spinning into light-headedness. The odor of photographic chemicals filled my nose. This was Wells' darkroom, where a dozen black and white forensic photos of naked dead women were tacked to the walls. All of them, victims of violent crimes.

Then a nightmarish twist caught my attention: there were photographs of the bodies of Arnie Bender, Mya Regis, Millie Bender and Kimmie Turner. In the photos, Wells was lying down or kneeling next to each one. His smile was cold and cruel looking, but his eyes seemed magnified with hot pleasure. Tacked to another wall were Mya Regis' missing green silk panties from the Griffith Park murder scene. They were labeled MYA. Next to them was a pair of red silk panties labeled KIMMIE, from the Rollins mansion murder scene. There was a photograph of Max, and one of me, then another one of Jewels and Woodhouse standing together. There were rifle-scope crosshairs drawn with red ink dead-center on each of our foreheads. Suddenly, my gut felt like a steel fist had plowed into it. I could barely breathe and my brain felt like it had swelled up and was pressing against my skull. I nearly lost my balance, but Woodhouse reached out, grabbed my arm and steadied me. I could hear him talking with Jewels. Their voices were muffled, like sluggish bird-wings beating the air.

Regaining my footing, I walked closer to the wall of photos. There was Wells in the rainy alley kneeling next to Arnie Bender's body, holding Arnie's bloodied head up by his hair, like a trophy kill. Wells had a ruthlessly smug expression. In his hand I could see a shutter release gadget for his camera. Next to that was a photo of him lying down with Mya Regis in the backseat of her green Lincoln. She was dead, her forehead was bloody. Wells was posing alongside of her with his hand on her exposed crotch. He looked coldly into the camera. I could see the handheld shutter release gadget in his other hand. It was the same with Kimmie Turner at the Robert Rollins mansion: in the photo, Wells was lying naked alongside a lifeless Turner. Blood had trickled down from her forehead to her nose. One of Kimmie's dead hands was positioned around Wells' erection.

Like a painful jab to the eye, there were photographs of Millie Bender lying on her couch. The photographs were displayed in sequential order. One showed Wells pouring white powder into a glass of whisky. Another showed Wells pinching Millie's mouth open and pouring the concoction down her throat. There was another with him lying next to Millie, her dress was pulled up. Wells' hand was on her exposed vagina. Another photo showed Millie's legs spread apart, panties pulled down to her ankles and Wells' face was buried in her crotch.

"No. You filthy bastard. No!" My voice bellowed outward like an explosion. Then I lunged at the wall, tearing at the photographs, cussing and yelling and cursing Wells. Jewels grabbed my arm and forced me outside of the darkroom, where I took off staggering down the hallway, back to Dave Wells' dead body. Pulling my Ruger from its holster, I took aim at Wells' throat, until a muscular young cop grabbed me from behind with a suffocating bear hug. He locked my arms to my sides then dragged me outside and threw me to the ground, and was trying to cuff me. My Ruger fell from my hand. I was thrashing around in the yellow ice plants, damning Dave Wells to Hell. Jewels and Woodhouse flew out the front door, like startled birds from a bush, and pulled the cop off me. Jewels hauled me to my feet, bawling me out with a raised voice that sounded like high-pitched radio static. Then Woodhouse shouted at me, condemning me, while sliding my Ruger into his coat pocket. In my current state of emotional confusion, his words popped and splashed like cantankerous bubbles in my face. With me in the middle, both detectives held my arms and walked me to my car, where I leaned back against the front door, trying to steady myself. With a shaky hand, I dug a pack of cigarettes out of my suitcoat pocket. Jewels grabbed the pack from my hand and popped a cigarette out. He lit the cig and handed it to me. I pulled a hard drag and looked up, releasing the smoke. The hot sunlight scorched my eyes, but the blue sky looked sinfully cold. I put my sunglasses on and just stood there, looking up and trembling. Inside my head, Dave Wells' voice was screaming: *Leave it alone, Joe. Walk away from it. It's not going to end well, Joe.* And from his suicide note left in my office, this line hit me like a blunt object to the face: *Jealousy is a bitter ambition. It loves to hate.*

Epilogue

Sinking into the hooch, I hit the bottom hard and stayed there. My gut burned with self-hatred. I was sickened from the obscene murders that Dave Wells had pulled off behind my back, and full of regret at not noticing his psychopathic illness.

For several days Max tried to put me back together, until she emotionally collapsed. She left Los Angeles again, to get out of the path of my self-destruction. She went back to Detroit, couldn't stand watching me gutting myself with whisky. I had piled a heavy load of self-loathing on top of myself. The crushing weight of it kept me nearly dead in the gutter. I stayed juiced up to the sixes and sevens, day after day.

The two detectives took turns watching over me. They would pull me off the floor, sit me up and make me drink water, tomato juice, and coffee, and they dumped my whisky down the drain. When they weren't around, I'd stagger back to the liquor store to restock. I didn't shave, didn't shower, didn't change my clothes. I stunk like a sick animal, until Jewels and Woodhouse dragged me fully clothed into the shower, and hit me with cold water. They made me wash myself, made me change clothes, shave, and eat.

Jewels finally brought in a doctor. The doc put me on sedatives to calm my nerves and to get me out of my head, and away from my self-destructive thoughts. Once the sedatives kicked in, I slept long and hard, without dreams.

It took me weeks to pull myself together.

After the overload of whisky was out of my blood, I called Max and told her that what Daniel McKenna had done was sick enough, but the amount of grief Dave Wells left behind dug out a hole inside of me, so deep and dark, that I felt trapped in there, dying.

The day after my phone conversation with Max, I went to the office in the afternoon. It was the first time in over a month.

The moment I stepped inside the phone started ringing. I ignored it and walked over to the window instead, and opened it all the way.

I just stood there at the open window, looking down at Hollywood Boulevard and Vine Street. Both were noisy streets, alive and vibrant. Something about that scene felt good to me. The phone kept ringing.

I sat down in the big pink-cushioned chair. The phone stopped ringing.

I thought about all the times Millie and Arnie Bender had sat in the office with me, talking about their plans of buying a house in Malibu. Thought about Mya Regis and Kimmie Turner, about how their lives were cut short by Dave Wells' demon. Thought about Scott Drum, Patty Walker and Sally Point, victims of Police Commissioner Daniel McKenna's deranged mind. Detective Woodhouse said later that the suicide note, left in my office typewriter, matched Commissioner McKenna's typewriter profile. I thought about Bryce Parker, who finally had the balls to stand up to his manipulative father, Daniel McKenna, and how emotionally used-up Parker must have felt to have ended his own life so tragically.

The phone was ringing again.

I stood up from the pink-cushioned chair and looked down at the street: traffic, people, life, and plenty of sunshine. Then I walked over to the desk to answer the call.

"Joe Stone, Private Investigator."

DOUBLE ON THE MURDER

a cocktail

Millie and Arnie Bender's Favorite Drinks

combined as:

DOUBLE ON THE MURDER

a cocktail

Scotch and ginger ale over ice

with a shot of bourbon on the side

and a water chaser

Savor the Scotch and ginger ale over ice,

until finished,

chase it with the shot of bourbon,

chase the bourbon with the water

ACKNOWLEDGEMENTS

Double On The Murder would not have existed in this final form without these readers, editors, and publisher:

Heike Helmer, for the unflinching hours she spent keeping the story's content in order.

Michael Grotsky, Julie Honan Johnston, Scott Waters, Julie Scornaienchi, Tamlyn S. Bright, and Karina Miranda. I am forever grateful for these readers and editors who scrutinized the many drafts of this novel. Their sound advice kept the story moving in the right direction.

And again, to writer Michael Grotsky, who encouraged me to turn a short story into a novel.

My unending gratefulness to the easy-going Craig Douglas, Managing Director of Close To The Bone Press, for believing in this story.

www.ingramcontent.com/pod-product-compliance
Lightning Source LLC
LaVergne TN
LVHW100513110826
845146LV00002B/621

* 9 7 9 8 9 9 5 0 8 4 3 0 3 *